THE SOUNDS
OF DEATH

A. A. PECORA

Order this book online at www.trafford.com
or email orders@trafford.com

Most Trafford titles are also available at major online book retailers.

Printed in the United States of America.

ISBN: 978-1-4669-4428-2 (sc)
ISBN: 978-1-4669-4426-8 (hc)
ISBN: 978-1-4669-4427-5 (e)

Library of Congress Control Number: 2012911326

Trafford rev. 06/27/2012

www.trafford.com

North America & international
toll-free: 1 888 232 4444 (USA & Canada)
phone: 250 383 6864 ♦ fax: 812 355 4082

CHAPTER 1

The room was warm and stuffy. Cody Thomas was standing by the window smoking his last cigarette. A crumpled, empty cigarette package lay on the windowsill.

The only sound that could be heard was a low hum originating from the tape machine, which was meant to record any activity picked up by a small "bug" that Cody had placed behind a picture in the room next door. He was attempting to gather information on a sleazy lawyer, who may have some ties to the mob and was cheating on his wife.

Cody could see no activity in the street three stories below. The city was not like itself this early in the morning, particularly in this neighborhood, where there are only old hotels, run-down apartment houses, and a few dilapidated warehouses. There were no people, no cars nor trucks, and the streets were cluttered with old newspapers and debris.

He had been holed up in this desolate flophouse for three days, waiting for the right moment. While investigating the wife of a client, Samuel T. Hollowell, Esq., Cody had discovered that

1

Hollowell was secretly bringing women to the Apollo Hotel which was certainly not the kind of place where he was likely to run into friends or business associates.

As Cody stared out the window, the reflection revealed a rugged, good-looking face with a five o'clock shadow and a three-inch scar running from the lower corner of the right eye back toward the earlobe. Plastic surgery was unable to completely hide the scar, which was the result of a street fight while on duty as a policeman. The dark skin and black hair betrayed Cody's one-eighth Native-American heritage. The cigarette dangled from his mouth. He stood six-foot tall with a well-developed body, which was pressed against the window frame. His right hand was jammed into the pocket of his rumpled slacks.

A brass clock sat on the dusty end table next to the bed, its second hand swept around the face in rhythmic jerks. Two larger black pointers moved almost imperceptibly, one indicating the hour and the other the minute. It was 3:00 a.m. Cigarette smoke hung like a pall over the tattered hotel room. The lamp on the table was not lit, leaving the room illuminated by only the blinking hotel sign outside.

A single bed covered with a sheet stained with what was most likely sweat and grime hugged the wall. The bedside table, on which the clock sat, also held a tarnished brass lamp with a tilted, dirty, fluted shade.

Across from the bed were two doors, one leading to the hall and the other to an empty closet. There was an old, broken wicker-back chair against the wall between the two doors. A small bathroom was off to the left.

The ashtray on the bedside table was filled to overflowing. A crushed cigarette butt smoldered half lit, its thin stream of smoke spiraling upward.

Against the wall, opposite the chair, stood a small black and white TV set with rabbit ear antenna sticking up in the shape of a V. Nothing in the room seemed to be meant for long-term use.

Another puff of blue-gray smoke exhaled from Cody's mouth and wafted across the room, accentuating the light, which intermittently streamed through the uneven blinds.

Hollowell had told Cody that he suspected his wife was running around on him and had hired him to follow her and gather evidence, presumably to be used in a divorce action. Cody subsequently came to suspect that the information was actually to be used by Hollowell as protection against his wife, in case she tried to divorce him and get a large settlement.

Hollowell also told Cody that his wife, Sarah, was out three nights a week with various excuses such as social club meetings, exercise groups, and the women's art society. Cody's job was to check these out and report any discrepancies to Samuel T.

After diligently setting up his investigation, Cody spent the next three weeks verifying each location Mrs. Hollowell visited. He discovered Mrs. Hollowell was doing exactly what she claimed.

At the gym, he found Mrs. Hollowell sweating along with her friends as they did their aerobics. When she finished, she'd shower and usually stop to have a cup of coffee with the ladies then immediately return home. When he checked out the women's social club and the art society, she was again doing what she was supposed to be doing. Cody noted suspiciously, however, that each evening when Mrs. Hollowell returned home, his client was never there.

Cody met with Mr. Hollowell to give him the preliminary report, thinking that he would be paid off, and their association would be ended. Instead, Hollowell insisted that Cody continue the investigation. Since he was being paid well, Cody was only too happy to continue.

It was then that Cody decided to set up surveillance on Mr. Hollowell. *It would be a kick,* he thought, and besides, it seemed ironic that the man who hired him would end up paying for his own surveillance. Since Cody had no other cases at this point, he readily agreed. Additionally, by gathering this information against Mr. Hollowell, Cody thought there might be an opportunity for a future paycheck from Mrs. Hollowell if she decided to start divorce proceedings of her own. Besides, he had come to dislike Samuel T. Hollowell, Esq. A lot.

This was the reason he had spent the last three nights in this crummy room, smoking cigarette after cigarette, and waiting. His routine was to arrive at the Apollo at around 7:00 p.m. and stay until 7:00 a.m. Nothing happened the first two nights, and Cody went home each morning tired and feeling grungy, like the hotel room he was using. When he got home, Joanna, his wife of two years, would be there with a hug and a kiss and no questions asked. She was Cody's second wife. His previous marriage had lasted only one year because Maryann, his first wife, couldn't accept his line of work and the hours spent doing it.

Early in their marriage, Maryann began to accuse him of infidelity. His crazy hours often kept them apart for days at a time. When he finally did get home, she would immediately begin questioning him regarding his whereabouts. She took no interest in his work and did nothing but complain about the lack of money and material things. Cody tried to make it up to her by spending money he didn't have. He eventually overextended himself with credit cards and loans, making things even worse.

Often, when he got home, Maryann wasn't there, and when eventually she did arrive, the excuses she offered for her absence were feeble. However, it was when she decided to take a separate vacation that things really fell apart. One day, he came home to find a note saying that she'd gone to a health spa for a week. She didn't even mention where the spa was located. When Maryann returned, they quarreled, and Maryann walked out. A few weeks later, he received the divorce papers, and that was the end of that.

Joanna was different. She was really excited by his work and understood and accepted the unusual hours and the frequent periods of financial insecurity. She never complained that he had to spend many late nights during his investigations.

Joanna Trombetti was working at the county courthouse as a stenographer when they met. Cody had been in court to testify in a case, when he noticed this pretty five feet two inches woman with flaxen hair and dark brown eyes who was recording the proceedings. She so captivated him that he made it his business to hang around until she was finished that particular session. He waited outside the courtroom, and when she came out, he walked over to her and calmly introduced himself. Cody did not lack courage, especially when it came to women.

She said she remembered him from the morning court case and a few minutes of small talk followed. He asked her to have lunch with him, she agreed, and they went to a nearby diner.

During lunch, he discovered Joanna was the oldest of three children. There was a boy two years younger and a sister four years younger. Joanna's brother, a CPA, was married with two children, two little girls. Joanna adored her nieces. Her sister had died tragically at a young age. When Cody tried to discuss the death of her sister, Joanna would refuse to go in to any detail and change the subject. Cody didn't press her for more information; he thought she would tell him when she felt the time was right. He also noted that Joanna had the slightest overbite. This small flaw didn't upset Cody at all; in fact, he found that he really liked it.

Mr. and Mrs. Trombetti were hard working people. Mr. Trombetti was a stonemason, and Joanna's mom raised her children to be honest and respectful. It was these qualities in Joanna that attracted that attracted Cody. He always felt that her honesty was her best quality and was the thing that most distinguished her from Maryann.

Things progressed steadily and rapidly from that day on, and three months later, they were married.

Suddenly, Cody was roused from his thoughts by the whirring of the tape recorder, which signaled there was activity in the next room. He picked up the frayed wicker chair, carried it to the table on which the tape recorder sat. As he moved across the room, the blinking light from the hotel sign streaming between the uneven slats of the wooden blinds reflected off his face.

Putting the earphones over his ears, he listened to the commotion in the next room. He could clearly hear a deep male voice that sounded like Samuel T. Hollowell. The words were slurred, and there was laughing. Because of the slurred speech, Cody was sure that the man had been drinking.

He listened intently in an attempt to hear the voice of the other person. It was a female voice, but it was very soft, too soft in fact, to be heard clearly. Besides, the man was doing most of the talking. He was loud and crude and was telling the woman to get undressed.

Cody could hear Hollowell stumbling about the room. Next, he heard the bedsprings squeak loudly, indicating that someone sat on the bed. First, one shoe, then the other hit the floor. Hollowell coughed and began to chuckle again as if he had thought of something amusing. Cody wondered why any woman would want to associate with this loud-mouthed boor, never mind have an affair. Then he remembered that Hollowell had lots of money and threw it around freely.

After a few minutes, Hollowell could be heard calling for the woman to come over to him. The muffled sounds of high-heeled shoes walking across the rug thumped through the earphones. Cody continued to listen for the next ten or fifteen minutes.

There were sounds of activity, which included the bed squeaking, grunting and groaning, and muffled coughing. It was not strange that the woman made little noise. Cody thought he could discern a couple of slaps, perhaps from a strap, which made him wonder about kinky sex. Maybe Hollowell liked to be dominated, or more likely, he would want to be the one in control.

Soon, the noise subsided, and Cody could hear only the sounds of the woman walking around the room, perhaps gathering her things. In a while, he heard the door open, and the high-heeled shoes echoing down the hall. Running to the door, he opened it ever so slightly, in an attempt to get a look at the woman. The single bulb at the end of the hallway failed to cast enough light for him to see her clearly in the shadows. She was about average height, but that was all he could make out before she opened the fire door and hurried through into the stairwell.

Cody closed the door and returned to the earphones. Listening carefully, he heard nothing more from the next room and assumed Hollowell was sleeping off his night of drinking and sex. At about 6:00 a.m., he packed up his recording equipment and left the room. After loading the equipment into his car, he drove home.

When he got home, about 6:45 a.m., he parked his car in the driveway and let himself into the house. He tried to be very quiet because he did not want to awaken Joanna. Then he realized she would have to be getting up soon anyway.

The sound of Joanna's alarm could be heard in the kitchen where Cody was starting to make some coffee. He heard her groan, and then the alarm was quiet. After a few minutes, nothing was stirring. He thought she might have rolled over and dozed off again, so he went upstairs to the bedroom, opened the door, and peeked in.

There was Joanna lying across the bed on her belly, completely nude, except for a pair of bikini panties. Her arm was stretched out toward the alarm. Cody laughed to himself and stood admiring her for a few minutes. He was dead tired, but he felt like getting undressed and making love to her right then and there.

Instead, he walked over and sat on the edge of the bed, gently placed his hand on Joanna's back, and slowly rubbed it up and down from her neck to her buttocks.

"Good morning, sweetheart, it's time to get up."

There was no response. Again he tried, "Hey, sleepyhead, it's time to get up."

Joanna let out a soft purring sound, opened one eye, looked at him, and smiled. "Do I have to?"

"You know it will take you an hour to get ready, and you have to be in Judge Woodengate's courtroom at 9:00 a.m."

She turned over, exposing her beautiful breasts to Cody. He immediately felt miserable because she had to go to work. He was about to suggest that she call in sick, but then thought better of it.

"Oh, all right. Let me jump in the shower." She inhaled deeply and sniffed. "Is that coffee I smell?"

"Yep, I put it on a few minutes ago."

"Great! Pour me a cup, while I get into the shower."

"Sure," he said, as he got up from the bed and went to the door. When he turned to look at her again, she was leaning over to turn on the shower. *Wow!* he thought. *How was I lucky enough to get her?*

He went downstairs quickly, poured the coffee, brought it up, and placed it on the table in the bathroom.

"The coffee's on the table. Hurry down, I have something interesting to tell you."

"Okay!" she replied in a voice loud enough to be heard over the noise of the shower.

Thirty minutes later, they were sitting at the kitchen table, and Cody was telling Joanna about his surveillance.

"Well, it finally paid off. My mark showed up last night with a woman."

"That's great, honey. By the way, who is this guy? You never did tell me his name. Oh, that's right. You're not supposed to, are you?"

Cody replied, "No, but you know, it's the sleaze bag that hired me to follow his wife. It turns out that the wife is okay, but the guy who hired me is a fraud and a cheat. I caught him with another woman last night."

"You caught him? Where? How?"

"Remember, I had that surveillance set up?"

"Yes, I do, but you never told me where or why you were even doing it."

Cody got up from the table and went to the counter to pour himself a second cup of coffee. As he stood there, he lit a cigarette and continued.

"At some run-down hotel in a crummy part of town. Anyway, after three nights, he showed up with a woman and was he loaded! They apparently had sex, and she left. He was still there when I left."

"Did you get a look at the woman?"

"I tried, but I couldn't see her clearly. I could just about hear her voice and not very well at that. I can tell you that I think something kinky was going on."

"Really! Tell me about it," said Joanna excitedly.

Cody eased back to the table and sat down as he went on with his story. "Well, there was a lot of slapping and hitting. And from what I could tell, the man seemed to be enjoying it. He was groaning and making all kinds of guttural sounds. It sounded very different to me. But I got the whole thing on tape."

"Crazy stuff, hon, but what are you going to do with it?"

"I don't know yet. I do know I'm going to drop this character as a client. But as to what I am going to do with the tape, I'm just not sure."

"Don't you think that it would be fair to give it to his wife?" Joanna asked with just the right amount of female indignation.

"Although she seems to be a nice lady, I wasn't hired by her, so I don't think I would just give it to her. I was thinking I might just hold on to it for future reference. One never knows. Then there is the thing about client confidentiality, even if he doesn't deserve it. Also, this guy is a pretty powerful individual and could cause me trouble and perhaps cost me my license."

"I guess I understand. Well, I'm off to court. I'll see you this evening around five thirty."

Joanna got up from the table and moved toward Cody to give him a good-bye kiss. After a quick peck on the cheek, she hurried out the door.

CHAPTER 2

Cody went upstairs to go to bed. He needed a few hours sleep. As he sat on the edge of the bed, he reviewed the events of the past few weeks and tried to decide what to do with his information. Maybe he just ought to go to Hollowell, tell him he was dropping the investigation, get rid of the tape and forget about everything. After all, the job he was hired to do was over. The rest of the material he had collected was not relevant to the original job for which he was hired, and the original client could, in fact, cause him trouble. As he lay back in the bed and closed his eyes, he had just about decided to destroy the tape and call the case closed.

It was 1:00 p.m. when he woke up. Habit had made getting up easy. He had mastered the ability to awaken and function quickly when he was a cop. Cody had been on the force for eight years before quitting. He left because he could no longer tolerate the lying, deceitful, sleazy individuals he had to come into contact with on a daily basis. This included some of his colleagues on the force, as well as the criminals. In fact, Cody had decided that some of the dishonest cops who were taking graft and falsifying evidence were just as bad as the characters he was arresting.

He remembered having gone to the captain of his precinct with information, which he had collected.

"Captain, after a lot of soul searching, I felt you had to know about this," he said, as he handed Captain MacTavish the packet he had prepared. It contained all the evidence he had gathered over the previous few months.

"What've you got here, Thomas?" The captain took the envelope from Cody.

"These are only some of the facts about what's going on at this precinct. This is what makes me ashamed to be a cop. Things like graft, drugs, and falsification of evidence. Something's got to be done about it, sir."

"Ah, come on now, Thomas, things can't be that bad, or I would've heard something about it."

Cody couldn't tell if the captain was really that stupid or if he was just putting on an act. Almost everyone else knew what was going on.

"It's all in the report—times, dates, names, all of it. When you read it, I'm sure you'll be convinced."

The captain sat quietly for a few moments, and then stood up from his chair. "Okay, thanks, Thomas. I'll look into this as soon as I can. Don't worry, I'll get to the bottom of this corruption if it exists."

"If it exists?" Cody blurted out. "There's no doubt about it. Something's got to be done, sir."

Cody had a definite feeling that the captain was going to ignore the whole thing. He made up his mind at that point that if the situation weren't addressed in the next few months, he would resign from the force.

Nothing ever came of it. No one was ever charged or even accused for that matter. The only thing that happened was that Cody's reputation was sullied. Although no one knew for sure he was a "turncoat," it was suspected, and he essentially became an outcast. The only person Cody could count on was Andy Perone, his ex-partner. Andy was a clean, honest cop whom Cody trusted implicitly.

Andy Perone was a second generation Puerto Rican. He was short, five feet four inches, and had thick black hair that he kept slicked back as best as he could. It was very unruly and fell over his eyes when he didn't have his hat on. Andy had dark brown, almost black, eyes that seemed to penetrate anything he looked at. His nose was small and came to a sharp point. His lips were two thin lines that were capable of spreading into a great smile or narrowing even further, leaving no doubt about his anger.

He liked wearing double-breasted suits and kept his shoes shined to a high gloss, a habit left over from his days as a street cop. When he spoke, it was with a slight Latin flavor, a remnant of his upbringing where only Spanish was spoken in the house while Andy was growing up.

Because things at the precinct hadn't changed, Cody resigned. He maintained a good relationship with Andy, however, and this association had been a great help to him in his work as a private detective. Andy could always be counted on for inside information such as an address, a phone number, or a license plate number. They often shared information about cases of mutual interest. Cody was even able to help Andy on occasion. Because of this relationship, Andy respected Cody's work, in spite of the fact that most policemen didn't really respect private detectives.

Cody got into the shower and washed quickly. He also shaved while in the shower, another habit he had acquired while on the force. After drying off and dressing, he went downstairs to make himself some brunch. While the coffee from the morning was heating, he went out front to get the newspaper. Glancing casually at the front page as he walked back to the house, the headline virtually jumped off the page: PROMINENT ATTORNEY, SAMUEL T. HOLLOWELL, FOUND DEAD.

Cody's mouth dropped open as he collapsed into the nearest chair as he entered the kitchen. He anxiously read the article that followed.

> Prominent city lawyer Samuel T. Hollowell was found this morning in an Old Town hotel room apparently suffocated to death according to someone close to the investigation. The police were unable to give any other details as yet except to say that there are presently no solid clues and that they are in the process of collecting evidence at the crime scene.

The article went on to describe Mr. Hollowell as a man who had his finger in numerous activities, intimating that not all were on the up and up. There were suggestions about dealings with the underworld since he had apparently defended some of the lesser-known criminals in the past. Additionally, there were suggestions about promiscuity and a shaky marriage. Cody thought, *The creep did not do as good a job of covering up as he thought he had.*

As Cody finished the article, he sat back to think and digest what he had just read. If Hollowell died last night, or more accurately, this morning, then he may have been listening to the murder. The event was most likely captured on the tape he had recorded. He went quickly to his equipment, set it up, and began listening to the sounds of last night, perhaps the sounds of death.

This time, he listened much more intently, trying unsuccessfully to make out the female voice. Next, he listened closely to Hollowell, wondering if the guttural sounds he heard could actually represent those of suffocation instead of sexual ecstasy.

After listening to the tape two more times, he decided to call Andy Perone. These tapes had to be turned over to Andy. Cody knew that if he kept this information from the police, he could be considered an accessory after-the-fact and could be in real hot water.

Cody picked up the phone and dialed Andy's private line at the precinct office. There was no answer. Thinking that Andy must be at the scene of the crime, he decided to go to the hotel, not only to see Andy, but also to get a line on what evidence may have turned up. He gulped down the tepid cup of coffee, grabbed his wrinkled jacket, car keys, and virtually flew to his car.

On the way to the Apollo Hotel, Cody went over the past few weeks for clues he may have ignored or missed. He couldn't think of anything that could have or should have tipped him off that Hollowell was about to be killed. The only thing he'd been aware of was Hollowell's promiscuous life with the ladies.

Maybe the lover Hollowell had brought to the hotel was the killer. He couldn't remember any sounds in the room after she left. Could someone have come to the hotel after he had left this morning? That's possible. Could someone have sneaked in while he was still there? Not very likely. He thought that he probably would have heard any activity in the next room.

Many thoughts were flashing by as he arrived at the hotel. He practically vaulted out of the car and ran to the front of the hotel. There was a patrolman there, only this "patrolman" was a woman. *A patrol*person, Cody thought to be politically correct.

"Hi! I'm Cody Thomas. I'm a private investigator," he said, showing the officer his identification card. "I'd like to see Lieutenant Perone. I have some information about the case he's investigating."

He tried to continue past the guard.

"Just a minute there, buster," she said, putting her hand on his chest. "This is a crime scene, and I can't let just anyone pass, you know."

Buster! thought Cody. *That's just what I need right now, a tight-assed cop to give me a bad time.*

"Look, officer, I've already told you, I'm a friend of the lieutenant, and I have some important information for him."

"Yeah, yeah, that's what they all say. What've you got to do with this case anyway? We've been here only a few hours ourselves."

"Look, just do me and yourself a favor and get Lieutenant Perone down here or let me go up. I'm telling you, I have important information here." He waved the tape in front of the cop's face, getting very frustrated. Just then, Andy stuck his head out from behind the door.

"It's okay, Casey. I know this guy." Then looking at Cody, "What're *you* doing here?" he said, emphasizing the "you."

"Oh, thank God!" Cody sighed, relieved that he wouldn't have to deal with the inflexible policewoman anymore. He inched toward Andy, holding up the tape. "I think I've got something here that will interest you."

"What's that, an audio tape?"

"Right on, buddy. If you've got a minute, I'll explain it to you."

"Okay, come on up."

Cody brushed quickly by the officer with a slight sneer on his face. Andy led him to an unoccupied room on the first floor and opened the door.

"All right, Cody. What could you possibly have on that tape that's so dammed important?"

"On this tape, my friend," Cody put the tape right up to Andy's face in order to emphasize his point, "I think I've recorded Samuel T. Hollowell's death."

"What the hell are you talking about? How could you have taped that?" Andy reached for the tape, but Cody pulled it back and took a step away from Andy.

"Because I was in the next room with a tape recorder."

"You were where?" said Andy in disbelief.

"In the next room, in this hotel, taping the . . . ah . . . what was going on."

Andy closed the door and put his hands in his pants pockets. He walked over and stood by the window. "Come on, Cody, what were you doing here? Were you following the guy for his suspicious wife?"

"It's a long story, but, yes, I was on a case, and it brought me to this hotel last night. As a matter of fact, I've been here for the last *three* nights. I was gathering some information for—are you ready for Mr. Samuel T. Hollowell? Part of that investigation," Cody knew he was stretching the truth when he continued, "includes this tape. It was recorded this morning, around 3:00 a.m. It was then that I heard Hollowell and a lady friend apparently getting it on. All of that, and some other tidbits, is recorded on this tape."

"Holy shit! I've got to hear this." Andy still seemed skeptical. "Well, let's get a tape player and listen to this thing right now."

As they walked out of the room together, Andy was still shaking his head. "I just can't believe it. It's too good to be true."

Walking to the front desk, Andy picked up the house phone and called the room in which the murder took place.

"Hello, Whitkowsky, this is Lieutenant Perone. I'm going back to the station for a while, and I'm leaving the investigation in your hands. Don't fuck it up, okay?"

Whitkowsky must have assured Andy and asked when he was coming back because Andy said, "I don't know, in about an hour or so. Just make sure you keep me informed about anything that looks interesting."

Andy nodded his head in response to a comment from the sergeant, hung up the phone, and turned to Cody. "You can never be too careful with these cases. So many guilty people have walked because the investigators fucked up. You remember that, don't you?"

Walking briskly, Andy led Cody toward the front door.

"How well I remember. Are we going to your office?"

"Yeah, but we better take two cars, in case—"

"Nah. Let's both go in your car. I want to come back with you anyway. I'd like to get a look at the crime scene if that's okay with you."

Andy's eyes opened wide, and he smiled wryly. After a pause, "What for? This is a police matter. There's no need for you to be getting in my way."

"Ah, come on, Andy, I won't bother anyone or get in the way. I promise. I'd just like to see the room one time. It'll be like old times."

After a little thought, Andy said, "Okay, but this'll be the one and only time. I don't want you to keep buggin' me after this."

"Gotcha!" Cody was getting excited. He was really anxious to get a look at that room. Even though the police would be collecting evidence, he felt that he might see something they had overlooked. He had always done a great job of finding hidden or obscure clues when he was on the force. Besides, he felt like this was his case, and come whatever, he was going to stay involved.

As they walked out the front door, Cody glanced at the cop standing on the step. His lip curled up in a sneer. He was thinking, *See, I told you I had some drag.*

The officer paid no attention, which, of course, irritated Cody even more. He hopped into Andy's car, and they drove off.

*   *   *   *

At the station, they listened to the tape over and over again. Andy didn't hear any more than Cody had heard. He leaned back in his chair and said, "I'm gonna give this tape to the lab. They may be able to enhance the sound and hear something more."

"That's a good idea. I was thinking the same thing myself. Can I get a copy of the report when they're finished?"

"What do *you* need that for? I told ya before, this is a police matter now, didn't I?"

"I realize that, but you know how it is. I kind of feel that I'm still a part of this thing, and after all, I am responsible for the best piece of evidence you've got so far, right?"

Andy got up from his chair and took the tape from the machine. Looking at Cody, he said, "Well, I guess so. But don't think you're gonna play a big role in this case. We'll take it from here. I'll give you a copy of the report on the tape, but that's all. Like I said before, I don't want you to keep buggin' me."

"Don't worry, pal, just this one thing," Cody said, smiling slightly. He knew damn well, as time went on, he would be back for more, and he knew that Andy understood that as well.

Cody felt he had to be involved. After all, he had come this far on the case, hadn't he? His detective's curiosity had been piqued. It was kind of like old times, when he was a detective, working on a case with Andy. The idea of dropping out at this point was unthinkable. Even though he would not be getting paid from this point on, he felt ownership in the case, and there was no way he could just stop abruptly. His old policeman's mind wouldn't let him. The thought of money caused him to say out loud, "Speaking of money, I've got some coming to me from Hollowell. I'll have to try to get it from his wife. I'll stop over to see her as soon as things settle down a little."

"Who's talking about money?" asked Andy.

"Oh, just thinking out loud. Let's get back to the hotel."

"Okay, let's go."

They walked through the busy station house, out to the sidewalk, and got into the car to head back. On the way over to the hotel, Cody, as subtly as possible, tried to find out what Andy already knew.

"What else have you got so far, Andy?"

"Hollowell was tied to the bed by his hands and feet. He must've liked that kinky stuff, ya know? And there was a silk scarf stuffed in his mouth."

"Hands and feet tied to the bed?" Cody repeated as if in disbelief. "I knew that guy was a creep. I guess that's how the woman was able to suffocate him."

"Yeah, that's one way, but he also may've been so drunk that he passed out. The room did smell like a brewery."

Cody took a cigarette from his pocket and pushed in the lighter on the dashboard. "What was he tied to the bed with?" he continued, asking questions nonchalantly so as not to get on Andy's nerves.

"Soft silk cords, you know, the kind that's used with draperies."

"Do you think they'll be easy to trace?"

"Probably not. You know that kind of thing is common."

"Maybe the woman brought them with her from home. All you'll have to do is match them up with the drapes, right?"

"Yeah, simple," said Andy, "but which woman and which drapes?"

"How about any signs of injury?"

"There was some blood comin' from his nose. Minor though, not a lot. We're writin' it off to the rough sex."

"This woman must be a tough customer."

Just then, the car pulled up in front of the hotel. The female cop was still on duty. They got out of the car and walked toward the dirty glass door and went in.

CHAPTER 3

Cody followed as Andy walked to the elevator, got in, and pushed the button to the third floor. As the elevator began to rise, Cody remembered that the woman had not used the elevator when she left. He said to Andy, "Did you talk to the guy at the front desk yet?"

"Two detectives are over at his house right now. He went off duty at 7:00 a.m. It was the morning man who found the body, actually, it was the cleaning lady—"

"I'll bet that scared the hell out of her." interrupted Cody.

"Yea," Andy continued, "she opened the door to clean the room and saw Hollowell on the bed. She said she let out a scream, and then called the deskman from the phone in the room—"

"That probably ruined any chance at fingerprints that might've been on the phone," again, Cody jumped in. This time he thought he noticed the familiar frown on Andy's face when he was annoyed.

"You know, Andy," said Cody, trying to get Andy's mind distracted a little. "I just remembered that the woman didn't leave by the elevator. She walked right past my door. I tried to catch a glimpse of her as she went by, but the light was so bad I could barely see her shape in the shadows, let alone any distinguishing features. She went down the fire stairs."

"That's great!" said Andy sarcastically. "That means that the deskman couldn't have seen her leave."

The elevator stopped, and the door opened. Cody and Andy exited and walked to the end of the hall where the murder took place. There was a lot of milling about by the coroner's assistants, criminalists, and detectives. They were lifting latent fingerprints and sifting dust and vacuuming with a Soderman-Heuberger filter. Everyone appeared as though they were trying to be extra careful about preserving the evidence.

It was about five and a half hours since the police arrived. The cleaning lady had found him at 8:15 a.m. or so, and the desk clerk immediately called 911. The first patrolman arrived at 8:23 a.m. It had taken a few hours to gather all the necessary people.

Because the criminalists and one of the coroner's assistants were still working on him, he was lying on the bed, naked and uncovered. The sight of Hollowell lying on his back with his hands over his head tied to the bedposts was a little unsettling to Cody. He had never quite gotten used to dead bodies.

Hollowell's head was twisted at a curious angle, his graying hair was in disarray, and his brown eyes were partially open and lacked any of the usual luster that is typical of life. Even though Cody disliked Hollowell and what he stood for, he felt embarrassed by the stark nakedness of the body, but he knew the lab people had their work to do before they could disturb the scene.

Hollowell's face was bluish-purple, and there was distinct lividity covering his chest and legs. A slight trickle of blood flowed from Hollowell's nose.

In order to get a better look, he moved a little closer to the bed, as disgusting as that was. Cody knew Andy would be watching him carefully, and sure enough, he heard in a half whisper, "Be careful, Cody. Remember what I told you. Don't disturb anything, and don't get in the way."

"Okay, boss! I just wanted to be sure it was Hollowell. Interesting shade of blue, isn't he?"

"Well, if he was killed at 3:30 or 4:00 a.m. as we suspect from the tape, then he's been dead around eleven hours now. I guess that'd make anyone look blue."

"You're right about that."

About that time, Sergeant Whitkowsky came over to Andy and said that the coroner was going to take the body.

"Did ya get enough pictures?"

"Plenty," Whitkowsky answered.

"And you were careful not to disturb any of the evidence, weren't ya?"

"Yep, we've been meticulous. Can I let 'im go now?"

"Okay," replied Andy, but the resignation in his voice suggested to Cody that he was more than concerned. Andy was always uneasy about his cases. He was a very precise cop.

The coroner's men untied the hands, which were encased in plastic bags, and also his feet, wrapped the body in a rubber sheet, and placed it in a large body bag. They were very careful not to disturb the bed sheet too much.

"Did ya check the body and the sheets for bodily fluids? If there are any, we may be able to test them for DNA."

"There was somethin' on the sheet. It was some kind of Fluid, all right, and there was a lot of it around. We couldn't tell if it was his or hers, but the lab people are aware of it."

"I hope so," said Andy.

Cody, by this time, had walked to the door leading to the bathroom. Because this was a corner room, it was slightly larger than the one he had used next door. The bathroom was a little bigger, and there was also a small desk against the wall.

He leaned in cautiously to look around. The sink and tub were dry, suggesting that no one had used them. However, it was approximately eleven hours after the fact, so they might well have been used and dried out by now. The toilet seat lid was down. Did the woman use it before she left? That might be something to inspect more carefully at a future time.

Cody would have liked to get at it right now, but he knew Andy would have none of that. He would have to figure a way to come back later even if that meant some of the evidence might be gone or tainted.

He turned, stepped back into the bedroom, and glanced around with a trained eye. There was the same kind of TV set, table, and chair as in the room next door. The desk had writing paper on it as well as a ballpoint pen. Cody was sure the detectives had dusted all those things for fingerprints. He casually walked over to the bed.

The criminalists had removed the sheets for complete examination at the lab. Cody walked to the head of the bed and looked at the space between the bed and the wall. He was wondering if anything had fallen in there. Trying to be as casual as possible, he noticed that one of the pieces of cord had somehow slipped between the bed and the wall. As he remembered, the police sometimes slipped up on an investigation. Cody felt he really wanted that piece of cord.

When he looked up, he saw Andy looking his way. In a voice sounding strangely like his father's used to sound when issuing a warning, Cody heard Andy warn, "Cooody! I'm watchin' you."

"Don't worry, Andy. I'm just looking around. I'm not going to touch anything."

"Yeah, I know. Just keep your hands to yourself."

Cody wondered how he was going to get that cord. He knew he couldn't get it while Andy was around. He would have to try to get back into the room after the cops had gone. But how? He would figure that out later.

He continued to examine the room carefully with his eyes. As he stepped away from the bed, he felt something small and hard press against the bottom of his shoe. He stood quietly and looked around. No one seemed to be paying any attention to him at that point. Reaching for the pack of cigarettes in his shirt pocket, he took it out and pretended to drop it accidentally. As he bent down to pick it up, he deftly moved his foot and quickly picked up the object as well.

It was small and metallic. Without looking at it, he quickly put the cigarettes and the object into his shirt pocket. He decided to look at it later.

28

After determining that there was nothing further that he could see under these circumstances, he turned to Andy.

"Thanks for letting me hang around for a while, Andy. I think I'll head on home now. It's almost time for my wife to be getting in. I like to be there when she gets home if I can."

"Okay, Cody. No doubt I'll be talkin' to ya, huh?" Andy said with a degree of sarcasm.

"Yeah, I guess so. I'll be in touch. Thanks again."

Cody couldn't wait to get to his car to look at the object he had found. While he was on the elevator, he took it out carefully and stared at it. It was a small gold clasp, which fit over the post of an earring for someone with pierced earlobes. The clasp was too small to contain fingerprints so he didn't worry about handling it. Maybe he would give it to Andy later, but not just yet. He wanted to try to solve this case alone, just to prove to Andy and himself that he was still a very good detective whether on the force or not.

While looking at the clasp, he was wondering if it could have belonged to the woman who was in the room or if it had been there for a while. It could even have belonged to a man, in this day and age. He'd just hold on to it for future reference.

The elevator door glided open, and he walked into the lobby. He walked directly to the door leading to the stair well and pushed it open. The cops probably hadn't looked there yet, since he had just told Andy about the woman using these stairs to leave.

Upon entering, the first thing he noticed was that there was a door leading to the outside. This is how she got out without the deskman seeing her. He also saw a way that he might use to get back into the hotel at a later time without being seen—that is, if it were left open. Cody walked over to the door, opened it, and looked around outside. He tried the knob on the outside and saw that it was broken and couldn't be locked. *That's a break!* he thought.

He slowly began climbing the stairs, carefully examining every inch. The stairs were dimly lit by just one light bulb at each landing. When he reached the flight leading from the third floor, he saw a glint of light on the second step. He moved toward it quickly, and as he got closer, his heart started to beat faster. It was a small diamond stud earring. He exploded with excitement. "This must be the earring that belongs to the clasp I found in the room," Cody said out loud with a grin on his face.

Although this kind of earring was very common, it could nonetheless be an important clue. He was still looking around the third floor landing when the fire door opened, and Andy and Whitkowsky came through. Cody looked at Andy with a silly grin, like Winnie the Pooh with his hand caught in the honey pot.

"I thought you were goin' home, Cody," said Andy.

"I was, but then I remembered that the woman used these stairs, so I thought I'd take a quick look around."

"Oh, you did, did ya? Well, I thought I told ya not to mess around. Did you find anything?"

"Nah! But I didn't look real good," Cody lied with a straight face.

"All right then, get lost, for real this time."

"Okay, I'm going, I'm going. See you later."

Cody hurried down the stairs and through the door leading to the lobby. He did not want to draw attention to the door leading to the outside, even though he realized Andy would probably discover it. He went out the front door to his car.

Withholding evidence could mean his license or perhaps even jail. Regardless, he couldn't let go of this case. Everything would eventually be given to Andy, but at the moment, he felt drawn in by what he had discovered. He surprised himself that he was willing to take such a risk.

Maybe his private work had become too routine, too mundane. He'd had only about five or six good weeks in the last year when he really used his brain and skills. At last, for a change, he felt alive. He had forgotten how much fun tough cases were. His car roared to a start, and he headed home.

CHAPTER 4

Cody arrived home at 4:30 p.m. He expected Joanna at around five o'clock or so. He went to the kitchen to clean up the morning dishes that he had left when he rushed out. Many possible motives began rushing through his head.

What would drive a woman to kill someone? Revenge? For what? Could she have been a client whom Hollowell had screwed over? He made a mental note to try to see Hollowell's office records. Cody was pretty sure, however, that the police would subpoena everything from the office. Even if Andy had taken Hollowell's files, Cody felt that he would have to see them somehow.

Could it have been one of Hollowell's hookers? If it were, would she have a good motive? Maybe robbery, but Andy hadn't mentioned that anything had been stolen. Cody made another mental note to ask Andy specifically about any theft.

How about a "woman scorned"? That's always a good motive. But what woman? One of his affairs, maybe? Perhaps one of his paramours found out about the others and got really ticked off and killed him. Cody thought he would have to determine the

32

whereabouts of each of Hollowell's ladies at the time of the murder. But first, he would have to find out who they were. Hollowell probably had a "little black book" somewhere. The Hollowell residence would have to be examined soon. The yet unpaid fee for his work was the best excuse he could think of to get to Mrs. Hollowell and the house.

What else? The paper had suggested that Hollowell had some connections with the underworld. Maybe the mob set him up with a female hit man. *A contradiction of terms,* thought Cody, *but an interesting thought nonetheless.*

Cody hadn't been this exhilarated in years. He was really getting excited now. All these ideas were racing through his brain when Joanna came breezing through the door.

"Hello, sweetheart! How was your day?"

"You won't believe it. This has been one of the most extraordinary days of my life."

"Really?" she said, kissing him on the cheek as she headed for the stairs. "Fill me in while I change my clothes."

"Well," Cody started to follow her up the stairs, "do you remember the surveillance I was telling you about this morning?"

"Sure I do."

"Well, those strange noises I heard might have been the sounds of death."

"What?" said Joanna in a tone a pitch higher. "I don't understand."

"I'm pretty sure the noises I heard were the sounds of a man dying, actually, getting murdered."

"That's unbelievable. You actually were listening to someone being murdered? Why didn't you stop it, or call the police, or something?"

They had reached the bedroom by this time. Joanna had her dress off and was facing Cody in her bra and panties. This sight distracted him to the point where he almost forgot what he was saying, but he struggled to continue, trying to explain.

"I didn't *know* he was being killed. Remember, I thought the noises were people having sex."

"Oh, that's right, I forgot. Well, what *did* you do?"

Cody walked over and sat on the bed. He was staring at Joanna intently, trying to keep his mind on what he was saying. "I went over to the hotel and talked to Andy Perone. I told him what I'd heard, and I gave him the tape."

"What did he say? I'll bet he was as shocked as I am."

"You can count on it. He was so excited he even let me look at the crime scene. I got a chance to get a look at the victim and the room, and to get some idea how the murder was committed."

"Who was the victim? Didn't you tell me this morning the man in the room was your client?"

"That's right. It *was* my client. I guess I can tell you now who he was, since he's dead, and his name is all over the paper. He was Samuel T. Hollowell, Esq."

"Samuel T. Hollowell! My goodness," Joanna cried out. I think I knew him. He's tried cases where I was the stenographer. Isn't that a coincidence?"

"Oh, yeah. Well, that's the guy, and he's deader than most of my stock investments."

Cody went on detailing all the events of the day. He told her about the drapery cords that were used to tie him up and about the earring.

"Why didn't you give the earring to Andy?"

"You know how I am. I hate to give up on a case, and this one's so juicy."

"But can't you get into trouble for withholding evidence?"

Joanna got up from the bed and walked toward the closet. She began hanging her dress with her back to Cody.

"Yeah, that's true, but I'm not even sure this earring has anything to do with this case."

"I know, but there's a good chance that it does, isn't there?" Joanna turned, facing Cody, and walked slowly to the bed and sat down.

"Possibly, but I'll just hold onto it for a little while, just until I see where, how, and if it fits. And I'll tell you something else, I'm going back to that hotel tonight and try to get that piece of cord if I can."

"You're what?" Joanna asked incredulously.

"You heard me. I've just got to see if I can solve this case, and that cord may become very important. Besides, it's no big deal. They've already got three other pieces."

"Okay, Cody. But now, you're starting to scare me. I wish you wouldn't get too involved."

"Look, honey, I'll just look around a little and see what I can turn up. Then, when I have it all figured out, I'll turn it over to Andy. I'll even let him take all the credit, okay?" he said with a smile that suggested he was really getting back into the joy of detecting.

"I guess there's no use in arguing with you. I never seem to win when it comes to your work."

"That's my girl. Don't worry, everything will be just fine. I should be able to get into the hotel easily enough, so getting the cord will be no problem."

Cody had been observing Joanna this whole time, and he could just about keep his mind on their conversation. He had wanted her badly since this morning. Putting his left arm over her shoulder and pulling her close, his right hand found her breast. Their lips came together in a long passionate kiss. As they fell back on the bed, Joanna reached up with her hands and began to unbutton his shirt. Within minutes, they were gyrating furiously around the bed in the "dance" of love.

When it was over, Cody languidly smoked a cigarette as he replayed the whole day once again in his mind. Then he began to outline his actions for the next few days. He noticed Joanna appeared to have fallen off into a deep sleep. Standing up, he looked back and marveled again at her good looks. After a short hot shower, while Joanna continued to sleep, he decided to go to the hotel. They could eat when he got back.

He dressed, went downstairs, and jotted a quick note to Joanna:

Sweetheart,

I've decided to pick up that little item I told you about. Don't worry about anything, including dinner. I'll stop and pick up Chinese. See you in a while.

Love ya,

Cody

He put on the same sport coat he had worn all day and went out to his car. His heart was pounding with excitement.

*　　*　　*　　*

Cody was anxious to get to the hotel so he could go over the room again, this time without Andy staring at him. When he arrived, he decided to park on a side street near the hotel, just in case there were any cops around who possibly might recognize him. No one was outside the entrance when he got out of his car.

The front of the hotel was baroque. It was covered with grotesque gargoyles and other figures, like many of the hotels that had been built around the same time. It was made from polished large white stones that had grayed over time. Years of wind and rainstorms had worn the gargoyles' faces so that they were even uglier.

There was a wide ledge that stretched from corner to corner and extended about eight inches from the wall. Above the ledge were the windows to the rooms. It was hard to tell from the ground exactly which windows belonged to which room. On each corner, there were large columns that reached from the ledge to the next floor. An old iron fire escape hung on the north side, beginning at the roof and ending at the first floor. It had a ladder that could be opened to reach the ground. The large sign, which extended from the first floor to the roof, spelled out the name of the hotel in bright blinking white bulbs, something like the marquees on Broadway.

Cody approached the front door, which was made from a solid piece of glass and swung inward when pushed. It was smeared with dirt and old fingerprints and obviously hadn't been washed in a long time.

For the first time, when he entered the lobby, Cody actually looked at it carefully. The lobby, like the rest of the hotel, was shabby and tired. There were two high-back red leather chairs against the right-hand wall with a small table between them. On the table were a couple of magazines. A dirty window, which was facing the street on the west side of the building, took up most of the other wall. In the middle of the lobby was a square support pillar with a padded circular settee surrounding it. It was dark maroon in color and was terribly worn. The hotel's desk was against the far right wall.

Sitting behind it was the night clerk whose face Cody knew from his previous visits here. Maybe he wouldn't have to use the broken fire door after all if he could do some business with the clerk.

The clerk, who had a thick growth of facial hair, glanced up from a girly magazine he was reading. He appeared as tired and worn as his surroundings. Standing about six feet three inches tall and weighing about 150 pounds, he looked like he could use a few good meals. His uncombed brown hair was thick and greasy. Thin wire-rimmed glasses with thick lenses were pulled tight against his nose. When he spoke, Cody could see his discolored teeth. His T-shirt had printing on the front that said "Apollo Hotel," and his khaki pants were wrinkled and stained. Appearance was obviously not one of his major concerns. Recognizing Cody, he said, "Where's your equipment, pal? Ain'tcha goin' back to your room?" As he said that, it was obvious that a thought popped into his head, and there was clearly plenty of room for that single thought. "Hey, wasn't you in room 313?"

"That's right," answered Cody.

"Did ya hear what happened in room 315, the room right next to yours?"

"Yes, I did. As a matter of fact, that's why I'm here. I'd like to ask you a few questions if you wouldn't mind."

Cody casually moved closer to the desk and put his hands on it.

"The cops've already drained me dry about that night, pal. I really don't know a whole lot about what happened."

"But you must have seen the victim ... uh ... Hollowell when he arrived, didn't you?"

"Yeah, I guess I did see 'im."

The clerk stood back from the desk, took out a cigarette, and began looking around for a match. When he couldn't find one, Cody took out his lighter, lit it, and held it up to the cigarette.

As the clerk inhaled, Cody went on, "How about the woman who was with him? Did you recognize her?"

"Nah, never seen 'er before."

"Wasn't Hollowell a regular here?"

"Yep! He came once or twice a month."

"Did he always have a different woman with him?"

"Mostly, though every now and then, he had a repeat. They was always knockouts though. He did okay for an old guy," the clerk said with a sneer that suggested he paid a lot more attention than he let on.

"How about the one that was with him last night? Was she a knockout, too? Can you describe her to me?" Cody took out a cigarette for himself and lit up.

"Let's see, she was every bit a knockout as the rest. She was mebbee five feet two or three inches tall, had light brown or dirty blond hair, and a terrific body. And, man, did she have the biggest boobs for a small broad, I'm tellin' you."

"Anything else? Did you see anything that was distinctive about her? Anything that stood out?"

"Yeah, din't I just tell ya?" he said with a wide leering grin as he opened his hands in front of his chest, clearly suggesting a woman's breasts. He obviously thought he made a funny remark because he then chuckled.

"That's not exactly what I meant," said Cody, trying not to get angry. *What a creep*, he thought to himself.

"I mean, like her clothes, or her walk, or something you might recognize if you saw her again."

"Ha! I'd sure know 'er if I seen 'er again. Don't you worry 'bout that. I wouldn't forget that body real soon, I can promise ya."

"Did you see her leave?"

"Nah, now that I think of it, I din't. And that's funny 'cause I din't leave the desk here all night. She must've got out by the fire 'scape or the fire stairs. I guess she din't want to be seen, considerin' what happened."

"Is there anything else you can remember?" Cody was impatient and wanted to get up to the room.

"Nah, not really."

"Okay, thanks for your help. Hey, listen, do you think you could let me into the room so I could take a little look around?"

"Ah, I can't, man. The cops shut off the room, and there's all kindsa tape across the door and everything."

"Listen, I'm an ex-cop, and if you'll give me the key, I think I'll be able to get in without disturbing anything. Nobody will know the difference."

"I told ya, I can't, man. I could get into big trouble, ya know?"

"Come on, be a sport." Cody took a $20 bill from his pocket and flashed it to the clerk. His eyes flickered, but he insisted he couldn't let Cody into the room.

"No way, man! The cops'd lock me up."

Cody took out another $20 and $10 and put the $50 on the desk in front of the clerk. He looked at it long and hard, reached out, and picked up the money. Then looking around as if to see if anybody had seen him, he reached behind and took the key off the rack. After he slid it across the desk, Cody picked it up, turned, and hurried to the elevator. Stepping in, he glanced back at the clerk who was busy trying to look busy.

Pushing the button to the third floor caused the car to lurch into action. On the way up, Cody wondered if the clerk would mention his visit to the police. He didn't think so.

CHAPTER 5

As Cody got out of the elevator, he immediately looked around, making sure there was no one there who might see him. He hurried down the hall to room 315, passing 313 on the way. Just as the clerk had said, there was yellow crime scene tape stretched from doorjamb to doorjamb. There was also a large twelve by twelve red police sticker placed right across the lock and the doorjamb. Cody knew that it would be impossible to get into the room without cutting the sticker. This, of course, would tip the police that someone had breached security. Cody looked around for another way in.

He saw the window at the end of the hall. Walking about fifteen feet to the window, he opened it and stuck his head out. The first thing he saw was the ledge, which projected out eight or nine inches from the wall. Then looking to the right, the window to room 315 could be seen. It was about six feet from where he was. He recognized that by getting out and inching along the ledge, he could reach it. Once he got there, Cody was certain he could open it and get into the room.

He wasn't sure if anything found would be worth this kind of effort, but he felt he had to try. He climbed out onto the ledge facing the wall. Holding his arms out wide and hugging the wall, he began to inch along the ledge. Fortunately, it was a calm night, and there was no wind. It took but a few minutes before Cody reached the window to the room. He could see that the lock was in the closed position. He thought that since this was an old hotel, the locks would be pretty simple to open. All he had to do was slip a credit card between the top and bottom windows near the lock and slide it across. Opening the lock was actually easier than he thought it would be. Cody pushed the window open and stepped into the room.

Cody waited for a moment, letting his eyes adjust to the dimness of the room. Like the room next door, the only illumination was from the blinking sign on the front of the building. After a few seconds, he moved toward the head of the bed.

He was hoping the piece of cord he had seen earlier was still there. It wasn't apparent at first glance. Had the cops seen it and removed it after all? Cody pushed the bed aside and pulled back the dirty shag rug, which over the years had loosened and crept up the wall. Then he saw the cord. It had slipped from the mattress, between the wall and the rug. Because the rug and the cord were similar in color, the cops, in their haste, had probably missed it. It wouldn't be the first time they had missed a piece of evidence.

He reached down and picked it up. It was a soft silky material and did look like drapery cord. The ends were finished with plastic tips, suggesting that it hadn't been cut from a long piece of cord.

It was more than likely from someone's drapes. Cody put it in his pocket and began looking around the room.

Using the small penlight from his jacket pocket, he went to the desk and began to look for anything that might help him. The desktop was clear. The police obviously had taken everything that could be of value. He quickly looked in the drawers, not really expecting to find much.

Then he went into the bathroom and noted that the toilet seat had been dusted for fingerprints. The police were thinking along the same lines as he was. He spent just a few minutes more, hastily looking about. Since he saw nothing more of interest, he decided it was time to go. Anyway, getting the cord was his first priority.

He went back to the window and climbed back onto the ledge. He closed the window and again inched his way across the ledge until he reached the hall window. Climbing back into the hall with a small sigh of relief, he closed the window and headed back down the hall. He didn't want to see the clerk again, so he decided to spend a little more time examining the fire stairs.

Using the penlight again, he examined the stairwell as carefully as he could. Between the light from the bulb in the stairwell and the penlight, he felt he did an adequate job and found nothing more of importance. When he reached the ground floor, he opened the door, which led to the south side of the building. One of the first things he noticed was an old office building across the street. It appeared to be partially occupied by the look of some of the windows.

He was surprised to find there were no people on the street or in the building since it was only 9:30 p.m. It would be highly unlikely that there would have been anyone around at three thirty or four o'clock in the morning when Hollowell's girlfriend left the hotel. He walked west to the back of the hotel, then north toward his car. Across the street to the west, there were a couple of old warehouses. This street was also dark and deserted. When he reached Fourth Street, he turned east and went to his car, got in, and drove off.

He began thinking about the piece of cord and the earring. How was he going to find the owner of each, even though he thought they probably belonged to the same person? While thinking about these things, Cody drove to the China Sea Restaurant and picked up some food for dinner. Joanna liked Chinese food a lot, and the China Sea was their favorite place. They usually had chow mien, eggs foo yung, and fried rice, which is what he ordered.

It was about 10:15 p.m. when he got home. Using the key, he let himself in quietly, just in case Joanna was still sleeping. When he walked into the kitchen, he saw Joanna brewing a pot of tea.

"Hi, honey!" he said, as he popped his head into the doorway.

"Oh, my gosh!" exclaimed Joanna, as she put her hand to her chest. She had obviously been deep in thought and had not heard him come in. "You startled me, Cody."

"I'm sorry, sweetheart. I didn't mean to scare you. I was trying to be quiet, in case you were still sleeping."

"I got up about seven thirty. When did you leave?"

"Just before then, I guess. Did you have a good nap?"

"Yes, I did. Did *you* sleep very long?"

"No, not at all. I was too anxious to get to the hotel. Look what I have." He took the cord out of his pocket and held it up to show Joanna.

"I was so worried while you were gone. I was afraid you would be caught or something."

"Nah, not a chance. I was very careful. I got in and out quickly, and no one will be the wiser."

"Did you find anything else while you were there?"

"Nope. I think Andy and his crew did a pretty thorough job, except for this cord. And this was just a fluke anyway. What's the matter with you, honey? You look upset."

"I guess I was just worried about you." As she said that, she looked away quickly.

"What's going on, Joanna? Why are you acting so queer?"

"Oh, Cody!" she sobbed, as she sat down on a chair, buried her face in her hands, and started crying.

"What is it, baby? You can tell me."

Joanna looked up into his face with tears streaming down her cheeks. She was sobbing deeply and trying to talk at the same time. Cody kneeled in front of her, put his arms around her, and tried to calm her down.

"Easy now, baby, easy. Stop crying, and tell me what's wrong. Nothing could be that bad."

"Oh, but it is," Joanna sobbed. "It is that bad."

"Tell me, then, so we can straighten it out."

"Cody, you're going to hate me. You're not going to believe me. Will you believe me?"

"Of course, I'll believe you, honey. Will you calm down now and tell me everything. I love you, baby, and I'll always love you, no matter what."

He was becoming more and more concerned. What could possibly be causing Joanna to act this way? After a few anxious moments, she answered, "Cody, it was me who was with Sam Hollowell last night." Joanna dropped her head again, so he was unable to see her eyes.

"What?" he shouted, his eyes wide with shock. "What are you saying? What do you mean it was you?"

His mind was racing with thoughts of Joanna cheating on him, going to bed with this creep, and then arriving at the unthinkable conclusion that Joanna had killed Hollowell. He continued to shout, "Joanna, what are you talking about? How could you have been with this guy? What were you thinking of? Why would you even think about something like this?"

Joanna finally looked at him. Her brown eyes were as wide as silver dollars just like a frightened deer caught in the headlights of an oncoming car. "Oh, Cody! Please don't look at me like that. Let me explain."

"Explain!" He was practically screaming. "How can you explain something like this? I thought you loved me. How could you do this to us? To our lives? To our plans? What were you thinking?"

"Cody, give me a chance to tell you the whole story."

He walked to the nearest chair and sat down without looking at Joanna. A familiar feeling of betrayal came over him. He knew he had to listen to her, but he was afraid of what he was going to hear, that he had been the brunt of a huge joke, that Joanna had fooled him into believing she really loved him, and even worse, that she was a murderer. That thought was unbearable.

Joanna was sitting silently with her eyes averted. He looked at her and said in a semicontrolled voice, "All right, Joanna, try to explain this to me so that I'll be able to comprehend it. I'll listen, but frankly, I can't see how I'm going to understand it."

"Honey! All I ask is that you give me a chance to explain. If, when I'm through, you can't understand and forgive me, I'll pack my bags and get out of your life forever."

By this time, Cody could see that Joanna was in better control of herself. He made every attempt to steel his emotions and braced himself for the worst. He said somewhat coldly, "Go ahead, I'm listening."

"I don't know exactly where to begin. Let me start with my baby sister. You remember me telling you that she died when she was seventeen years old, don't you?"

He nodded and mumbled that he did. She continued, "Well, I never told you how that happened, did I?"

Again, Cody nodded in agreement.

"She died of an overdose of cocaine. She was the sweetest kid you'd ever want to know until she met a wild boy at school. She fell in love with him or so she thought. He got her started using drugs by telling her that if she didn't, he would leave her. Before she knew it, she was hooked. Once that happened, he dumped her anyway."

Cody didn't respond, he couldn't, and the shock was still sinking in.

"She became a walking zombie from that point on," continued Joanna. "Nothing we could say or do helped. She refused to go to a rehab center. Even our priest, whom she loved, couldn't get through to her. She was so ashamed but couldn't help herself. Eventually, she ran away from home. A few months later, she was found dead in a hotel room. Do you want to know what hotel, Cody?"

Cody, whose head was down, looked up. He was about to answer when Joanna continued, "The Apollo Hotel, Cody. Does that ring a bell? Yes, the same Apollo Hotel where Samuel T. Hollowell was found dead. The same Apollo Hotel to which Samuel T. Hollowell took his lovers and his hookers."

Cody thought he could see where Joanna was heading with her story.

She proceeded to recount the events as if these had just occurred. "You see, she had become a prostitute in order to make money to feed her habit. She had become one of Hollowell's regulars. He liked them young and beautiful, and she was both of those. He also supplied her with drugs, of which he had a seemingly endless supply. He kept her coming back for more. That was his favorite trick. You see, as long as he gave her drugs, he didn't even have to pay her."

Cody was staring straight at Joanna now, his anger and hurt subsiding a little. He was beginning to see the connection. He had seen hundreds of young kids strung out on drugs during his years on the force. He knew that they often had no control over their lives once the drugs took hold. It was easy to see why Joanna would be angry. It was easier to see why she might want revenge.

"So you decided to get revenge," he said.

"Yes! I found out that she was one of his regular girls. So for the last year, I've been trying to find a way to expose him for the lowlife that he was."

"Why didn't you come to me for help? You must have known that I would have done anything to help you."

Joanna got up and began pacing back and forth, wringing her hands.

"I had already been setting things up with him when I met you. Then, I was afraid to tell you because it might spoil our relationship. Besides, I felt this was something I wanted to do. I needed to destroy this animal myself."

"So you murdered him?" he asked, still not able to believe what she was saying.

"That's just it, Cody. I didn't murder him."

"Wait a minute! You say you were with him last night."

Cody jumped up from his chair and walked quickly across the room. He was trying to comprehend what he had just heard, but his mind was not working well at this point.

"Yes, I was."

"But he was killed last night or this morning. I heard it."

"Yes, that's true. But I didn't kill him. He was alive when I left. I swear it."

Cody's thoughts shifted back to his first wife. Although she had left for a different reason, she had betrayed him. She had not honored their marriage vows. Now, he felt betrayed again, by another wife, by Joanna. His mind snapped back to the present.

"I heard you leave about 3:30 or 4:00 a.m., didn't I?"

"Yes, that is about the time I left. But I tell you, he was still alive at that time. And I'll tell you something else, he wasn't tied to the bedposts when I left."

"Are you trying to tell me that someone else went into that room after you left, tied him up, and then killed him?"

"That's what must have happened."

He was trying to believe her, but he was having a hard time. More questions followed in quick succession.

"But I was there until about six o'clock and heard nothing going on."

"Then someone must have waited until you left and gone in and done it. He was lying on the bed, drunk as a skunk, and high on cocaine when I walked out. I went down the fire stairs so that clerk wouldn't see me, got a cab, and came home." Joanna was talking faster and faster as if she had to get the whole story in before Cody walked out or something. "I knew I had to get home before you did, so I wouldn't have had time to kill him, although God knows I wanted to badly enough. So I left him like he was."

Joanna walked back to her chair and sat down again. Cody, turning to her, asked, "But you had planned to kill him, hadn't you?" He was trying to understand a side of Joanna that he had never seen nor even suspected.

"Yes, I think so, although I'm not sure. I just knew I had to do something to get even. I would have asked you, but since I had already compromised myself, I was afraid.

"If you hadn't planned on killing him, what did you think you were going to do?"

"Originally, my plan was to try to take pictures of him in a compromising position."

"Pictures, what the hell were you going to do with pictures?" Cody was thoroughly confused now and somewhat incredulous.

"Oh, I don't know, perhaps send them to his wife, or to his office, or to the newspaper, somewhere, I don't know, anywhere they would do him the greatest harm. I did bring a camera with me last night, but I didn't use it. I was so upset, I ran right out."

"Why did you have to fuck him?" he said, the anger spilling out again. He couldn't control himself.

"I didn't do that either," Joanna cried out, once again burying her face in her hands. "I only pretended I would, in order to get him to the hotel."

"But didn't I hear you undressing?" His anger and disbelief spewed out again. "And I heard him get undressed and saw him naked on the bed."

"He still had his pants on when I left. I don't know how he got undressed or how or when he was killed. Cody, you've got to believe me."

By this time, Cody was thoroughly confused. Even though he was angry, he still wanted to believe her. He felt that he still loved her, and because of his feelings, he wanted to help her because she was going to need it.

"All right, Joanna, let me get my thoughts together." He walked slowly across the room, tugging on his earlobe, his mind trying to sift through all the information it had just received.

Joanna was the woman in the room. Hollowell was killed in the room. Joanna says she didn't do it. He was inclined to believe her. If that was the case, then someone else had to have done it. Who?

Why? He remembered the earring and the drapery cord. The earring certainly wasn't Joanna's because she didn't have pierced ears. There were no drapes in this house; therefore, the cord must have belonged to someone else.

That Joanna was probably telling the truth about the murder seemed more reasonable to him now. But what was the truth about her having sex with that creep Hollowell? He wanted to believe that she hadn't.

Cody looked at her from across the room. She looked so fragile and helpless as she sat sobbing. He knew she would never cheat on him purely for the sex. She might go through with it, though, to draw Hollowell into some compromising plot because of his role in the death of her kid sister. Cody knew he would have to put that behind him for now. She needed his help.

He decided to worry about it later since the immediate problem was this murder and who did it. Another question crossed his mind, and that was how to let Andy Perone know about this.

Joanna was definitely the woman in the room. Andy, undoubtedly, would find out about Joanna. It would be harder on Joanna if he did. Should he get a lawyer and bring Joanna to the station before Andy did find out? Would Andy be as anxious to believe Joanna as he was?

He suddenly realized he was dead tired. His mind wasn't working as smoothly as usual.

"Okay, Joanna, I want you to know that I do believe that you didn't kill Hollowell. I also want to believe that you didn't have sex with him. So let's relax a little, get something to eat, and decide what we're going to do next. Okay?"

"Okay, whatever you say."

Joanna leaped toward Cody and threw her arms around him. She buried her face in his chest and began crying again. Pulling her tightly against him, his feeling toward her still there, he kissed her on the top of her head.

*   *   *   *

They had finished eating, although neither of them ate very much. Not a whole lot had been said during the meal. Cody was still trying to decide what to do, and Joanna was probably trying to understand what she had gotten herself into. It was now 11:30 p.m. They were both very tired.

"Let's go to bed now and sleep on this mess. Our minds will be clearer in the morning, and we'll be able to think better."

"Yes," Joanna agreed, "we'll both feel better in the morning."

They went upstairs, undressed, and got into bed.

CHAPTER 6

Cody woke up first. He hadn't really slept well anyway, tossing and turning throughout the night. Each time he woke up, his mind was filled with thoughts of Joanna being in the same room with Hollowell, of the noises he had heard, of the murder, of the murderer, whoever that was. He turned his head to look at Joanna. She was still sleeping. Getting out of bed, he went downstairs and started brewing some coffee. A few minutes later, Joanna came into the kitchen in her shorty pajamas. He always thought she looked great in those.

"Good morning, sweetheart," yawned Joanna.

"Hi," said Cody subdued. He had not quite gotten over the news of last night.

"How do you feel this morning, honey?" asked Joanna.

"Okay, I guess. I just didn't sleep very well, that's all. How are you doing?"

"All right. Can you pour me a cup of that coffee?" Joanna walked over to the counter with her cup.

"Sure," he said as he poured the coffee. "I've been thinking about our next move. It seems to me that we ought to get hold of Andy and tell him the whole story."

"Why?" Joanna snapped. "He'll never know I was there. Anyway, since I'm not the one who killed Hollowell, why do we have to tell him anything?"

Cody went to the table and sat down. As he was lighting up a cigarette, he said, "Because, in the first place, it's the right thing to do. In the second place, it's precisely because you didn't do it that we should tell him. And in the third place, he's likely to find out anyway. He is a good cop. If we don't come forward, it will look like we have something to hide.

"But he'll put me in jail, won't he?" Joanna was obviously upset by that thought.

"There's nothing to be afraid of. You're innocent, aren't you? And besides, if he does arrest you, we can always get you out on bail."

Cody felt sure Andy would help Joanna. They had been partners, hadn't they? Besides, he was sure she was innocent.

"Do you really think so?"

"He probably won't even put you under arrest. He'll review the facts and just ask you to stick around town. But if we don't tell him and he finds out on his own, it'll really look bad."

"How can he find out? I didn't leave any clues."

"What about fingerprints? Did you remember to clean up any of the prints you may have left?"

"How would he know they were my prints?"

"Have you ever been printed?"

"Oh, I hadn't thought of that," said Joanna. She looked up suddenly, as if she had just remembered something.

"I was fingerprinted when I took the job as court stenographer. Anyone who works for county must be fingerprinted. I had forgotten about that."

"Well, the police will be able to trace them with no trouble at all. That's why we have to go to Andy first."

"I guess you're right. But I can't help being afraid anyway. The thought of being locked in a jail cell has always been one of my biggest fears."

"I know, but don't worry, I'm going to get to the bottom of this. Now, let's go over all the facts. Try to remember them as accurately as possible. How many times were you with him?"

Joanna turned away from Cody and poured herself another cup of coffee. He could see that she didn't want to look at him directly. And every time the subject of Joanna and Hollowell came up, his mind conjured up thoughts of the two of them in bed.

"Just a few times, once or twice for a drink after work, and occasionally, after court, kind of a come-on thing, you know, just to get him interested, and then last night."

"What did you talk about?"

"Most of it was nonsense. He was trying to impress me. He talked about his cars and his boat and the fact that he had a lot of contacts, both legal and illegal."

"What kind of illegal contacts? Did he tell you who he knew or where he got his cocaine?"

He stood up and walked to the window. His sixth sense was telling him there might be a connection between Hollowell's murder and drug dealers. A likely scenario would be that Hollowell had pissed them off, and they simply killed him.

"No, he didn't mention any names that I can remember, although he did hint that he had some underworld connections."

"What exactly did he say about the underworld?"

"Well, he said that he had defended some mob boys and that they occasionally paid him off with drugs or, sometimes, tips about sporting events so that he could bet on them and make some money." Joanna looked up as if trying to recall more of their conversations.

"He also said that they had connections in the courts. Wasn't he arrogant to tell me all that? I guess he thought that I would be so impressed that I wouldn't say anything to anyone."

His head snapped around to face Joanna again. If Hollowell had associations with people who could control the courts, he thought that could possibly spell trouble, down the line, for Joanna.

"Did he say that they controlled some of the judges? Did he mention any names?"

"He never told me any of their names. Do you know that he even bragged about his being married? He seemed proud of the fact that he was cheating and was getting away with it."

"Yeah, I know. Remember, the creep was so cocky that he had me following his wife. Now, didn't you say that he was high on cocaine last night?"

"Yes! I saw him snort some, after we got into his car to go to the hotel. He even offered me some, but I turned him down. Why?" Joanna asked curiously.

She is so naïve, Cody thought. *It was easy to see how this fast-talking shyster could dupe her.*

"I was just wondering if the mob might have had something to do with this thing. You know, when you fool around with those type of people, you can sometimes get hurt. It's possible that he somehow screwed up, and they set him up." Cody was really getting into it now. The thoughts were emerging one after another.

"At first, I thought it was a woman who killed him. But now that I know you were the woman who was with him, I'm not so sure. It could have been anybody who went there after you left and did him."

The mob connection was appealing to Cody more and more because they had the power, the means, and probably the motive.

"But you did find an earring."

His mind quickly filtered the facts, as he knew them, and the earring and the drapery cord still bothered him.

"Yeah, that's true, but, but hell, they could've been planted as decoys, or maybe they sent a woman to do it."

"You mean, a hit woman?"

"Why not? Haven't you said yourself that some people will do anything for that white powder? Did you notice anything unusual when you left the hotel?"

"No, not really. I was so anxious to get out of there that I went out the fire stairs door and rushed to the corner to flag a taxi cab."

A cab? wondered Cody, *In that neighborhood? At that hour of the morning?*

"Didn't you have trouble getting a cab? That area is so deserted, I would have thought you'd be waiting there all night."

"You know, I never gave it a thought, but a cab did pull up almost immediately."

"What kind of cab was it?"

"It was a Yellow Cab."

"Can you remember anything else about the cab?"

"I remember the number of the cab."

"Really! How the hell can you remember that?" he wondered how she could recall the number in her state of anxiety.

"Because it is the same as our ages, 3528. And the driver was a foreigner, an Arab or Greek, someone with a swarthy complexion and a thick accent."

This excited Cody. At least it was somewhere to get started. He walked back to the counter and poured himself a second cup of coffee.

"This is great. I have a place to start. Someone must have had the cab waiting there for you so he or she—let's say he for the sake of argument—would know when you left. He would also have to know when I left. So he must have been nearby."

"So you think this whole thing was planned?"

"No doubt about it. And carefully! The killer must have known about my surveillance and Hollowell's date with you." Cody was rolling now. "If I can find the cab driver, maybe he can tell me who hired him to pick you up. I'll get right on it, as soon as we go see

Andy. Why don't you go take your shower, and I'll try to reach Andy at his office."

"Okay," said Joanna, obviously still not sure she wanted to do this, "if you think it's the right thing to do."

"It's the only smart thing to do, trust me. Now, go get your shower."

Joanna quickly left the kitchen and went upstairs, while Cody went outside to get the morning paper. He hurriedly scanned the front page for any news about the murder. There, at the bottom of the page, was an article reporting the ongoing police investigation. It included the fact that the police claimed to have no significant leads.

Cody wanted to see Andy first. He also thought he would contact Harvey Whitcomb, a lawyer friend of his. It would be necessary that a lawyer accompany Joanna when they went downtown. He felt sure that Andy would go easy on Joanna out of deference to him, but he wasn't going to take any chances.

After taking care of Joanna, he would go to the Yellow Cab dispatch station and try to locate that cab driver. That shouldn't be too hard since he had the cab's number and a fairly adequate description of the driver.

Once he determined where that information might lead him, he would have to make it his business to go to see Mrs. Hollowell. He had a few things to talk to her about: number one, the fee, which the victim had never paid him; number two, he would like to get access to Hollowell's office to see what he could find out about his business dealings and maybe about his girlfriends. Since Mrs. Hollowell appeared to be a lady, she might be cooperative.

It was 10:30 a.m. as he contemplated calling Harvey Whitcomb before he called Andy. He decided to take a shower before he made all the calls. He was reading the paper as Joanna came back into the kitchen. He told her of his plans for the day and reminded her to call in sick or something since they would probably be tied up all day. He also told her about calling Harvey.

"All right, honey, I'll do that right now. But why do you think I'll need a lawyer?" she asked anxiously. "You said you thought Andy would go easy on me."

"I do, but it doesn't hurt to be cautious. The law is a funny thing, and I'd like to have a smart lawyer there to help us. I'm going up and take my shower now. You relax until I'm finished, and then we'll get started."

Cody had been in the shower stall for about five minutes when he heard Joanna calling to him from the bedroom. Her voice sounded frightened. He turned off the water and opened the shower stall door. At that moment, Joanna rushed in, crying hysterically.

"Cody, come quickly! Andy's here to arrest me."

"What! Andy's here? Take it easy a minute. Let me dry off and put something on. Wait here with me."

As he was drying, his mind was racing again. Andy must have found Joanna's prints at the hotel. *That was quick,* he thought. But then, with the computer programs for fingerprint comparisons they have now, it doesn't take long to match prints. And since Joanna's prints were on file, it wasn't all that surprising after all. He finished drying as quickly as he could, put on his jockey shorts and robe, grabbed Joanna by the hand, and went downstairs.

"What's going on, Andy?" asked Cody, as he and Joanna walked into the kitchen where Andy was waiting with two uniformed policemen.

"Well, Cody, I've some distressing news for you. We've found Joanna's fingerprints all over the murder scene at the Apollo Hotel. Can you or Joanna explain that?"

"I think we'll be able to explain it to your satisfaction. Just give us a minute. And would you mind asking your bodyguards to wait outside." He was a little annoyed that Andy felt it necessary to bring two cops along with him.

"Okay, fellas, wait outside for me. I'll call when and if I need ya."

Andy then turned to Cody and said, "It's strictly procedure, Cody. You know the drill. You ought to be thankful that I came personally. Ordinarily, I would've just sent the uniforms."

Then, turning to Joanna, he said, "Joanna, I must make you aware of your rights. You have the right to remain silent . . ." Andy droned through the rest of the routine, which he had repeated so many times before.

Cody thought, *At least he's not going to handcuff her.* That would be the last straw.

"Geez, Andy, this is Joanna and I. Don't we deserve to be treated a little differently?"

"You know I can't give special treatment to anyone. It would look funny to the internal affairs boys. Besides, this is a murder case, and there's a lot of noise from upstairs on this one."

Cody's thoughts jumped back to what Joanna had said about Hollowell's connections with the mob, and their connections to the judicial system, and the police department. He could remember from his days as a cop that, on occasion, some very specific orders would come from administration.

One particular case came to mind. It was when he and Andy were investigating a murder that appeared to be an open and shut case. Andy had come to him and said, "Word just came from upstairs that we'll have to be extra careful on this one."

"What do you mean, 'be extra careful'? We've practically got this thing sewed up right now. You know as well as I that it was that smalltime hood, Sam Varrella."

"Yeah, I know. But we'll have to just take it a little easy. Somebody must have some big time juice upstairs. I've been told to slow down."

"Come on, Andy, when did we ever pay attention to that kind of crap?"

"Sometimes you just have to listen," Andy replied.

"Sometimes you just can't make waves, ya know? Anyway, what's the big deal? This guy is nothing in the scheme of things."

This kind of thing was not common, but it did suggest that Andy, although honest, could succumb to pressure. Andy might play the game, particularly if it meant a promotion.

Cody, returning to the present, said to Andy, "Will you just give me a chance to call our lawyer?" clearly becoming more annoyed.

"Okay, but hurry it up," snapped Andy.

Cody thought that Andy must have been given some very specific orders to cause him to be acting like this.

"I thought we're supposed to be friends," Cody said half sarcastically.

"We are, but orders are orders."

Cody shook his head in his confusion and quickly went to the phone to dial Harvey Whitcomb, a long-time friend and associate. Cody had done a lot of investigation work for Harvey over the years and knew he was a good defense attorney. He could be counted on for help at any time.

Harvey was a tall thin man with thick curly brown hair. He wore thick black horn-rimmed glasses and usually wore a very conservative Brooks Brothers suit. Cody often used Harvey for his sounding board while working on a case. Harvey was the voice of reason, while Cody's thoughts would fly off in all directions.

He had known Harvey since his days on the force. They had met while Cody was testifying at a murder trial. Harvey was a young assistant district attorney at the time. That was twelve years ago. Harvey still had that same unruly hair, wore the same kind of horn-rimmed glasses, and still dressed conservatively.

He was a graduate of Yale Law School. Even though he was a New Yorker, he still retained a hint of the New England accent he had picked up while at school. He was a good lawyer and a good man. Cody trusted him.

A female voice answered at Harvey's office, "Law office of Harvey Whitcomb. Can I help you?"

"Hello, Thelma, this is Cody Thomas. Is Harvey there?"

"Oh, hi, Cody. He's not here right now, but I expect him any minute. Do you want me to have him call you?"

"Aw, shit!" spat out Cody. "I really need him badly. Can you have him come right down to the police station, as soon as possible?"

"The police station!" exclaimed Thelma. "Are you in some kind of trouble?"

Cody was in no mood to be answering any questions right now. He responded to Thelma in a terse and somewhat annoyed tone, "Yes, I am. Just tell him I need him Desperately, okay?"

"All right, Cody, as soon as he gets in. What station?" Thelma was being more professional and less personal. This made Cody happier.

"The thirty-ninth precinct."

"All right, just as soon as he gets here."

Cody heard the phone click. He put the receiver down and turned to Joanna, who, by this time, was clearly petrified.

"He'll be right there, honey." Then he turned to Andy. "Let me throw on some clothes, and we can go."

"As quickly as you can, we've fooled around long enough."

Andy was really uptight, Cody thought, not like the former partner he remembered. Andy also appeared uncomfortable, like it wasn't something he was relishing.

He must really be under some pressure. But why was pressure being applied? Was Hollowell that important? Who could be pulling the strings?

Cody finished dressing and returned to the kitchen where Andy and Joanna were waiting. He looked at Andy.

"Okay, let's go." He reached out and took Joanna's hand as they walked out the front door. He could feel that her hands were cold and sweaty. His anger and disappointment had subsided as he said gently, "Don't worry, Joanna, Harvey will meet us at the station and straighten this whole thing out."

"I hope so. I don't think I could stand being in a jail cell," she replied. Cody could feel her hand squeeze his, even more tightly than before.

CHAPTER 7

When they reached the station, Cody got out of the car first. He turned and gave Joanna his hand as she slid toward the door. As they reached the main room of the station house, Cody looked around anxiously for Harvey. He was hoping that Harvey had gotten to the station before them.

The room was large and was bustling with considerable activity. There was the high desk behind which the sergeant sat. He was busy directing traffic and telling other cops and their prisoners where to go. Harvey was nowhere to be found.

Cody began to panic because he knew Joanna would disintegrate quickly if Harvey didn't arrive soon. Andy directed them across the large room, toward the elevator. They stepped into the car and rode to the third floor where Andy took them to a small interrogation room.

Cody was quite familiar with these rooms, having used them many times himself. Inside the room were two chairs and a large table with a microphone on it. One wall was composed essentially of a large window. Andy motioned to Joanna.

"Sit down, Joanna. Make yourself comfortable."

"Comfortable! Are you kidding? How can anyone be comfortable in a place like this?"

"Well, I mean as comfortable as possible. I just need to ask you a few questions. Cody, you'll have to leave."

"Can't I wait in here with Joanna until our lawyer gets here? She's not going to answer any questions until then anyhow."

He felt since Andy was following the book, he would be a careful as possible. There was no sense in letting Joanna answer any questions in her present state of mind. Besides, it certainly appeared as though someone was anxious to let Joanna take the fall for this case.

"I thought you were gonna be able to explain everything rather easily. Why do ya think your lawyer has to be here?"

"Yeah, I think we can, but since you're being so tight-assed about this, I thought we had better be careful."

Cody spit that comment out without a smile, hoping that Andy would see just how ridiculous his attitude appeared.

"Look, Cody, I don't mean to be a prick, and I'm sorry to upset you and Joanna, but this guy Hollowell must've had some big time drag downtown. The commissioner called the captain this morning and told him to get a move on. When he found out we had prints, he wanted action fast. I asked him to let me handle the arrest personally because we're friends."

"Well, friends shouldn't treat friends the way you're treating us. This has upset the hell out of Joanna. You know she's not capable of this kind of thing, don't you?"

"Sure, I do. But like I said, her prints are all over the crime scene. How'd they get there, and why are they there?"

"We'll explain that in due time."

Just then Harvey came in through the door breathlessly. He had just run up three flights of stairs. His hair, always unkempt, was even worse now. There were small beads of sweat on his upper lip.

"Cody, I got here as soon as I could. What the hell's going on here? What have you gotten yourself into now? Wait, don't say anything yet. Who is this?" he said, pointing his thumb at Andy.

"That's Lt. Andy Perone of the thirty-ninth precinct, Homicide Division."

"Homicide? What have you got to do with a homicide? Excuse me, Lieutenant, but may I talk to my client alone please."

Andy stood up and began walking to the door, saying, "Sure, you can."

"What about this microphone on the table? Is it turned on?"

"No, it isn't."

"Well, can you get it out of here anyway, or give us a room with a little more privacy."

"What's the matter? Don't you trust us?" Andy asked, with half a smile on his face. He knew damn well that this lawyer was not going to allow any chance of someone overhearing his conversation.

"You can use the consultation room down the hall. There are no electronic devices there."

"That's fine," said Harvey, obviously more relaxed since he took control of the situation. He turned to Cody and Joanna. "Let's go."

They left the room quickly and walked down the hall to the consultation room. After entering the room, Joanna sat down, but Cody and Harvey remained standing—Cody because he was nervous, and Harvey because he hardly ever sat down.

"All right, Cody, tell me exactly what happened. Who was killed, and how are you supposed to have done it?"

"Harvey, it's not me who's under suspicion, it's Joanna."

"Joanna? Holy cow! What are you talking about? How can Joanna be accused of murder?"

Cody began to recount to Harvey the whole complicated mess from the beginning. He included the business about Hollowell's darker side. Harvey was somewhat familiar with him, mostly by reputation, although he had met him on occasion at various functions. When Cody was finished, Harvey spoke.

"We can talk to the lieutenant now. Joanna, you'll answer only the questions I say you can answer. Don't volunteer any information unless I say it's okay."

"All right, Harvey. But I'm so frightened. What do you think they'll do to me?"

"More than likely, they'll want to put you in jail until the arraignment, when they will formally charge you with the murder. Then we'll be able to ask for bail."

"Do you mean I'll have to stay in here? In a cell? Overnight?"

Joanna was clearly panicking now. Cody knew he was going to have to get her out as soon as possible.

"Well, only as long as it takes to raise bail. This is a capital murder case, and they usually do that under these circumstances," replied Harvey.

"Oh, Cody!" Joanna broke down crying again. "I guess I can make it overnight, but you must do something as quickly as possible. Otherwise, I don't think I'll be able to stand this too long."

"Try to put up with it for tonight, honey. I'll talk to Andy, okay?"

He was skeptical about Andy being helpful; nevertheless, he would try to play on Andy's friendship. Hopefully, he could convince Andy that Joanna would not disappear, and he would let her go home.

They left the consultation room and walked back to the interrogation room where Andy was talking to a uniformed policeman.

"We're ready to answer your questions now, Lieutenant." Harvey was completely in charge now.

"All right, let's get started."

Andy seemed a bit friendlier. Cody sure hoped he was anyway.

*   *   *   *

Andy led Joanna and Harvey into the interrogation room. Harvey said to Cody, "Don't worry. I'll take good care of her. We'll probably be tied up for a couple hours. Where can I reach you when we're done?"

"I'll be doing a few things. Why don't I come back in two hours? If you're finished sooner, you can just wait until I get back, okay?"

"Okay. We'll see what we can do about bail at the arraignment."

"Great! You know how Joanna feels about spending time in a cell."

After Harvey and Joanna went into the interrogation room, Cody hurried down the stairs, instead of taking the elevator. As his first order of business, he was going to try to find the cab driver. He hurried through the large entry hall to the front door and out to his car.

As he drove to the Yellow Cab dispatch building, his thoughts drifted back to Joanna. He knew she couldn't have killed Hollowell, but after due consideration, he was less than confident that she hadn't had sex with him. The fact that Joanna had even considered any kind of retaliation definitely surprised Cody. He didn't think she was capable of that kind of mindset. Cody seriously doubted that she would have been able to carry out the act, when it came right down to it. Upon further reflection, he decided she wouldn't have.

He thought to himself, *If not Joanna, then who?* If he could find out who sent the cab to pick up Joanna, at least he would know if it had been a man or a woman. Then he would see Mrs. Hollowell and try to get into the old man's office records.

In Cody's mind, the murderer was probably somehow connected to the mob. After all, they usually didn't think twice about killing somebody, especially if it had something to do with drugs or money. But he couldn't get that earring and the drapery cord out of his mind. These things made it look like a woman. However, strangling was not a female thing. She certainly would have to have been pretty strong and pretty vicious. Or maybe, she was just angry.

Cody parked the car in front of the dispatch building and got out. He walked in and located the head dispatcher who was seated in a cage, behind a screen. There were about ten cabs parked in the garage in various stages of repair. He went up to the cage and introduced himself to the dispatcher.

"Hi, I'm Cody Thomas. I wonder if I could get some information about one of your drivers?"

"What kinda information?" asked the dispatcher, obviously annoyed. "Who are you anyway? And why should I answer your questions?" he said sounding like a pompous fool.

Cody kept his temper under control. He knew he had to stay on the right side of this guy, so he calmly answered.

"I'm just a customer whose wife lost her handbag in one of your cabs the other night. I'm trying to find the cab and the driver to see if he knows anything about it."

"Oh," the dispatcher responded with a little less hostility. "Do you know the guy's name?"

"No, but I know the cab number and the time she was in his cab."

"Give me the number, and I'll see what I can do for ya."

"The number is 3528. He picked her up at around three thirty or four o'clock in the morning, near the Apollo Hotel at Fourth and Walnut, in Old Town."

"Give me a minute to look at the time sheets. But I'm still not sure if I should do this."

The dispatcher, who was downright scruffy looking, with a day-old beard and a dirty shirt, stared at Cody for a moment, and then chuckled to himself as he typed the information into the computer.

He stared intently at the screen until he found the time and cab number. "Here it is. The guy's name is Agit Mustafa. He picked her up at 3:45 a.m. But you wanna know something, he was dispatched there."

"You mean, he was sent there, specifically to pick up a fare, at that time?"

"Yup, that's exactly what I mean."

"Who sent him? And who ordered the cab?" Cody was getting truly excited now. This looked like it might be a hot trail to follow.

"Ah, let's see, that would be the 11:00 p.m. to 7:00 a.m. dispatcher. His name is Joe . . . uh, Joe Johnston."

"Would he know who ordered the cab?" Cody kept firing the questions. He felt this information could lead him to the killer or killers.

"He might. But then again, he might not. Maybe he don't remember but maybe wrote down the phone number of the people who called in."

"Is there some way I can talk to either one of them?"

"Let's see. Johnston lives over on the West Side. I don't know exactly where. We hardly see each other at all. And I don't know anything about Mustafa. He just hired on last week. You know, these guys come and go like the wind."

"Can I get the address from the personnel office?"

"I don't know. They probably won't give out anybody's home address without permission. But you know what, I got an emergency number for Johnston."

"You do? That's great! Can you let me have it?"

Cody knew when he said that, this guy would try to yank his chain again, and he was right.

"I'm not supposed to give that out, ya know. It's a private number."

Cody took some money out of his pocket and let him see it.

"Are you sure you can't let me have it? I promise I won't tell anybody where I got it."

He unfolded a $20 bill and slid it toward him. The dispatcher took the money, wrote the number on a scrap of paper, and pushed it toward Cody.

"'Ey, there's no point in you coming back no more 'cause I got nothing else to say."

"Thanks for the help. I might be back, if I can't locate Johnston or Mustafa."

"I'm telling you, there's no use in coming back, man. I got nothing else to give ya."

"Well, you never know. See you."

Cody looked at his watch. An hour had passed since he left Joanna and Harvey at the station. He thought he had time to look up Johnston's address in a phone book and maybe even get over to see him. After all, he was more important than Mustafa. Johnston could know who made the call or, at least, the number of the person. That would put him on the right track.

He went to his car and began to drive until he found a public phone. Pulling up to it, he got out of his car and walked to the tattered phone book. Quickly leafing back to the Johnstons, Cody ran his finger down the list of names until he found Joseph. Then he followed across until he found the number the dispatcher had given him. After locating the address, he quickly jotted it down.

He decided to try the number and see if Johnston was home. He got back to his car and used his cell phone to make the call. The phone rang on the other end seven or eight times, but there was no answer. He wondered if Johnston was sleeping and couldn't hear the ringing, or if he was just out. Clicking off the phone, he decided it was time to go to the station to see if Andy had finished with Joanna.

CHAPTER 8

When Cody arrived at the station, Harvey and Joanna were no longer in the interrogation room. Torn between anger and anxiety, he hurried to Andy's office, which was in the back of a very large square room, perhaps forty feet by forty feet. The walls were covered with corkboards filled with information about wanted criminals. There were fifteen to twenty desks, which were used by the detectives, scattered through the room without any specific decorative idea in mind. The desks were a mixture of neatness and sloppiness according to the personalities of the detectives using them. There were detectives in various stages of activity: some on the phone, some at the many filing cabinets lined up against the walls, some drinking coffee, and others just talking about who knows what.

This room was familiar to Cody since he had spent eight years of his life working out of one of the desks that cluttered the room. The hustle and bustle was unchanged, and the sight and smell brought back many memories, both good and bad.

Suddenly, Cody was transported back to the days when he worked in this same room. He was standing in front of a filing cabinet looking at a file on a local thief, Willy the second-story man. Cody had been given a cold case file that had been sitting around for a year or so. Someone had broken into a house and taken money and jewelry and disappeared. Now, after all this time, some of the jewelry began turning up in pawn shops around the city. Cody had immediately thought of Willy since this was his kind of job. After rereading the file and noting where Willy hung out, Cody was out the door hurrying to a bar, which Willy was known to frequent. Cody was lucky that day because he found Willy, brought him into the station, and after some routine questioning, was able to elicit a confession. For this, Cody was promoted to the detective bureau, which is where exactly he wanted to be.

Returning to present, Cody looked around at the faces of the detectives working there now; he wondered who, if anyone, was on the take. Cody could see Andy through the large glass window in the wall, separating him from the rest of the detectives. As Andy looked up, he saw Cody and waved him in.

"Where's Joanna?" Cody had his hands on his hips as he stood in front of Andy's desk.

"She's with your lawyer in the consultation room. Sit down, Cody, and relax a little."

As he sat down, he noticed that Andy seemed less uptight, so he decided to be less abrasive.

"How did the interrogation go? Are you satisfied with Joanna's explanation?"

"I was only able to get bits and pieces since your lawyer allowed me very little latitude. She admitted she was in the room with Hollowell, but claims he was alive when she left."

"Yes, that's true. What else do you need? You don't really think she could've killed him, do you?"

"Look, Cody, she's your wife, and I can understand your willingness to believe her story completely. But look at this through my eyes. It's not so clear-cut. We've got all kinds of things, some of which are hers, like fingerprints, and we have other things that we should be able to match up, like hair, fibers, lipstick traces, footprints, and some stains that look like bodily fluids. And so far, we're not able to put anyone else in the room. How do you expect me to ignore that kind of evidence?"

When Cody heard Andy say "bodily fluids," he recoiled and almost lost his train of thought. The fact that bodily fluids were found suggested that Hollowell probably had sex with someone on that bed. And Joanna was there. The pictures his mind conjured up were so repulsive that Cody quickly tried to push them from his thoughts. Distractedly, he said to Andy, "Does this mean you're going to charge her?"

"I really don't have a choice, Cody. If this weren't your wife, you'd see that I have no choice."

"When will she be arraigned?"

"This afternoon, in Judge Richter's court."

"Do you have any idea how much the bail will be?"

"I don't know. That'll be up to the assistant district attorney and the judge. It is a capital case, ya know. The bail could be substantial."

"But she's innocent, and she's never been in trouble before. I could guarantee she won't run away. You know I don't have big bucks, and she'll never be able to stand it in jail."

"It's not up to me. If it were, I'd let her go home with you."

Cody was getting frantic. Not only had the thought of Joanna screwing Hollowell been brought back to his consciousness, but he was also forced to wonder again about her committing the murder. If she'd lied about the sex, she could be lying about the murder too. As he turned to leave the room, he asked, "What time is court in session?"

"It starts at two o'clock."

Andy seemed much more like his old self, which made things a little easier to accept. "Try to relax, pal. I'll do my best to help when I can. I don't know what I'll be able to do, but I'll try, okay?"

"Thanks. I'll count on that. See you later."

Cody left Andy's office and went as quickly as he could to the consultation room. As he walked there, his mind summoned pictures of Joanna and Hollowell together in that sleazy hotel room. They were thoughts he'd never dreamed of having about Joanna. His first marriage was a bust because Maryann couldn't accept his work and lifestyle. But this was an entirely different matter.

He really hadn't known that much about Joanna before they were married. They had a whirlwind affair and quick marriage. Because he was so in love with her and so pleased he had won her, nothing else had seemed to matter.

Now, he was faced with her possible and probable infidelity, and he was having difficulty handling it. He hadn't believed she could be a murderer, but he wasn't so sure about it now. Could she have done it? The thought was repugnant to him. He tried to dismiss it from his mind as he walked in and saw Harvey consoling Joanna.

She was crying loudly and sobbing so deeply that her body virtually shook. Cody walked quickly to her and pulled her to her feet. His first thought was to confront her with his newly revived suspicions, but then he held back and decided to wait until they were alone.

"Don't cry, Joanna. We'll get this all straightened out, don't worry."

He said this more with a professional attitude than that of a husband who was concerned about his wife. He didn't want to sound indifferent, but he couldn't help himself.

"Oh, Cody," Joanna sobbed, as she lifted her head up and looked into his face. "What are we going to do? Andy and Harvey think I may have to stay in jail."

"Only until I can post bail. That probably won't even be a couple of hours, then you'll come home with me."

With that said, he turned and walked away from Joanna. He couldn't get the thoughts of her killing that old scumbag out of his mind. The idea of her having sex with him was so outrageous it took all his willpower not to grab her and shake the truth out of her.

As he turned back to look at Joanna, she asked, "How did I ever get into this mess? What was I thinking of?"

Cody walked over to the table in the center of the room and leaned on it.

"Harve, what do you think the bail will be set at?"

"It all depends on the judge's attitude. If he feels that there is a big risk of Joanna leaving town, or if he feels strongly about her guilt, he could go high, perhaps five hundred thousand to a million. But my guess is, he'll go easy and make it one to two hundred thousand."

"It's one thirty now," Cody said, glancing at his watch. "Court starts at two o'clock. What'll we do for the next half hour?"

"It will probably take that long for that detective to print Joanna and formally book her. Then we can all go over to the courthouse. You might as well call Perone and get the booking over with."

"Okay, I'll get him," Cody said, walking toward the door. He looked back and saw Joanna leaning forward with her face buried in her hands, crying loudly. As she looked up at Cody, he could see the giant tears streaming down her face with her eyes red-rimmed and widened with fear. Her shoulders were hunched forward, giving her the appearance of someone who had done hard labor for many years.

She sniffed back a stream of thin clear liquid running from her nose, which was irritated from her frequent rubbing. Reaching into her handbag, she pulled out a tissue and began trying to clean herself up, but the tears continued despite her efforts.

Cody was torn between his anger and the sorrow he felt for her. He walked over to her and touched her shoulder gently.

"Try to hang on, Joanna. I'll get us through this mess somehow."

Joanna stood up and buried her face in his chest sobbing. "I know you will, but I'm just so frightened."

"Of course, you are. I'm going to get Andy. You try to relax now." Then, looking at Harvey, he continued, "Keep her calm while I'm gone."

"Okay," Harvey replied as he moved closer to Joanna.

*　　*　　*　　*

Joanna and Harvey stood behind a table facing Judge Richter. An assistant district attorney stood behind a tall lectern to the side of the judge. The bailiff read the charges, murder in the first degree, as well as other related charges. The judge asked in a rather bored tone, "How do you plead?"

Joanna replied, "Not guilty," so softly as to cause the judge to say, "Speak up, please. The court can't hear you."

"Not guilty," said Joanna a second time, this time a little louder, but with an equal amount of timidity. Harvey was supporting her with his arm around her waist.

"What are you suggesting in the way of bail, Counsel?"

"Your Honor, my client has never been accused of any crime, let alone a felony. And she certainly has never been convicted of anything. She has strong ties to the city: a husband, a family, and a job with the court, I might add. Therefore, I would ask the court to release my client on her own recognizance."

"What do the people have to say about that?"

"Your Honor, this is capital murder," said an assistant district attorney. "A man has been killed, and there is sufficient evidence against this suspect to warrant no bail at all. We would, therefore, suggest to the court that she be remanded to the city jail until the trial."

"Don't you think that's a little harsh, in view of the fact that she has no record? However, I am sympathetic to the people's feelings. Bail is set at $300,000. Next case." The judge banged his gavel and sat back.

Joanna's mouth dropped open; she appeared to be in a state of shock. The tears, which had ceased, were again rolling down her cheeks. A uniformed policewoman came up to her and took hold of her arm. Cody jumped up to Joanna and put his arms around her to try to quiet her.

"Don't worry! I'll get the money and have you out of here just as soon as I can."

"But where are you going to get that kind of money?"

"I'll get a bail bondsman. We only have to come up with 10 percent of the bail. I can put the house up as collateral. It won't take me long. Just try to stay calm until I get it done."

"Okay, but hurry, please."

Cody watched Joanna being led away by the policewoman. He knew he had to get her out as quickly as possible, so he wasted no time in heading to a bail bondsman. There were many of them located close to the courthouse. These guys were available all the time for just such emergencies.

Cody went directly to the nearest building that housed these characters, about half a block away. It was a dirty, dilapidated old stone building common to the neighborhood. It was ten stories high and had twelve windows across the front, presumably representing two for each office. The gray stones were stained from the years of car exhaust, dirt, and rain. The window frames had probably not been painted in five years, and they looked it. There was an old rusted fire escape extending from the roof to the first floor. That, too, was clearly untouched for some time. The sight of the building did not bother Cody, however, since his only thought at this time was to get Joanna out of jail as quickly as possible.

For no good reason, he picked out the name of Myron Metz from the directory on the wall. His office was on the second floor.

Since the elevator looked very old and run-down, Cody decided to use the stairs. Reaching the second floor, he walked down the hall to room 204. The door had a window made of smoked glass with the name "Myron Metz, Bail Bondsman" printed in fading black lettering.

As he walked in, an old mahogany desk, which was near the back wall, was immediately visible. It was covered with piles of papers and magazines. Sitting behind the desk was a fat short bald man with a half-smoked cigar in his mouth. The smell of stale cigar smoke saturated the room. The office, the man, the smell, and the whole idea of being there sickened Cody.

"What can I do for you, friend?" he asked, as he looked up from the daily racing form.

"I need to get bail for my wife," Cody replied. He was a little unsure of himself since he had never been in this situation before. He had never had to get anyone out of jail. His job was to put them in.

"How much do you need?"

"$300,000."

"Wow! This case must be a whopper. What did your wife do, murder somebody?"

"As a matter of fact, it is a murder charge. But she didn't do it."

"Yeah, I know, everybody is innocent. You'll have to put up $30,000, you know."

"I know, and, yes, she is innocent," Cody said indignantly. He wasn't in the mood for witty repartee with this fat man, who reminded him of Sidney Greenstreet from an old Humphrey Bogart movie.

"Okay, okay. What have you got for collateral?"

"Our house. The market value is about a hundred and fifty thousand."

"Is there a mortgage on the place?"

"No, I own it free and clear."

"Well, I'll need to see the paid-up deed, you understand, before I get the money."

"Oh, I didn't know that. Okay, you get the necessary papers drawn up while I go to my safe deposit box and get the deed. I want to do this as quickly as possible."

"All right, pal. I'll be here waiting. I'm open until midnight."

Cody quickly rushed out the door and down the stairs. He drove like a madman to the bank. The day he had planned had gone awry. His agenda had to change now. First, he had to get Joanna out of jail and home. Then, he definitely must go to talk to Mrs. Hollowell. He not only needed information, he also needed the money that Mr. Hollowell owed him.

Because of Joanna's predicament, he felt that getting at Hollowell's office records was his top priority. He had to find out more about his former client's business associates, and most of all, his girlfriends and his possible connection to the mob. These last two, he felt were the most fertile areas, which might produce the murderer or murderers.

He didn't think the police were going to do much investigating since they thought their case against Joanna was so tight. Maybe he ought to talk to Andy first about the results of the autopsy and the tape enhancement. That information might give him some leads that could help. *Okay then,* he thought. Andy would be his first stop after Joanna, then Mrs. Hollowell. After that, he would decide what or who was next.

CHAPTER 9

Cody had gone to the bank, back to Metz's office, over to the courthouse, put up the bail, and picked up Joanna in what seemed like minutes. They were on the way home, and Cody could contain himself no longer.

"Andy said they found a lot of evidence in the hotel room."

"I know about the fingerprints. What else could they possibly have?"

"They found things like hair, fibers, traces of lipstick, and . . ." Cody turned to look directly at Joanna so he could observe her reaction, "bodily fluids."

He said this with such coldness that Joanna looked at Cody, and then turned away. She put her head down and said, "What do you mean, 'bodily fluids'?"

"Come on, Joanna, you know what bodily fluids are, don't you? Things like tears, saliva . . ." Still not taking his eyes off her, he continued, with his teeth clenched, "semen and vaginal fluids."

"So what do you think that means?"

"Let's not act naïve, Joanna. It means that in all likelihood Hollowell had fucked somebody."

Cody's voice was half an octave higher by this point. He was beginning to tremble as he always did when angry. It was his signal that he was ready to fight.

"You don't think it was me, do you?"

"Just who the hell else could it have been? There was a lot of noise while you were there, and I heard nothing else after you left. Who else? Tell me, please. Give me a hint."

Joanna began to sob again. She sat quietly for what seemed to Cody to be an eternity. He thought he could hear her mind working.

Finally, she looked at him and said, "Okay, it *was* me. I did have sex with him. I'm sorry I lied to you. Please don't hate me for it."

"Why did you do it?" His frustration was gushing out like water from a fire hydrant. "Why did you have to go that far? Couldn't you just have carried out your plan without the sex?"

While Cody was still staring at her, the car was slowly veering to the other side of the street. There was a car about two hundred yards away. Joanna must have caught a glimpse of it because she shouted, "Look out! You're going to hit that car!"

Cody jerked his head back in time to see the other car and quickly turned the wheel. The car lurched back to the right side of the street with its tires screeching. It rocked back and forth a few seconds with the back of the car fishtailing, and then straightening out. After the car was under control, Cody turned back to Joanna and demanded, "Go ahead, Joanna, explain it to me."

"I don't know that I can. You must know that this had nothing to do with lust or love, don't you?"

Cody didn't answer. He couldn't. He wasn't quite sure what he thought. All he knew was that he felt terribly betrayed. So he just waited for her to continue.

"All I knew was I had to get even with him for his responsibility in my sister's death. Once I was in that hotel room, all rational thought disappeared. I felt trapped, and once he started to undress, I don't know, it was like I was sleepwalking. Before I knew it, it was over. Frankly, between the drugs and alcohol, I was shocked that he could even think about it, let alone perform. I can't even remember it. It's like a bad dream."

How could Cody rationalize what had happened? He couldn't understand his feelings. There was hurt, anger, and confusion, most of all, concern about what else went on in that room. After a long pause, he said in a low, controlled voice, "What do you expect me to say, Joanna?"

"I guess I just want you to say that you understand and that you still love me. I didn't mean to hurt you, sweetheart. You know that, don't you?"

His rage was subsiding somewhat, but he still wasn't sure he could forgive her right now. The real question was would he ever be ready to forgive her. Clearly, there was a need in his life that only she fulfilled. But would he ever be able to forget, let alone forgive?

"Right now, I'm so angry and confused that I shouldn't say anything. But you must understand my feelings. I would have trusted you with my life, but now, I have to deal with this and with the idea that you may have killed him too."

"What! You can't be serious! Yes, I did have sex with him, but I swear to you that I didn't kill him. You must believe that."

He looked at her with a mixture of resignation and despair. "Okay, you want me to believe that. But didn't you also ask me to believe that you didn't fuck him? I don't know what to believe right now."

"Cody, if you believe nothing else, please believe this—I did not kill him." She said the last part with emphasis, punctuating each word.

The car pulled into the driveway of their house. Cody stepped on the parking brake and got out of the car. Joanna didn't wait for him to open her door and got out of the car by herself. They walked up onto the porch, and Cody quickly opened the door with his key.

It was about 6:30 p.m. A lot had transpired since Cody had awakened that morning. He found out his wife had screwed, and perhaps killed, another man. She had been arrested and charged. He had put up their house for bail and found out that possibly Andy was not as good a friend as he'd thought he was. His investigation hadn't gotten very far, and he was dog tired. But there was no way he could stay in the house with Joanna right now.

Deciding he would try to talk to Andy tonight, he walked to the phone as Joanna went upstairs. He dialed Andy's office number and heard the ring on the other end. After a few rings, Andy picked up the receiver.

"Hello, Lieutenant Perone speaking."

"Andy, this is Cody. I need to see you tonight. Can I come right down to the station?"

"Tonight? Can't this wait 'til tomorrow?"

"Not really. I have some important things to go over with you, some new information."

"What kinda new information, and why can't it wait?

"I have to see you tonight. It's really important. You've got to do me this favor."

There was a long pause on the other end. Finally, Andy said, "Okay, for Joanna's sake. But don't try to pull this shit too often."

"Thanks, buddy. I'll be there in fifteen or twenty minutes."

He hung up the phone and called to Joanna, "I'm going to see Andy Perone at the station. Don't wait up for me. I don't know how late I'll be."

He waited a while for a response, but didn't hear one, so he opened the door and walked out onto the porch. After waiting on the porch for a minute, to see if Joanna had decided to answer, he continued to the car. The motor roared into action when he turned the key, and the car lurched forward quickly.

He arrived at the thirty-ninth precinct and went up to Andy's office. There wasn't as much hustle and bustle at this time of the day. He hurried back to Andy's cubicle and saw him sitting at his desk. When Andy saw him, he waved him in. Cody entered the office. "Thanks for seeing me, Andy. I really appreciate it. There are a few things I'd like to know. That is, if you don't mind giving me the information."

"I don't know how much I can give. Besides, you said you had some new information, didn't you?"

"If you'll tell me about the autopsy and anything you've got on the tape, I think I've got something that'll interest you."

"Oh, I see. We're going to trade information, huh? Okay, who goes first?"

"You go ahead, will you? I need to listen to some good news for a change."

Andy thought for a moment, and then said, "Okay, but you'd better not be pullin' my leg. The autopsy's not completed yet, that is the toxicology and microscopic. But the gross exam is done. You'll be surprised at one of the findings."

Cody leaned forward and put his hands on Andy's desk. His mind flashed back to the hotel room and the body lying on the bed. The only thing unusual that he could remember was the blood coming from Hollowell's nose.

"Well, what is it? Don't keep me in suspense."

"Hollowell wasn't strangled. He was shot."

"Shot! No shit! Where? The only blood was from his nose and not much at that."

"That's just it. The bullet went up his nostril and into his brain. It was a small-caliber pistol, so the bullet never exited the head. It rattled around in there and sort of mashed up the brain, and there was only minor bleeding."

Cody was surprised indeed to say the least. This put a different light on the subject. Maybe this was a mob hit after all.

Andy continued, "We think it was a twenty-five millimeter, probably an Italian Beretta."

"Wow, that is a shock. It really puts a different slant on things, doesn't it?"

"You bet it does. Do you or your wife own a gun?"

Cody was taken aback by the question. Andy obviously still considered Joanna the prime suspect. He felt himself beginning to tremble, and his anger was rising. Then he remembered that Joanna had bought a gun right after they were married because there had been trouble in the parking garage near the courthouse. She had gotten a permit for it. He didn't own one. It really wasn't necessary for his usual kind of work.

"You know I don't own one. But, yes, Joanna does, for protection."

"I'm glad you told me because we had already checked on it and saw her permit registration. It's a 22-caliber job, isn't it, Cody?"

"I think it is." He knew damn well what it was because he had helped her pick it out.

"But you said it was a 25-caliber bullet, didn't you?"

"Yes, we think it is. But you see, the bullet shattered into tiny fragments, and we can't be entirely sure. It could be a 22."

Cody was really upset at this point. Things were looking worse and worse for Joanna. And yet, he was still finding it difficult to believe she could do this thing. In deep thought, he pulled on his earlobe. But she had lied about the sex. Could she have lost her head completely and killed him? Maybe she doesn't remember. What's that thing called, "irresistible impulse"?

He just found it hard to believe that she had killed willfully. Joanna was not the type. It was even more imperative to find out what really had happened in that room. He thought back and didn't remember hearing a shot.

"If the bullet was shattered as you say, then it will be difficult to be sure exactly what gun it came from, won't it?"

"Yes, but we do know it was a small-caliber gun, and a 22 is a small-caliber gun. Therefore, by inference, and with the rest of the evidence, we can sure make a hell of a case."

Cody could see no point in talking to Andy anymore. Andy's mind appeared to be made up, and frankly, he probably would have felt the same way if he were still a cop. He got up and began making his way to the door.

"What was that new evidence you said you had?"

Cody had intended to give Andy the earring. He had thought it would help point the finger away from Joanna. But he could see now that Andy would not be easy to dissuade. He would probably say there was no way of connecting it to the crime, so Cody decided to keep it for future reference.

"Oh, it was nothing compared to what you have. I just thought you'd like to know that Joanna took a cab from the hotel that night," he lied.

"We knew that. She told me that during the interrogation. What're you giving me? You must've known she told me that."

"I guess I forgot. Well, I've got to go now. Thanks for seeing me."

Cody hurried through the door as Andy called after him. "Who do you think you're bullshittin'? Come back here, Cody. What're you trying to pull?"

Cody turned his head as he continued to walk through the large room, "That's it, Andy, no shit. I'll see you later. Thanks again."

He could see that Andy was furious, as he practically sprinted between the desks scattered around the room. He was kind of pleased with himself that he had made Andy mad. After the way Andy had been acting, he deserved to be fooled.

As Cody reached his car, it was about 7:30 p.m. He thought about Joe Johnston and decided to give him another call. Johnston did not go to work until 11:00 p.m. Using his cell phone, he made the call. Again, the phone rang eight or nine times with no answer. *Where the hell is this guy?* he thought. He clicked off and decided to go home, get some sleep, and start fresh in the morning.

When Cody got home, Joanna was not downstairs. He could hear no activity upstairs and became a little concerned. Quickly, he ran upstairs into the bedroom. His heart jumped when he didn't Joanna in the bed. Where was she? He called out to her, "Joanna! Joanna! Are you here?"

"Yes, I'm back here," he heard a soft, almost imperceptible voice coming from the back room, which he used as an office. He rushed back to the room and pushed open the door. Joanna was sitting on the sofa in the dark. She was in her robe and had a drink in her hand. She quite obviously was crying.

"What're you doing back here?" he asked, realizing she was frightened.

"I just wanted to be alone in the dark. Besides, I didn't think you'd want to sleep with an adulteress and a murderer." She said this sadly but with a touch of sarcasm.

Sitting down on the sofa next to her, he remembered how much she meant to him. He put his arm around her, and she put her head against his chest. After a moment, he said, "You'll have to give me some time to sort this out. I'm trying as hard as I can to understand. I do know this much though. I want to believe you and will stick by you until I get this solved. And I *will* get it solved. This, I promise you."

"Until you get this solved? Does that mean you'll leave me when this is over?" Joanna's voice was quivering with fear. He could sense that the thought of him leaving her was almost as frightening to her as the thought of going to jail. It was like a second sentence hanging over her head. Nevertheless, he couldn't answer because he really didn't know the answer right now.

He sat silently in the darkness, trying to separate his feelings. Joanna looked up into his face and smiled, despite her tears. Leaning down, he kissed her, gently at first. There was no mistaking his physical need for her. Even in this state of confusion, he desired her, as always.

He kissed her more forcefully. Joanna responded and within minutes, her robe was opened, and he was fondling her breasts. His head bent to kiss her breasts. Joanna's heart was pounding in his ear.

She reached down and opened the belt buckle and slipped his zipper down. But to his surprise, Cody was not responding. He was clearly not ready for her advances. She tried fondling him, and then kissing him, but Cody could not muster a response. His eyes were closed in forced concentration, but try as he might, there was no reaction. He fell back on the couch in frustration. Nothing like this had ever happened before. He was always ready but not this time.

Joanna looked up at him and said, "What's wrong, honey?"

"I don't know," said Cody. "I just can't get excited."

"Why? This has never happened to you before."

"I know. It must be everything that's happened. I can't get my mind to concentrate."

"It's my fault, isn't it?" cried Joanna, as she sat up in the chair. "It's because of what I have done. I have ruined our entire relationship, haven't I?"

"Oh, maybe I'm just worn out. This has been a very confusing and chaotic day. Perhaps it not so unusual that I can't respond. I know it has happened to other guys, particularly when they are tired and worried." Despite his attempt at a logical explanation, Cody was apprehensive. Never going through anything like this before, he felt inadequate and helpless.

"No, I know it's because of me. How can I ever repair the damage I have done?" said Joanna, as she got up and began to walk out of the room.

"What we need is a good night's sleep. This will straighten itself out tomorrow. I am not really worried about it," he lied. Cody was extremely anxious about his failure. He wondered if he would continue to have trouble having sex with Joanna in the future. Was this going to be their fate from now on?

"Let's go to bed, and we'll see how things are in the morning."

"Okay," said Joanna. "But I know it's all my fault. I don't think I'll get any sleep at all."

Cody got up from the chair, and after fixing his pants, he put his arm around her shoulder. They walked to the bedroom with Joanna softly crying.

Cody was trying to erase all thoughts of the last few minutes, but he couldn't clear away this disappointment.

CHAPTER 10

When Cody awakened in the morning, Joanna was already out of bed. He stretched his arms and yawned. Last night was still vividly in his mind. He tried to clear away those depressing thoughts with only partial success.

After a quick shower, he dressed and went downstairs. Joanna was sitting in the kitchen, drinking coffee, and reading the paper intently. She looked up and smiled weakly at him as she handed him the front page. As he took the paper, he could tell last night was still weighing heavily on her. He poured himself a cup of coffee and glanced at the front page. The headlines were concerning the president's visit to Russia. However, further down the page, in bold print, he saw,

CAB DISPATCHER FOUND MURDERED IN HIS ROOM

A Yellow Cab dispatcher was found murdered in his apartment early this morning. Joseph R. Johnston did not report to work at his usual time, and when he didn't answer

his phone, the company called the police. When no one
responded to their knocks, they broke in and found Johnston
in his bedroom, apparently shot in the head. He had been dead
approximately twenty-four hours according to the coroner.

The article went on to say that the police had no significant
clues as yet but were gathering evidence. It also mentioned that the
homicide division from the twenty-eighth precinct was handling
the murder investigation.

Cody looked at Joanna, who was reading another section
of the paper. "Did you notice this article about the Yellow Cab
dispatcher?"

"No, I didn't. Should I have?"

"This is the guy who dispatched the cab that picked you up the
night of the murder. I've been trying to get in touch with him all day."

"How do you know that?"

"I went to the dispatch office when Andy was interrogating you.
I got his phone number there. I figured that he'd be able to tell me
who sent the cab to pick you up."

He hung his head and let out a soft sigh. This was his one chance
to find out who sent the cab. Now, that lead was gone. Maybe he
would try to see Mustafa, the driver, but he didn't think that would
lead anywhere.

"What'll you do now? Do you have any more leads?"

"I have a few. There's Mrs. Hollowell and the old man's office,
which I must get into somehow. I've also got to go to the twenty-eighth
precinct to see what I can find out about Johnston."

At this point, Joanna got up and walked over and sat on Cody's lap. She gave him a kiss on the cheek and said, "You know, after last night, I feel guiltier about what I've done. Now, it has affected our lives more deeply than I could have ever imagined. How stupid I was."

He kissed her back and tried to help Joanna by saying, "Let's put last night behind us for now. I've got many things to do today, and I can't be worrying about something that's not likely to happen again." He said that with a certain amount of false gallantry. He smiled at her and gently pushed her to her feet.

"Let me get busy now. I've got a lot to do today."

"Where are you going first?"

"My first stop is to see Mrs. Hollowell. I'd like to talk to her a little and get paid for my previous services. In fact, I'm going to call her right now to see if she'll see me."

He picked up the phone and dialed the number, which he had memorized while dealing with her husband. The phone rang a few times, and then a female voice answered. "Hollowell residence, who's calling please?"

"My name is Cody Thomas. I'd like to speak to Mrs. Hollowell."

"May I tell her why you're calling?"

"It is regarding a job I did for Mr. Hollowell, and I'd like to see her."

"Just a moment, please. I'll see if she's at home."

Cody waited impatiently. He wanted a cigarette but didn't have one, which made the waiting seem that much longer. After what seemed to be an hour, the voice came back on the phone and said, "Mrs. Hollowell can see you today. What time will you be arriving?"

"I can be there in fifteen or twenty minutes."

"Just come up to the gate and buzz the groundskeeper. He'll be expecting you."

"Okay, that's great. Thank you."

He hung up the phone and said to Joanna, "She told me I can come right over."

They walked arm in arm to the door and kissed again. He walked to his car, got in, and waved to Joanna as he pulled out of the driveway. On his way to Mrs. Hollowell's, he planned his approach. From what he knew about her, he didn't anticipate her being too much trouble. Thoughts about Hollowell's involvement in the drug scene ran through his head. Getting involved with the mob and drugs could be a dangerous business.

If he could get a couple of names from the files, then maybe he could gather some information from one of his old informants. Maybe there was some news on the street.

He didn't think Sarah Hollowell could help him with facts about the old man's collection of women. She was probably unaware of Hollowell's adventures with the ladies. But then, he thought, she isn't stupid. She probably did know. If he could only find a telephone number or something, it might lead him in the right direction.

Good judgment would be important when talking to Mrs. Hollowell about any of these things. He didn't want to turn her off by being overbearing or obnoxious. Just as important right now, he needed to get his money. That subject might be very tricky.

Just about that time, he pulled up in front of the Hollowell house. But this was more than a house. It was an estate. A seven-foot high stone wall surrounded the property. There was a large iron gate that opened to reveal a curving macadam driveway. In the middle of the driveway, there stood a massive concrete fountain with a large bronze fish spewing water from its mouth.

In the center, there was a naked water nymph holding a wine pitcher also pouring water. Both the fish and the nymph had that rich green patina that comes with age. The driveway surrounded the fountain.

The house was a three-story stone building with many gables. The roof was made of slate shingles. He estimated between fifteen and twenty rooms in the place.

Cody stopped in front of the gate and reached out from his window to pick up the phone attached to the wall. He pushed the button and waited for a response. A few seconds later, a male voice answered, "Hollowell residence. Can I help you?"

"My name is Cody Thomas. Mrs. Hollowell is expecting me."

"Oh, yes, sir. One moment, please, I'll open the gate."

A buzzing sound signaled the opening of the gate. It began to swing inward, toward the house. Cody turned his car into the long driveway and proceeded to the house, passing the fountain and parking his car against the curb. He walked up to a pair of huge double doors with large brass knockers.

Surveying the house as he walked up to the doors, he whistled softly and thought, *It's good to be wealthy.* The knocker made a sharp metallic sound as he rapped on the door. The door opened and a middle-aged woman dressed in a uniform stood before him.

"Mr. Thomas?"

"Yes, that's right," he answered, almost intimidated by the opulence of the foyer.

"Come in, please," said the woman as she stood back to give him room to pass.

"If you'll wait here, please, I will announce you."

He nodded. The foyer appeared to be bigger than the entire downstairs area of his house. In the center was a beautiful table with carved legs, on which sat a giant vase filled with fresh flowers. There were two staircases leading upstairs, one on either side of the foyer.

The doors to at least five bedrooms were visible beyond the large carved wooden railing, which ascended from the marble tiles that made up the floor. The railing ran across the open upstairs hallway to the other staircase and down again to the other side of the foyer.

From where Cody was standing, he could see a set of double doors to the right and another set to the left. Both sets were closed. Forced by habit, he studied the area for a security system. A motion detector was visible in one corner of the foyer, and in the other corner was a video camera. The house was obviously monitored by a sophisticated alarm system.

As he was admiring the house, one set of double doors on the right side of the foyer slid open, and Mrs. Hollowell emerged in front of what looked to be a library. She came toward him, holding out her hand in greeting. Cody had a chance to look at her more carefully. He had seen her only from a distance during his surveillance. She was indeed an attractive woman. She stood about five feet six inches tall, looked to be about 120 to 125 pounds, and appeared to be in great shape. He suspected she must be because she worked out at least three nights a week at the gym. Her brunette-colored hair was worn pulled back in a ponytail, and her skin showed no wrinkles at forty-five years of age, a very attractive forty-five years of age. She wore a man-tailored white shirt with the collar opened. He noticed that she wore a very expensive pair of ruby stud earrings and a ruby pendant that was tasteful without being gaudy. This was indeed a very classy lady.

"Mr. Thomas? I am Sarah Hollowell. Won't you please come into the library where we can talk?" She said this while stepping aside to let Cody through the doorway.

"Thank you," he said, as he passed by her into the large room, which had a ceiling at least twelve feet high. The walls were covered from floor to ceiling with bookshelves, filled with hundreds of books of varying sizes and colors. Their content extended from fiction to psychology to history and even some how-to books. He thought these people must be avid readers. His being in awe of the place made him feel ashamed. He thought it strange that he saw no law books.

There was a heavy wooden desk off to the side with a large high-backed red leather chair sitting behind it. Next to the stone fireplace, which stood six feet high, were two small sofas facing each other. A coffee table sat between them. There was a lectern against one of the walls, which held an open book that Cody could not see clearly, but he thought that it might be a bible.

"Won't you sit down, Mr. Thomas?" She motioned toward one of the sofas. "Can I get you some coffee or tea or perhaps something stronger?"

He walked over and sat on the sofa nearest him.

"A cup of coffee would be great, thank you."

Mrs. Hollowell walked over to the desk and pushed a button that was one of eight, which studded that corner of the desktop.

"Now, you said you had done some work for my husband, didn't you?"

"Yes, ma'am, I did."

"Oh, please, don't call me 'ma'am.' It makes me feel like some old spinster schoolmarm. Why don't you call me Sarah?"

"All right, ma . . . uh, Mrs. Hollowell."

"Sarah, please," she corrected him again.

"Sarah. Yes, I did about three weeks of surveillance work for him."

"I see. Was it for one of his cases?"

"Ah . . . yes, that's it. It was one of his cases."

He saw no need to tell her the truth about the surveillance. It wasn't going to help anything, and it might only cause her pain. Besides, keeping the reason to himself might be the perfect excuse for which to get her permission to look into Hollowell's files.

"Were you able to complete the assignment, then?"

"Yes, I was. But you see, Mr. Hollowell didn't get a chance to pay me before he . . . ah . . . died. Oh, and also, let me offer you my deepest sympathy."

"Thank you, Mr. Thomas."

"Cody. Please call me Cody," he interrupted.

"All right, then, Cody," she replied softly.

Besides being extremely attractive, Cody thought she was a lady, a very sophisticated lady. It was the way she carried herself and the way she walked and talked that impressed him.

Just then the uniformed maid came into the room carrying a tray with the coffee. There were also some biscuits and butter on the tray. She set it down on the table and left.

"May I pour you a cup, Cody?"

"Here, let me do that," he said, as he jumped up from the sofa and reached for the coffeepot. He poured her a cup, handed it to her, and then poured one for himself. As she sipped her coffee, Cody noticed that she took it black with no sugar. He was not surprised.

Then she asked, "What is the fee for your services?"

"My fee is $50 an hour. My surveillance totaled seventy-two hours, so that adds up to $3,600."

He did not include the time spent observing Hollowell. After considering it, he thought that would have been a little unethical and greedy.

"Well, I'm sure my husband would have paid you from his office accounts. Have you prepared a bill?"

"Yes, I have it right here," he said, pulling an envelope from his inside coat pocket.

He was about to hand it to her when she said, "Would it be too much trouble to ask you to mail it to the office?"

"Well, you see, ma ... ah ... Sarah, I kind of need the money now. Expenses, you know."

"Oh, I see. Let me think a minute. All right, I'll call the office and tell the manager that you'll be right over. She'll see that you get a check. How's that?"

"That would be just great."

And he thought this was a terrific way to get into his office. All he had to do was get her to approve it. He wondered how he should go about it. His mind quickly ran through many ideas. Then he hit upon what he thought was the right one.

"Listen, Sarah. While I'm there, would you ask the office manager to let me go through some of your husband's files? You see the surveillance I was doing for your husband involved some shady characters and between what I discovered and what may be found in your husband's files, I might have some protection, if they decided to come after me. I would be able to turn it over to the police and keep them away from me."

This was said with such conviction that he was sure she would agree.

"I also feel, well, sort of an obligation to help find your husband's killer. After all, I was working for him when he died."

This was stretching the truth, but he wanted desperately to get her to help him.

"Well, that's quite nice of you, but it's really not your obligation. And you must know that the police have already been to Samuel's office."

"Yes, I thought they might have, but they may not be looking for the same kinds of things I am. Or perhaps your husband kept certain information in a separate place that you or his office manager might not know about."

"I surely don't know any secret places, but perhaps Olivia does. And since you were working for Sam anyway, I guess I don't mind if you look around down there."

He was elated. Now, if only he could find something worthwhile that could help Joanna.

"Thanks, Sarah. That could be a big help. Do you think you can call the office now? I'd like to go right over."

"Yes, I'll do that for you. Did you do a lot of work for my husband?"

"No, as a matter of fact, this was my first assignment."

She picked up the phone and dialed the number.

"How did he find you?"

"It was through a friend of mine who had done some things for him. He was too busy, so he suggested me for the job."

"Hello, Ms. Hastings? This is Sarah Hollowell. Yes, fine, thanks. Ms. Hastings, a Mr. Cody Thomas will be coming to the office today. He did some work for my husband before he died but hasn't been paid as yet. He will bring his bill. Would you be kind enough to make him a check and have one of Mr. Hollowell's partners sign it."

Mrs. Hollowell listened for a moment, and then asked Cody, "How much did you say the bill was?"

"$3,600."

Mrs. Hollowell repeated the sum to Miss Hastings.

"Please don't forget about the files," he reminded her in a loud whisper.

"And also, please let him have access to the files of the cases he was working on. Thank you." She looked at Cody. "Will that help?"

"Yes, it will, tremendously. Thanks a lot. I'll go there right away. You've been wonderful to give me all this help. May I come back again, if I need anything else?"

Cody admired how she handled herself. She appeared to be a strong self-reliant woman. He wondered how she ever got involved with the old man. They just didn't seem to belong together.

"I don't see why not." Although she agreed, Cody thought she looked a little unsure. He attributed this to Hollowell's death and all that was going on her life right now.

"Thanks, Sarah. I'll be seeing you then."

"Okay, Cody. I hope everything works out for you. Good-bye."

She walked him through the foyer and to the front doors. He opened the door and walked out to his car, waving to Sarah Hollowell as he got in.

As he drove away, he thought Mrs. Hollowell was being very helpful, but after all, he was trying to find her husband's killer, wasn't he?

CHAPTER 11

While driving to Hollowell's office, Cody was considering his alternatives for getting as much information as he could from the files. First, he would have to come up with some names of people in the mob with whom Hollowell might have had some arrangements.

He knew many smalltime hoods from his days as a cop, but would they be the ones Hollowell knew? If Hollowell was in deeper than Cody thought, he might have dealt with some of the big boys.

Oh, well, he thought, I'll just pick a name I remember and go from there. He thought for a minute and decided on Sal "the Cook" Cuccinata. He was a middleman—high enough to be able to afford a mouthpiece like Hollowell, but not so high as to be able to avoid exposure as some of the bigger names did. He had seen the Cook's name in the paper often and even thought he might have remembered it in association with Hollowell. He wasn't sure, but it was worth a try anyway.

Going back to see Mrs. Hollowell would be necessary, especially if he had no success at the office. He was sure Hollowell had an office of some sort at home, where he might have kept some things, secret things.

Also, a visit to the twenty-eighth precinct to find out more about Johnston's murder was absolutely necessary. That was an interesting twist. Why was he killed? Was it because he knew who had dispatched the cab for Joanna? If so, then Hollowell's murderer was a smart cookie. He was covering up his tracks. Was the death coincidental? *Not likely,* he thought, *that would be too much of a coincidence.*

The paper said he was shot in the head. It didn't mention "gangland style," but you never know. He shook his head. This was getting "curiouser and curiouser," as Alice in Wonderland once said.

Would there be any profit in trying to find that Mustafa guy? Would the dispatcher have told him who ordered the cab? Probably not. After all, he was just the driver. He just went where he was told to go. He certainly would have logged the trip on his way sheet. That would at least prove that he was dispatched for Joanna. Maybe he would try to find him if all else failed.

Thinking through this problem made driving around the city easier. When Cody arrived at Hollowell's office building, he parked in the subterranean parking lot and took the elevator up to the lobby. When the elevator door opened, Cody was looking at a large area, which was filled with people hustling in all directions. He walked across the terrazzo floors to the elevators on the far wall of this area. These elevators serviced the regular floors in the building. Hollowell's office was on the seventeenth floor.

The offices took up the entire floor. Besides the five partners, there were thirty or forty other lawyers associated with the firm.

What an operation, Cody marveled. *No wonder Hollowell lived like he did.* Approaching the receptionist's desk, he said, "My name is Cody Thomas. I'm here to see a Ms. Hastings."

"Just a minute, sir. I'll ring her." She picked up the interoffice phone and pushed a button. A few seconds later, she said, "Ms. Hastings, there's a Mr. Thomas here to see you." Then she hung up the receiver. "She'll be right out, sir."

A few minutes later, a strikingly attractive blonde with a magnificent figure appeared, as if Scotty from the Starship Enterprise had beamed her down. She moved with a marvelous grace and ease that belied her height. She was easily five feet nine or ten inches with breasts that were large but proportionate for her size. She wore a short skirt that showed off her perfectly shaped legs and a silk shirt that buttoned at the neck with a large button.

Around her neck was a stylish gold choker necklace, and on her earlobes were matching clip-on earrings.

There were no rings on her fingers, and her nails were red to match her lipstick. Cody couldn't help but marvel at her attractiveness. There was one flaw, however, which he noticed. Her hair, which was bleached blond, was unevenly colored, causing it to appear to have many different shades. They ranged from golden blond to almost white. Cody thought it strange that this woman would allow something like this to happen, proving that no one is really perfect.

He immediately wondered if she was one of Hollowell's girlfriends. If so, he had to give the old man credit. She approached, extending her hand.

"Mr. Thomas? I am Olivia Hastings, Mr. Hollowell's private secretary and administrative assistant. Won't you come back to my office so I can give you your check?"

Cody shook her hand and nodded in silent agreement. He followed her through a door, which led to a large room filled with desks to accommodate the many staff people it took to run an operation of this size. After what seemed to be a city block, she stopped at an office, opened the door, and stepped aside to let him go in first.

It was a professionally decorated office with a standard desk and chairs. He walked over to one of the chairs and waited for Ms. Hastings to get to her desk.

"I have the check already prepared for you," she said, as she reached down to the desk and picked it up. She handed it to him with a pleasant smile.

"Thank you very much," he said, reaching into his inside jacket pocket and pulling out the bill for his services.

"Here's the bill. I'm sure you'll want this for your records."

"Yes, thank you. You know, I'm not familiar with your name. You haven't worked for Sam ... ah ... Mr. Hollowell before, have you?"

"No, as a matter of fact, this was my first assignment for him."

"What were you investigating?"

Cody thought that Hollowell must have kept him a secret from the office because of the nature of the investigation. He probably wanted to keep his plans about divorce from Ms. Hastings, in case she might get ideas about taking up where Sarah Hollowell was about to leave off.

After thinking about it for a moment, he decided he would tell her. Maybe that would rattle her a little, and she might let something slip, particularly if she were one of his playmates.

"This was sort of a personal matter. He had me following his wife. I guess he was trying to gather evidence for a divorce."

There, he thought, *let's see how you handle that piece of information.* He looked at her intently to note any change in expression or body language. She looked at him with an expression of surprise, but not exactly the look he expected. She said with a sarcastic chuckle, "He had you following his wife? That sweet woman? You must be kidding me. Mrs. Hollowell is one of the nicest people you'd ever want to know."

"Yes, I know. I met her today for the first time, and I agree with you. She is very nice, indeed. Nevertheless, he had me follow her. Of course, nothing came of the investigation, as you might have expected."

"I'm not surprised. How long did you follow her?"

"My surveillance took a couple of weeks but a total of about seventy-two actual working hours, as you can see from my bill."

"Oh, yes. I can see that now," she said, as she looked down at the bill. Cody wanted to try to get on with his investigation, so he asked her about looking at some files.

"Did Mrs. Hollowell tell you that I wanted to look at some of Mr. Hollowell's files?"

"Yes, she did mention it to me. And frankly, I don't understand why. You must know the police have been through them already, and they didn't seem to find anything of importance."

"I thought they might have been here. But I'm looking for something entirely different. I'm trying to find a connection between Mr. Hollowell's murder and the Mafia." He decided to tell her this, thinking it might get her to help him. He didn't expect the kind of response he got, however.

"The Mafia? What makes you think they're involved?"

"Didn't he handle some mob business?"

"The only thing I can think of would be the few times he was hired to defend a couple of them on minor violations. But he certainly wasn't a 'mob' lawyer, as they say." Cody could see she was agitated and assumed she was trying to protect her boss. Or was it more than that?

"Well, you see, I'm trying to get some evidence pointing to them as possible conspirators in his death."

"Why are you interested in this whole thing anyway?"

Then, as if a light went on in her head, an all-knowing look spread over her face.

"Thomas! Didn't I read in the paper that was the name of the woman who was arrested for his murder?"

"Yes, it is," he said, feeling kind of stupid because he had been found out. "She's my wife. But she didn't do this thing, and I'm trying to prove it. That's why I need your help."

He felt he had to come clean at this point because it was obvious she was beginning to put two and two together.

"How can I possibly help you? From what I can understand from the newspapers, there's a lot of circumstantial evidence that points to her."

"Yes, there is, but you can help me by letting me see Hollowell's files. I may be able to find something the police missed because I'm looking in a different direction."

Cody decided to change his approach. He now felt that, by being direct, he would get better cooperation from her. His experience as a detective told him that being direct and pretending he had more information than he really did have often caused the defendant to be more cooperative.

"Besides, there is some evidence that points to the mob."

"I can't see how you suspect the mob. Mr. Hollowell only defended some smalltime hoods."

"There's some evidence that he was involved with cocaine. And you must be aware that the mob deals in cocaine."

He kept his eyes on her, trying to detect any sign of breakdown. She must have been acquainted with Hollowell's personal habits, being his administrative assistant. He just had to get at Hollowell's files and dig around a little.

"Cocaine! I never knew anything about Mr. H. and cocaine. How could he be involved?"

"He was using it the night he was killed."

"Oh . . . er . . . I didn't know that. But how does that prove he might be involved with the Mafia?"

"It doesn't directly. But I hear he had plenty of the stuff. I guess he could have bought it, but it's possible that he could have been on the import end or the production end. He did travel a lot, didn't he? He could have been a 'mule.'"

"A mule! What the hell is a mule?"

119

"A mule is someone who transports the stuff, either into the country or around the country."

"I don't think Mr. Hollowell could or would be involved in something as despicable as that. He was a kind and generous man."

Now Cody felt it might be the right time to let her know about Mr. Hollowell's extramarital affairs, if she wasn't already aware of them.

"Did you know that your boss was running around on his wife?"

There was a long moment of silence. Ms. Hastings was obviously uncomfortable. When she replied, her voice was higher and more strident.

"And just how do you know this?"

"Because while I was following his wife for him, I stumbled on the fact that he was cheating on her. Maybe he wasn't such a great guy after all, huh?" Cody said sarcastically.

"Mr. Thomas, I don't think I want to discuss this any further with you. I'll let you see the files, only because Mrs. Hollowell said it was all right. You can follow me."

She got up from her desk, walked to the door of the office, and jerked it open. She looked at Cody as if she wanted to throw him out the door. Instead, she walked on through. Jumping to his feet, he followed hurriedly so she wouldn't get away.

She led him to a large room with shelf after shelf of files from floor to ceiling. The sections were divided up according to each lawyer so that each one had an area that was exclusively his. In each section, the files were in alphabetical order.

"Is this the only area where files are kept? I mean, could the lawyers possibly keep very personal or private cases here?"

"There are small filing cabinets in each lawyer's private office for more personal matters, but Mrs. H. never said anything about those files. Besides, the police have already been through them."

Cody suspected that the kind of information he was interested in would be in those private files. He decided he would have to get into them somehow. Ms. Hastings left him alone in the file room, and he began to scan the files for names he might recognize.

He wanted a cigarette badly. Since he hadn't bought a pack in the last twenty-four hours, he wondered if this would be a good time to try to quit. He had tried many times before but never had the courage. Maybe he could pull a Kojak and begin sucking lollipops. The idea sickened him. He hated candy. Well, he would figure it out later.

Anderson, Barnes, Bigalow, Charles, Cantarro were some of the names he passed as he fingered through the files. When he pulled up the next folder, he saw a name that rang a bell. It was Lola Dupres. He remembered that name from his days on the force.

She was a well-known madam with a string of high-class women who catered to the affluent. These women were the $1,000–$2,000 a night call girls that only the rich could afford. Could this be where Hollowell got some or most likely all of his women?

He wrote down her address and phone number. *Another place to look,* he thought. He continued to peruse the files. Another name jumped out at him, Gino Buononotti, better known as Good Night Gino. The name had a kind of double meaning. His last name meant

121

"good night" in Italian, and he was well known for putting people to sleep, permanently.

Cody pulled out the file and read through it. It seems Hollowell had defended Buononotti on a tax evasion charge and got him off. Buononotti was also involved in prostitution, loan sharking, and drugs. This might be a good place to start looking, as far as the mob was concerned.

He spent about an hour looking through the files but found nothing else of real interest. Still, there were those private filing cabinets in Hollowell's consultation office. How to get at them was another problem. Maybe he would have to come back at night and break in.

He would worry about that later. He had some modest leads to follow up for now. He wanted to go to the twenty-eighth precinct and find out more about the Johnston killing. And he would look up Lola. That should keep him busy for a while.

As he walked down the hall and into the large staff room, he casually looked around for Hollowell's office. He didn't see it. It must have been somewhere in the back.

He walked over to Ms. Hastings's office and knocked on the closed door. He heard her say, "Come in," and opened the door. Putting his head inside, he said, "I just wanted to thank you for your help and say 'so long.'"

"Oh. It's you," she snapped back. "Good-bye, Mr. Thomas. And I want you to know that I didn't appreciate the things you said about Mr. Hollowell. I've been sitting here stewing about it since I left you."

"I'm very sorry I've upset you. I didn't mean to. I guess I can't forget my days on the force."

"An ex-cop! I should have known. You guys must take courses on how to be rude."

"Not really. You just get that way because of the people you're forced to deal with day after day. Anyway, I wanted to thank you, and I apologize for upsetting you."

Cody thought it best to try and stay on her good side in case he needed her in the future.

"Okay, but I hope you haven't told Mrs. H. any of this."

"No, I haven't. Thanks again, and maybe I'll see you again."

He pulled his head out of the room and closed the door, not wanting to give her a chance to refuse to see him again.

He walked past the receptionist to the elevator, which took him to the lobby. The elevator to the garage was on the other side of the lobby. When he reached it, he took it down to the garage and walked to his car. He was off to the twenty-eighth precinct.

CHAPTER 12

When Cody arrived at the twenty-eighth precinct, it was about 1:30 p.m. He parked in the lot behind the building and went in the front door. This precinct was not very different from the thirty-ninth where he had worked. There was a large room, the desk sergeant, a lot of uniformed cops milling about and criminals, lots of criminals, both male and female. He walked over to the desk sergeant.

"Excuse me, Sergeant, can you tell me who's handling the Johnston murder?"

The sergeant, seated behind a desk which was two or three feet above the floor Cody was standing on, peered over the desk and replied, "Just a minute, my friend. Who are you?"

"My name is Cody Thomas. I'm a private detective," he said, while opening his wallet to show his license.

"A private detective. What do you have to do with Johnston?"

"He was involved in a case I'm working on. I'm just trying to find out about his murder to see if there's any connection between it and my case."

The sergeant still appeared somewhat annoyed. After giving the request a few moments deliberation, he replied, "You guys are always comin' to us for help. I don't think you could exist without the police force."

Cody smiled back at him and just waited patiently. Finally, in a semidisgusted tone, the sergeant said, "That's being handled by the homicide boys upstairs. Sgt. Dan Wilson is the lead detective."

"Is he around? I'd like to see him if I can."

"I don't know. You'll have to go upstairs and find out."

Cody thought that the sergeant was being tight-assed like everybody else. He asked himself why the cops felt such disdain for private detectives. It must have to do with an outsider moving into their space. Cops feel that all crime is their domain.

"Thanks a lot, Sarge," he replied sarcastically.

Hurrying to the elevator, he took it to the fourth floor and got out. He walked down a long corridor to a large room filled with desks, not unlike the thirty-ninth precinct. There was no one he recognized from his past, which made him happy. He wasn't anxious to run into anyone he knew.

He walked up to the nearest desk where there was a detective busy typing a report in triplicate, no doubt. He had done many of these himself in a previous life.

"Excuse me, Detective, can you point out Sgt. Dan Wilson?"

The detective looked up for a moment, and then looked around the room. He turned back to Cody and said, "That's him over there by the filing cabinet, the one with the thinning brown hair."

Cody looked over to the filing cabinet and picked out Wilson.

"Thanks very much." He walked toward the balding detective.

When he got to where Wilson was standing, he put out his hand. "Sergeant Wilson? I'm Cody Thomas. I'm a private detective. I understand that you're in charge of the Johnston investigation."

Wilson hesitatingly put out his hand. Cody could tell Wilson was less than enthused to meet him, but he didn't think he saw any signs of recognition in his eyes.

"Yeah, that's right. What can I do for ya?"

"This fellow, Johnston, was involved in a case I'm investigating, and I'm looking for any connection between his death and that case. Would you mind giving me some of the details that you've gotten so far?"

"What case are you investigatin'?"

Cody hesitated for a second or two before answering. He was afraid Wilson might make a connection between him and Joanna. But then, he thought, there were so many murders being investigated right now that he probably wouldn't make the connection.

"The Hollowell murder. You see," he went on without hesitation, "I was working for Hollowell on another matter when he was killed. So I kind of have a vested interest in it. I just want to see if there are any similarities."

"Oh, the Hollowell case, I'm somewhat familiar with it. A Lieutenant Perone contacted me about it."

Andy was really on the ball. *He must have drawn the same conclusion as I,* thought Cody. After all, Joanna did tell him about being picked up by the cab the night of the murder. He decided to go on.

"You have talked to Andy, then? I should've known he'd contact you. He's such a good cop. I've known Andy for some time now. We've worked together on other cases."

Since Cody knew Andy was a good cop, it was really no surprise that he had made all the right moves so far. But Cody wondered again whether Andy was just being a good detective or if anyone was pushing him. Cody had suspected many years before that Andy was not moving quickly on an investigation they were working on together because of pressure from someone with some pull. He hoped that Andy was not being forced to pin this murder on Joanna. There was no reason to think Andy was crooked, but he knew pressure from higher-ups could affect Andy's attitude.

"Yes, he is a good cop, and honest too."

He wondered if that last comment was meant for him, but Wilson continued without further reference.

"If Andy thinks you're okay, I guess I can give you what we have so far. According to what we know right now, Johnston was shot in the ear with a small-caliber pistol. He apparently died instantly."

"Do you know what caliber?"

"We can't be sure, but it looks like a 22. The bullet exited his head and entered the wall next to the bed. Then it was dug out, probably by the killer."

"What was the time of death?"

"Between 8:00 p.m. and midnight last night."

Cody did some quick calculations and determined that was about the time he called, after taking Joanna home from jail. He also concluded that, since he was out of the house at that time, Joanna could have had the time to kill Johnston.

He was irritated that he continued to find reasons to suspect Joanna. And if he did, then certainly Andy would.

"Did you find anything else at the scene?"

"Yeah, some unusual things. First, he was found naked in bed. Second, he was tied to the bedposts. And third, he had a silk scarf stuffed in his mouth."

"Just like Hollowell," Cody blurted out. The same modus operandi, the same small-caliber pistol, the same kind of silk scarf, this guy probably knew something about who called for Joanna's cab. And that's why he was murdered. It sure sounded like a cover-up. This couldn't be purely coincidental.

Sergeant Wilson jolted him out of his thoughts. "Yeah, that's what Perone and I were thinkin'."

Then Wilson seemed to put two and two together, and continued, "Hey, wait a minute. Did you say your name was Thomas?"

"Yeah. And before you ask, yes, it is my wife who's the suspect," Cody said, almost happy that it was out in the open.

"Yeah, Perone told me the wife of his former partner was the prime suspect. How the hell could that happen, man? What was she doin' there, anyway?"

"It's a long story, Sarge. Just believe me when I say she is innocent." Cody heard himself saying these words, and then wondered why he kept suspecting otherwise.

"Look . . . ah . . . Thomas, I'll leave that up to Perone. I've got enough trouble with my own cases, particularly Johnston's. I don't have a whole lot more right now. The lab boys are analyzing most of the stuff. Why don't you give it twenty-four hours or so to see what we come up with, okay?"

Cody thought that Wilson seemed less willing to share information now that he knew who he was. He wondered what else Andy had told Wilson. He decided to try to remain on Wilson's good side.

"Okay, Sarge. And if I come up with anything significant, I'll be sure to let you know. Can I get back to you in a couple of days?"

"Yeah, yeah, sure you can," said Wilson, but with a lot less conviction than Cody wanted to hear.

"Thanks. I'll be in touch, then."

As Cody walked away from Wilson, he wasn't sure if he would get much more information. But if Wilson thought Cody was going to give up, then he didn't know him very well. Cody wasn't the kind of guy who got discouraged too easily. He hurried back to his car. There were a few more things to do today.

While sitting in his car contemplating his next move, he decided it had to be Lola Dupres. He felt there was a definite connection there. Why else would Hollowell have a file on her? It wasn't his style to defend prostitutes. Maybe Hollowell got involved with her through Buononotti. After all, Gino ran the prostitution racket in the city, and Hollowell definitely knew Good Night Gino. Maybe he could get to Gino through Lola.

He took out his cell phone and punched up Lola's name, which he had entered at Hollowell's office. Maybe he should call first and set up an appointment. That might be the best way since barging in might cause her to be less than cooperative. Acting like a potential customer might actually work better. He dialed Lola's number and waited for someone to answer. Someone, probably Lola, would be there.

She had been in business in the city for a long time. Even though this address was well known to the cops, they never closed it down. Lola paid off, and he knew it.

After the third ring, someone answered. "Hello, Quality Escort Service," a soft feminine voice whispered into Cody's ear.

"Uh . . . yes . . . I am interested in getting some company this afternoon," he replied, feeling a bit nervous.

"Yes, sir. We have many beautiful ladies, any of whom I'm sure can fulfill all your needs. What kind of lady are you interested in?"

"Well . . . er . . . frankly, I'd like to speak to Lola. Is she there? You see, she was recommended to me by a friend."

"This is Lola. And who recommended me? I don't do the escort thing myself."

Lola's voice took on a different tone. She clearly was acting suspicious. Being in the business for so long made her extra cautious. Cody was afraid he might give himself away before he could see her.

"Are you a cop?" Lola asked suddenly. She knew he would have to tell her if he was. That was the law. The police couldn't entrap prostitutes.

"No, I'm not. I was just told that I should deal only with you. That you would make sure I would be . . . ah . . . satisfied."

"Who told ya that?"

"Some guy I met in a bar. I'm from out of town, and I am looking for some female company. This guy I was talking to mentioned your name and gave me this number," he said quickly.

"Some guy in a bar, huh! Did he give you my address as well?"

"Yes, ma'am." Cody was trying to sound like a hick from the sticks. He just wanted to get into her place. He would try to convince her to talk to him afterward.

"What's your name?"

"Cody Thomas."

He knew he had to give her his correct name because she would ask for identification sooner or later. Besides, what difference did it make if she knew?

"All right, Cody, you can come on over. Just give four raps and wait for me to answer."

"Okay, I'll be there in ten or fifteen minutes."

He clicked off and put the cell phone down next to him on the seat. *Well,* he thought, *that's a start. At least, I'll be able to see her. Getting any good information might be something else again.*

He immediately headed for Lola's place. It would be interesting to know if Hollowell used Lola to get his women and if there was any connection with Buononotti.

Handling this part would be tricky; he knew he had to take his time and be sure to get this right. One thing he knew for sure was that he didn't want Gino and his people ticked off at him. That could be very dangerous. They wouldn't hesitate to kill him if they thought he was a threat to the operation.

Cody was feeling a little nervous. He wanted a cigarette badly. *What a time to try to quit,* he thought. He reached into his pocket for a stick of gum, unwrapped it, and put it into his mouth. After a few minutes, he knew that chewing gum wasn't going to help. He would have to find another substitute.

CHAPTER 13

The car pulled up in front of the three-story brownstone in Fredrickson Village, a very old section of town. At one time, it had been for the very rich, but over time, the rich moved out, and the area became run-down. It wasn't exactly the slums, but "nice" people no longer lived there. Now, smalltime hoods, drifters, and "ladies of the night" mostly inhabited the neighborhood.

The brownstone was an apartment house with worn white marble stairs leading up to the old wooden double doors. Cody glanced down at the address written on the piece of paper: 1223 Fredrickson Avenue, Apartment 1C.

He walked up to the front doors and looked at the names and apartment numbers on the large mailbox on the wall. There was no "Apartment 1C" on any of the mail slots. Cody looked at the address again to make sure he was at the right building. It was 1223.

He walked back down the steps and began to walk toward the alley that separated this building from the next. An elderly man dressed in a wrinkled dirty suit was coming his way. As he came toward Cody, he asked, "What're ya lookin' fer, buddy?"

Cody was taken by surprise. He stopped and looked at the old man for a minute, and then said, "I'm looking for an apartment supposedly at this address. Apartment 1C."

The old man smiled a toothless smile and said, "I thought so. A lotta guys can't find that place. It's 'round the back, through that alley," he said, pointing to the alley a few feet away. "I can't see how that joint does any business at all. If it wasn't fer me, nobody would find it."

Cody chuckled to himself. He reached into his pocket, pulled out a $5 bill and offered it to the old man. "Thanks, pal. Don't know what I would've done without you."

The old man took the bill and shuffled away. Cody walked to the alley and turned into the shadows. He had walked about fifteen yards when he came to a door on the side of the building. On the door was a brass 1C, worn and discolored. Below the number was a small peephole.

Cody rapped four times. In a few minutes, he could make out an eye looking through the peephole. A voice came through the door.

"Who's there?"

"It's Cody Thomas, ma'am. I called a few minutes ago. I'm here to see Lola."

"Let me see some I.D., please."

He took out his wallet and pulled out a credit card. He couldn't use his driver's license because he had told her he was from out of town. The eye in the peephole scanned the credit card. A moment later, the door opened, and there stood a woman, who was about as tall as Cody.

She was dressed in a loose-fitting multicolored dressing gown that hung to the floor. Her hair was bleached blond and frizzy with a cheap comb stuck in the back. The makeup she wore was thick and gaudy. A cheap pair of glasses clung to her nose as she peered over the rims. A cigarette dangled from her mouth, and her one eye was half closed to protect it from the smoke that was coming from the cigarette. On her feet were dirty faded silver slippers with white pompons on the insteps. She stepped aside and motioned for Cody to come in. He hoped the women who worked here looked better than Lola.

The apartment surprised Cody with its lavishness. The living room was large and expensively furnished. Covering the floor was a beautiful wall-to-wall white shag rug. Two large brown velvet sofas sat against opposite walls. They looked like they were brand new. There was a large glass coffee table on the floor between them, on which sat a crystal vase with fresh flowers. A square porcelain ashtray was filled with cigarette butts.

There were two straight-backed brocade armchairs against another wall near the large flat screened TV set. The walls were covered with white-on-white wallpaper. Two sizeable and expensive-looking oil paintings hung on the walls above the sofas.

The TV was on, showing one of those corny soap operas. Cody was very impressed with the place, considering what the building looked like on the outside and what Lola looked like on the inside.

Since Lola had catered to a rich clientele over the years, it was probably necessary that she keep it in the very best of shape. Cody remembered that her girls were expensive, so Lola could afford the furnishings.

"Sit down, Mr. Thomas. Now, just what kind of company were you interested in?"

She had no sooner said that than a middle-aged man came through a doorway that led to the back of the apartment. Cody assumed there were bedrooms back there.

"All finished, Charley?" Lola said to him with a big smile. "Was everything okay?"

"Just great, Lola, as usual. I'll see you next week, at the same time."

He put on his jacket and walked to the door with Lola in close pursuit. She opened the door for him.

"See ya next week, then, Charley. Take good care of yourself." Charley said "See ya," and left. Lola then turned her attention to Cody.

"All right, let's get back to you. What's your pleasure?"

"Well, I'll tell you, Lola. What I'm really interested in is some information."

Lola's expression changed dramatically. Her smile drooped, and her eyes squinted.

"Information? What kind of information? What're ya talkin' about? Just who the hell are you? I thought you said you weren't a cop."

"No, I'm not a cop. I'm a private investigator, and I'm trying to get some information on Samuel T. Hollowell. He was a customer of yours, wasn't he?"

"A private 'eye.' Why you sneaky son-of-a-bitch. Lyin' your way in here like this. I'm tellin' you nothin'. Get the hell outta here."

It didn't take a genius to realize that he had made a mistake in handling Lola. He knew offering her money wasn't going to help. She obviously didn't need his measly few dollars. He decided to try gaining her sympathy. Hookers and madams had a well-known reputation for being softhearted.

"Please, wait a minute, Lola. I'm in real trouble, and you may be the only one who can help me."

"Don't gimme that bullshit. I don't deal with private 'dicks.' You guys are nothin' but trouble."

"Lola, listen for a minute, will you, please. My wife is under indictment for murdering Samuel Hollowell. And since I found your name at his office, I thought you might be able to help me. Won't you at least listen?"

Cody paused for a minute for dramatic effect. Staring sad-eyed into Lola's eyes, he thought he detected a little softer attitude.

"Look, Mr. . . . . er . . . Thomas, or whatever your name is, how the hell do you think I can help ya? What are ya lookin' for?"

"I'm just trying to find out who spent Hollowell's last few hours with him. I know he was with a woman. If I could find her, she might be able to give me a clue of some sort."

"What makes you think she was one of my ladies?"

Good, Cody thought. *At least she isn't throwing me out.* His experience as a cop had taught him that as long as someone was willing to talk, he was in pretty good shape. So he continued, "Well, I don't know that for sure, but I know that Hollowell liked pretty women, and I'm told that yours are the finest in the city. Besides, as I said, I found your name in his files."

"There's no doubt 'bout that," said Lola, referring to the remark about her girls. She was obviously pleased that her reputation was still considered the best. "But why should I give you any information at all?"

Cody could see her tough attitude returning. He decided to take another approach.

"Basically, two reasons. One, because I can see that you're a nice person and just might want to help me, and two, because if you don't, I may just have to get my friends downtown to harass you. And you know that wouldn't be good for business."

He could see by Lola's expression that he had hit her where it could hurt the most. She knew that even though she paid off, the police had to make a show of "doing the right thing" every now and then. And even if things slowed down for only a week or two, she would lose plenty of money. Cody knew she wouldn't want that. After a few minutes contemplation, Lola said in a subdued voice, "Okay, what exactly do ya want from me?"

"Can you tell me if Hollowell had a date with any of your ladies three nights ago?"

"Three nights ago? I'll hafta look on the computer. Wait a minute."

She walked to the large desk situated in the corner of the room across from the two sofas. She began to type in some information. Just then, the fancy French phone rang. Lola picked it up.

"Quality Escort Service. Can I help you?"

Cody could tell that Lola recognized the voice on the other end.

"Oh, it's you. Is it that time of the month already?" She obviously wasn't happy to be talking to this person.

"Yes, it's ready. Send your boy over any time."

She put the phone back on the cradle and appeared distracted. She looked over at Cody and began typing again. The phone rang once more. Again she said, "Quality Escort Service. Can I help you? Oh, hello, Bill." Her voice softened noticeably. "Are you calling for Helga?"

The person on the other end of the line must have answered yes, because Lola said, "Well, she's available. Do ya want me to send her to the usual place?" A brief pause, and then she said, "Okay, sweetheart. She'll be there in 'bout half an hour."

Lola placed the receiver of the French phone down and picked up a small handheld organizer. She punched in some keys until she apparently located the information she was looking for. She dialed a number and waited. Soon, someone answered, and she said, "Helga? It's me. Yeah! Your friend, William the Conqueror, called. He's interested in seein' you today. I told 'im you'd be there in 'bout half an hour. Is that all right? Good! Don't forget your playthings. Bye."

Cody's ears had perked up like a dog that that just heard his master's whistle when he heard Lola talking about playthings. Was Helga the lady who tied people to the bed?

"All right, now, let's get back to you."

Lola began working the computer again. When she found the date in question, she ran the list of clients. A few seconds later, she looked up and said, "I don't see Hollowell's name in here for that night. He wasn't with any of my ladies."

139

Cody's heart sank. He was hoping that Lola would find Helga's name. But instead, he was left with the prospect that Joanna was the only one in Hollowell's room that night. *There must have been someone else there,* he thought.

"I said, he wasn't with any of my ladies," Lola repeated because Cody was lost in his thoughts.

"What? Well . . . ah . . . I was hoping he was. I'm really in a bind now. He must've been with someone other than my wife."

Cody let that slip out quite accidentally.

"Your *wife*? You mean *she* was with Hollowell?"

"Uh . . . yeah, she was. That's why I'm here. I've just got to place someone else in that room that night, so I can get her off the hook."

"And you're lookin' for one of my girls? Why, you lousy bastard. And I'm tryin' to help you? Get out. Get the hell out, right now. I don't care who you know downtown."

She walked to the door and opened it. Cody knew that this visit was over, so he walked dejectedly out the door, which slammed shut behind him. As he walked to his car, he remembered Lola's phone conversation with someone who was told to come over at any time. Who was that? Was it one of the mob boys collecting their piece of the action? Was it the payoff to the cops who protected Lola's spot?

Cody had to know. He decided to wait in his car to see if he could recognize the collector, whoever it was. Crouching low in the front seat, he waited. It wasn't long until that craving for a cigarette gripped him. It was stronger than ever. He reached into his pocket absentmindedly, expecting to find a pack. When he realized one wasn't there, he searched frantically for something, anything, to satisfy his craving. He found only an old cough drop. He took off the paper covering it and popped it into his mouth. Would this help? He didn't think so.

He tried not to think about it. Instead, he thought about the case, about Joanna, Sarah Hollowell, Olivia Hastings, ah, Ms. Hastings. Could she have been one of Hollowell's dates? She sure seemed ready to protect his reputation. He would have to talk to her again, and he would do that soon.

While waiting for about four and a half hours, he had seen six cars drive up and park. Six men had walked into the alley. These were well-dressed distinguished-looking men who stayed an average of three-quarters of an hour, came out, and drove off.

The seventh car, however, a large black Cadillac, pulled up with two swarthy young men in the front seat and parked for only a few minutes. A short broad man dressed in a dark blue pinstriped suit and walking with a definite swagger disappeared into the alley. Cody thought he detected a bulge under his left arm.

As Blue Suit came out of the alley, he looked around furtively, pulled down on the brim of his hat, and continued on to the Cadillac. Behind the wheel was another man. This one also wore a hat with the brim snapped down over his brow. His suit, however, was a flashy gray plaid, and he wore a bright red tie. His face wore the same scowl as Mr. Blue Suit.

These probably were the "bagmen" for the mob. They must be picking up their monthly skim. Cody had to know whom they worked for, so he decided to follow the car. As the Cadillac pulled away from the curb, Cody started the motor of his own car and eased into the traffic about two or three car lengths behind. His heart was pounding with excitement.

At last, he might be getting somewhere. If these were Gino's men, as he suspected, this would confirm the mob's connection with Lola. Since Lola hadn't denied that Hollowell was a customer of hers, Cody felt that suggested Gino, Lola, and Hollowell were somehow associated. Hollowell's relationship with these people was probably more than just as a consumer. Cody was feeling better already. This was something he could get his teeth into. However, he knew he had to be careful. Gino didn't fool around.

CHAPTER 14

The Cadillac pulled up in front of a small restaurant on a side street. Cody stopped a block behind and watched the two men enter through the front door. After allowing a few minutes for the men to get settled, he drove his car slowly past the restaurant and tried to see what was going on inside.

Printed on the window, in large white letters, was the name of the restaurant, "La Cuccina Famiglia." Because the letters obscured his view, Cody was unable to see inside. Since he wanted to know with whom these men were meeting, he parked his car at the end of the block and walked casually back toward the restaurant.

In front of the window, he pretended to read the menu that was taped there. After a few minutes, he opened the door and walked into a large room, which had many tables. They were covered with white linen tablecloths. The walls were covered with a dark red flowered paper and had what looked like original artwork hanging at various intervals. Cody thought that some local artist probably did these paintings. There were prices on the frames. The floor was made of white tiles, which were stained by food and foot marks from years of use.

There was a long bar to the right which ran half the length of the wall. Like many bars, the back wall had a large mirror. Shelves containing many different kinds of liquor were attached to the mirror.

A bartender was standing behind the bar, indifferently pushing a folded white cloth napkin across the top of the bar. He stared intently at Cody, making him feel very uneasy. Cody stood by the door waiting to be seated.

There were people at only three tables. A man and woman at one; a man, woman, and child of about six or seven at another; and in the back, against the far wall, were four men. Two of the men were the ones from the Cadillac. They had their backs to the door. Facing Cody were two other men.

One was a large man appearing to weigh 250 to 300 pounds. He wore a gray suit with the jacket open. Cody could make out a strap, which undoubtedly held a shoulder holster. The fat man was eating pasta.

The other man was well built with neatly combed graying hair. His skin was tanned and without wrinkles. When he smiled, his teeth were white as the clouds in a clear afternoon sky. His eyes were dark brown, almost black, and seemed as though they could look right through you.

He wore light tan slacks and a dark blue sport shirt, open at the collar. The sleeves were buttoned at the wrists. His shoes were shined to a high polish so that they reflected the white tablecloths nearby. He was a good-looking man who knew how to dress and clearly cared about his appearance.

A newspaper was on the table in front of him. He was talking to one of the men who had just sat down. *He must be "The Man,"* thought Cody.

Staring hard at him, Cody tried to remember what Gino looked like. He had seen him last, maybe, ten years ago. Gino was younger then, naturally, but the features were essentially the same. That was Good Night Gino in the flesh.

After a few minutes, Cody looked over at the bartender and said, "Do you seat yourself?"

The man behind the bar, who had not taken his eyes off him, slowly walked around from behind the bar toward Cody, with a menu in his hand.

"Smokin' or nonsmokin'?" he asked in a deep gravelly voice. Cody looked around and saw no one smoking. He chuckled to himself and thought, *This guy must be kidding.* He answered, "Nonsmoking."

The bartender gestured toward a table near the door. As Cody sat down, the bartender threw the menu down in front of him. *What a personality,* thought Cody, while quickly glancing toward the rear table. He opened the menu so as to appear like any other customer.

"Whaddya want t'drink?" asked the same deep voice.

Cody, who was distracted, looked up at him and stuttered, "Ah ... a beer, a light beer." He wanted to get back to observing Gino and the boys.

As the bartender left the table, Cody could see the fat man eyeing him. He didn't want to appear to be staring back, so he dropped his gaze to the menu and pretended to read it. Although he was straining to hear, he couldn't make out the whispers from the back table.

When he looked up again, he could see the man in the blue suit take a brown paper bag from his suit pocket and place it on the table in front of Gino. *This guy is really a "bag" man,* mused Cody. The bartender brought his beer.

"Whaddya want t'eat?"

"I think I'll just have an antipasto and a cup of pasta y fagioli," he said, using the correct Italian instead of the Americanized, "pasta fazool."

The hulking bartender turned away without a word and walked back past Gino's table, which was in the direction of the kitchen. As he went by it, Cody could see him glance at the fat man, which forced his eyes off Cody for that moment. The fat man's expression seemed to ask, "Who the hell is that character?" as he tipped his head toward Cody ever so slightly. The bartender shrugged and continued into the kitchen.

Obviously, these people were very careful and suspicious of anyone they didn't recognize. Cody knew he had to be composed and not give himself away. From then on, he glanced in their direction only occasionally.

His soup and salad were served, and he ate them rather quickly. No one else came into the restaurant. Those who were there had finished and left, leaving Cody alone except for the men in the back. The bartender didn't offer another beer as he dropped the check on the table. It was obvious that Cody wasn't wanted anymore.

"Ya c'n pay me now," said Mr. Personality.

"Do you take credit cards?"

"No. Cash only."

"Oh, wait just a minute."

Cody reached into his back pocket and pulled out his wallet. He opened it, took out a $20 bill, and handed it to the bartender. The check came to $12.50. He said to Cody, "D'ya want change?"

Cody contemplated a minute and said, "No, that's okay. Keep it."

Since he was the only one left in the place, he didn't want to wait until the bartender made change and came back. He was trying not to be conspicuous at this point.

"T'anks. Come again," said "The Hulk," a remark which Cody felt he clearly didn't mean.

As he got up to leave, Cody looked to the back again, one last time, and saw that Gino had his eyes fixed on him, the fat man too. He hoped he didn't appear to be as nervous as he actually was. Getting out of there as quickly as possible was his first priority.

He hurried to the door, opened it, and stepped out onto the pavement. As he closed the door, he breathed a sigh of relief. The fact that he was shaking made him realize just how scary these guys were. When he walked past the window, he noticed that Mr. Blue Suit had moved closer to the window and was observing him. He tried to act as nonchalant as he could.

He walked the one block to his car, got in, and started the motor. As he pulled away, he wondered if he had been too suspicious looking. Was he that out of place? Are they that smart, or are they just very cautious? *Probably just cautious,* he thought. At least, he hoped so.

It was now 7:30 p.m., and he realized he was tired. It had been a busy and relatively fruitful day. Since he hadn't spoken to Joanna at all, he dialed their number on the cell phone. The phone rang six or seven times, but there was no answer. Where was Joanna? She should be home. He disconnected and sped home.

* * * *

All the way home, Cody's thoughts were spinning out of control. Where was Joanna? Why wasn't she home? Was she out on another date? If so, with whom? Was she hiding evidence? Was she killing someone?

He couldn't stop the flood of suspicion, no matter how hard he tried. When he arrived at the house, he didn't see Joanna's car in the driveway. He bolted from the car and onto the front porch. Fumbling with the key, it took him a few seconds to put it into the lock. When he finally opened the door and stepped into the family room, there were small beads of sweat on his forehead. He called out, "Joanna! Joanna! Are you in here?"

He was hoping against hope that she was there even though the car wasn't. Racing up the stairs, he went directly to the back room office where she had been the other night. She wasn't there. The bedroom was empty too.

He slumped down on the bed. Not knowing what was happening, his thoughts flipped back to his first wife. She, too, had been gone when he came home late one day. That led eventually to their divorce. Now, Joanna was out. Doing what? Just then, he heard a car drive up.

He went to the bedroom window and looked down. Joanna's car was pulling into the driveway. He rushed out of the bedroom and down the stairs. The door was opening as he reached the family room. When Joanna saw him, she appeared a bit startled. She opened her mouth, about to say something, but he blurted out, "Where the hell were you?"

"What?" Joanna's mouth dropped open. "Where was I? I was waiting for you at the diner."

"You were waiting for me at the diner? What diner?" He was confused. What was she talking about? He had not been at any diner.

While he was trying to organize his thoughts, Joanna said, "The Rosemont Diner at Ninth and Federal. I went there to meet you."

"I was never at the Rosemont Diner tonight or any other night for that matter. I never called you to go there, either."

He could see Joanna was puzzled. Her face was screwed up in a perplexed frown.

"I didn't say you called. I said I was told to meet you there. Someone, who said she was the bail bondsman's secretary, said there was a problem with the bail, and I was to meet you and him at the diner."

"Metz! He doesn't even have a secretary."

"Metz? Who's that? She said the name was Schwartz, Arnold Schwartz."

"I don't know anyone by the name of Schwartz. Our guy's name is Metz, Myron Metz. What are you trying to pull, Joanna?"

He knew he was being hard on her, but he was feeling deceived again. Were all women liars? Why did Joanna have to screw around with Hollowell? His feelings right now were so jumbled; he was trying to deal with them, but he couldn't reconcile them.

"What am I trying to pull? Are you saying you don't believe me? I'm not making this stuff up, you know."

"Look, Joanna, I'm trying like hell to understand this, but can you blame me for being suspicious? After all, you're the one who was fucking around."

Cody knew he was being hurtful, but he couldn't help himself. He saw the tears welling up in Joanna's eyes. A low blow had been struck, and he knew it. She turned away from him and ran to the kitchen. He stood frozen for a moment, trying to decide if he should believe her story, because if he didn't, there would be no justification for his staying around.

He wondered why she would make up something like this, something that would be very easy to check out. She did appear genuinely confused. And hadn't she eventually confessed about Hollowell and appeared truly sorry?

Trying to clear his mind of all his suspicions, he walked slowly toward the kitchen. He wanted to make a real effort to listen to Joanna and understand what had happened. When he reached the kitchen, Joanna was sitting in a chair with her arms on the table and head buried in her hands. She was sobbing softly.

He walked over to her and touched her on the shoulder. She didn't respond. He sat on a chair next to her and put his hand on her back. Again, no response. Sitting quietly, he waited. Finally, she sat up, looked at him, and said, "Cody, I am going to leave the house tonight. It's obvious that you no longer trust me, and I don't see the point in us staying together."

He was staggered by Joanna's statement. He had never thought, even for a moment, that she would consider leaving. Memories of his first wife walking out on him flooded back. The same feelings of desolation gripped him. He didn't want to go through that again. And besides, down deep, he wanted to believe Joanna.

After thinking about her story, he supposed it could be true. It had to be true. He looked at her intently.

"Listen, Joanna. I don't want you to leave. I'm sorry I blew my stack. I really didn't mean to hurt you. But you must try to understand my feelings too. So much has happened over the last few days. It's been a little rough."

"Rough on you? What about me? Don't you think it's been rough on me?"

Cody listened and knew she had a point. He was going to have to stop throwing things up to her every time he got upset. There must be a way for him to control himself better.

"I know it's been hard on you too. I'm going to try to do a better job of controlling my emotions."

"I hope so. You must believe that I love you and wouldn't consciously do anything to hurt you either. What went on between Hollowell and me was an aberration. I wouldn't consider ever doing anything like that again with anyone for any reason. You must know that."

"I do know that."

Those words came out, but did he truly mean them? He knew he must if he wanted to keep the marriage together.

"I hope you do mean it, Cody, because I don't think I can take another assault from you. It just hurts too much."

"I'm going to try my best. I promise. Okay, now, let's go over what happened today."

Joanna seemed to feel better, as she began to tell the story again, this time with more detail.

"First of all, I waited all day for you to call me. When you didn't, I became more and more frightened. Then, about four thirty or so, the phone rang. I thought it was you. When the voice on the phone said I was to meet you, I didn't question it. I just followed the directions."

"Did you recognize the voice at all?"

"No, I don't think so. I really didn't pay too much attention to it."

He was wondering who would try to lure Joanna out of the house and why.

"Okay, go on."

"Anyway, she said I was to meet you at the diner with the deed to the house. I said okay and hung up. But I couldn't find the deed."

"No, you couldn't have, because I already gave it to Metz."

"Oh, I didn't know that. No wonder I couldn't find it. I decided to go anyway because I didn't know what was going on with the bail, and I was scared.

"When I got there, you weren't there, so I waited. I waited for three hours, not knowing what I was supposed to do. When you didn't show up, I phoned the house and your cell phone. There was no answer from either phone. I didn't know what to think. I just decided to drive home, and you know the rest."

"Yeah, I know the rest," he said, remorsefully. "I must've been in the restaurant when you called."

"What restaurant?"

"It's a long story. Speaking of restaurants, are you hungry? You must be. What do you say we go out and get something to eat, and I'll tell you all about my day."

"That sounds great."

They walked hand in hand to the front door and out onto the porch. Cody felt more at ease with himself now. He didn't really know why, but he did. Perhaps he was basically satisfied that Joanna was telling the truth, and that was enough right now.

CHAPTER 15

After having dinner at a local restaurant, they returned home and went to bed. Cody had filled Joanna in on the events of the day. She had asked a lot of questions about the brothel. She was nervous about the restaurant "boys" as she put it. Although he'd told her not to worry, that everything was under control, secretly, he too was concerned about them.

When Cody awoke the next morning, Joanna was already up. The smell of coffee and bacon was in the air. He was hungry and felt like having a big breakfast. After taking a quick shower and shave, he put on fresh clothes and went downstairs.

As he entered the kitchen, Joanna turned from the range and smiled.

"Good morning, sweetheart." Her tone suggested that she had put aside the conversation of last night, which made him happy. He wanted to try to forget it too.

"Good morning," he replied. "Did you sleep well?"

"Great! And you?"

"Like a baby. What're you cooking?"

"I thought I'd give you a treat, so I'm making you pancakes and bacon. How's that?"

Cody felt like he used to when they were first married. She would often get up early and cook him a big breakfast. Somehow, she didn't do that much anymore. Cody thought, *This is terrific, just like old times.*

When he came back from getting the morning paper, Cody sat down at the table and put some sugar in the coffee Joanna had poured him. He was about to read the front page when there was a knock on the front door. They looked at each other in surprise, and then he said, "Who can that be at this hour of the morning?"

It was 8:30 a.m. Cody went to the door and opened it. He was startled to see Andy Perone standing there with two uniformed cops. One was a female.

"What the hell are you doing here, Andy?"

"I'm afraid I have some more bad news for you, Cody. Joanna's bail has been revoked, and I'm gonna have to take her in again."

Cody was dumbstruck. He just stood there staring at Andy, at first not knowing what to say. Finally, he was able to say, "What is this, some kind of joke? Why would her bail be revoked?"

"There's been another murder."

But before Andy could get any further, Cody interrupted. "Oh, do you mean the Johnston killing? I know about that. What's that got to do with Joanna?"

"This isn't about the Johnston murder. This is about Lola Dupres. She was killed last evening."

"Lola Dupres?"

Cody was in a state of total shock. His mind and body were transfixed with confusion and bewilderment. When he got himself under some control, he continued, "How in hell did you connect Joanna with Lola Dupres's murder? What is this, some kind of witch hunt?"

"We found Joanna's brooch at the crime scene, that's how."

Again, Cody found himself speechless. Finally, he said, "Joanna's brooch? Wait a minute, Andy. How do you know it's Joanna's brooch?"

"Because it has an inscription on the back that says, 'To Joanna, 6/17/94, Love, Cody.'"

Cody remembered that inscription. It was on the brooch he had given her on their wedding day. There was no doubt that it was Joanna's.

"What time was she killed?" he asked.

"Between 5:30 p.m. and 8:30 p.m. last night. She was found in a motel just off Federal Street in Old Town."

Cody's mind immediately flashed back to last evening and Joanna being out of the house during that time period. Could she have been deceiving him when she told him the diner story? Could she have been lying about everything?

His first reaction was to rush in and confront Joanna with this latest development. Then he thought this whole thing sounded too cut and dry. Like someone was going out of his or her way to set up Joanna. He needed time to think this through; however, he didn't have time. Andy was here and was going to take her away.

"Where was Joanna last night between those hours?"

Cody knew that as soon as he told Andy that Joanna was out of the house, he would essentially be incriminating her. But what else could he say? He knew Andy would find out sooner or later, if he didn't already know.

"Ah . . . she was waiting for me at a diner."

"You mean she was alone and out of the house?"

"Yes, but we can explain the whole thing."

By this time, Joanna had come into the family room from the kitchen. When she saw Andy, she rushed to Cody and clutched his arm.

"What are you doing here, Andy? Cody, what's going on?"

Cody could feel her shaking as she clung to him.

"Joanna, I'm gonna have to take you in again."

"Take me in? What's he talking about, Cody? Why am I being arrested again?"

"For the murder of Lola Dupres," Andy said, in a cold and professional tone.

"Lola Dupres? I don't know anyone by that name. I didn't kill anyone. Cody, tell him it wasn't me. This must be some mistake."

Joanna was clearly panicking. Cody thought he had better not let her say anything else before she got herself in deeper.

"Take it easy, honey. Don't say any more. We'll get Harvey. He'll take care of this." He turned to Andy and said, "I want to call our lawyer."

"Okay. Tell him to meet you at the precinct."

Cody went to the phone with Joanna clinging to him, like a vine to a tree. He dialed Harvey's number and waited. Once again,

Thelma answered, "Law office of Harvey Whitcomb. Can I help you?"

"Thelma, this is Cody Thomas. Is Harvey there?"

"No, Cody. He's in court today. Can I help you?"

"I need him now. Can you reach him at all?"

"I can try his cell phone, but he usually has it turned off when he is in court."

"Will you do that, please. It's urgent. I must speak to him immediately." There was enough stress in his voice to convey that message to Thelma without him saying it.

"Okay, Cody. I'll try to reach him right now. Maybe court isn't in session yet. It's not nine o'clock yet."

"Good! Have him call me at home."

As he said that, he turned to Andy with his hands slightly outstretched and his head pushed forward as if to be pleading. "Could you give me just a few minutes?" Andy's face tightened as he shrugged his shoulders and shook his head disgustedly.

"He'd better call back in two or three minutes, or we won't be here."

"Thanks!" Cody turned to Joanna. "Go upstairs and get dressed, honey."

"This officer will go with her," said Andy, pointing to the female cop.

"Is that really necessary, Andy?"

"Yes, I'm afraid it is."

There was no explanation coming from Andy. It was just going to be that way, and Cody knew it. He nearly had to shove Joanna to get her to go. She was immobilized with fear. It seemed like hours until the phone rang. Cody rushed to pick it up.

"Hello, Harvey. Thank God! Harve, I need you right now. I know you're in court, but can you postpone the case somehow? You've just got to. Joanna's in big trouble, and you must meet us at the thirty-ninth precinct. They've revoked her bail." After a short pause, he said, "They're accusing her of another murder."

As Cody was pleading with Harvey, Joanna came downstairs and ran to his side again. She was ashen. Her fear was so intense, she wasn't even crying. Cody continued talking to Harvey.

"Yeah, we're leaving right now. How long before you can be there? Make it sooner, please. Okay, we'll see you there. And Harve, thanks."

He hung up the phone and put his arms around Joanna, trying to ease her fears.

"Harvey will be at the station in about half an hour. Don't worry, honey, we'll get this straightened out."

The policewoman came over to Joanna with her handcuffs prepared. Cody glanced at Andy with a pitiable look on his face, silently imploring him not to cuff Joanna. He knew that Andy got the message when he told the officer to forget it for now. It appeared as if Andy was showing some class for the first time since this whole mess started. Cody put his arm around Joanna, and they walked out the door. Joanna got into the police car first, and they drove off to the station.

* * * *

159

They were at the station for about thirty minutes before Harvey arrived. Once again, he was breathless and frazzled. They went to the consultation room and tried to sort through the facts. Cody informed him of the charges and what little he knew about the murder. He also told Harvey about the brooch.

That's what really bothered Cody. How did Joanna's brooch get to the crime scene? He had asked her, and she replied that she didn't know. She said that it had been at home in her jewelry box and that she hadn't worn it for months. In fact, neither of them had seen the brooch for a long time.

Harvey looked a bit unsure, and Cody wondered if he had some doubts. He said to him, "I'm going to go talk to Andy for a while. I'll see if he'll tell me anything useful."

"Okay," replied Harvey, "but don't be too optimistic."

He left and hurried to Andy's office, a place that was becoming very distasteful to him. When he arrived, Andy was sitting behind his desk working on some papers. Andy's office was really nothing but a small cubicle in the back of the larger room that housed all the detectives in the precinct. It had a large window separating Andy from the rest of the crew. He could look out on them, and they could see him.

His desk was neat, and everything was in the right place. It was just like Andy's personality, by the numbers. Cody knocked on the door and walked in. Andy looked up and appeared somewhat irritated.

"I'm kinda busy right now, Cody. I really can't talk to you."

"I just need to bother you for a minute or two. You can listen to me, for old times' sake, can't you?"

"I told ya before, you can't keep usin' that gimmick, Cody."

Andy was really sounding like a hard ass again. Cody thought the pressure must be on again. But he persisted.

"Okay, then, listen because it's the fair thing to do, because you happen to like Joanna a little, or because I don't have anywhere else to turn, whatever reason you like best. Just give me some time, will you?"

Andy sat back in his chair and exhaled through his partially closed mouth, making a whistling sound.

"All right, go ahead."

"Thanks, pal," Cody said sarcastically. Then with a sense of urgency, he began to try to make Andy see the light, his light.

"First of all, don't you think it's very convenient that Joanna's brooch was found right there? I mean, really, would she be dumb enough to do that?"

"She might not have realized that it came off. She could've been in a big hurry, right?"

"All right, then, what's her motive?"

Cody was asking these questions, not only to get information, but in an attempt to understand what was happening. The web of circumstantial evidence surrounding Joanna was getting thicker and thicker.

He wanted to believe she was innocent. Yet every time he began trusting her again, something new and incriminating popped up to weaken his resolve. Once again, Joanna appeared to have had the opportunity to kill somebody. However, if her story about the diner was true, then someone must be setting Joanna up as the killer. While Cody was mulling this over, Andy broke the silence.

"I'm not sure about that just yet, but I haven't talked to her about it, either. And you even said she wasn't in the house at the time of the murder."

"Yeah, that's true, but it's too obvious. It looks like a setup to me. She was called by someone claiming there was a problem with her bail and that she was to meet me at the Rosemont Diner."

"The Rosemont Diner? Is that where she was? That's on Federal Street, not far from the motel where Dupres was killed."

Cody immediately felt a twinge of remorse. He had just put Joanna in an area close enough to commit the murder. But then he realized that Andy would have found out about it sooner or later. Trying to direct Andy closer to his own thoughts, he said, "Yeah, don't you see it? It's a perfect setup. They not only got her out of the house, but they put her in close proximity to the murder. It's all too perfect, Andy. Can't you see it?"

"Perhaps, but what about the brooch? How do ya explain that?"

"I'm not sure yet. But Joanna hasn't worn that thing in months. Check the clasp, I think it might be broken."

Cody was beginning to see the whole plot more clearly now. Hollowell was killed for whatever reason. Joanna happened to be there. She would be a perfect patsy. Then, Johnston was killed to make sure he didn't tell who hired the cab. Now, Lola is murdered. She had to be killed because she knew Hollowell, and perhaps also knew whoever else was mixed up in this whole case. Again, Joanna would be the perfect pawn. Get her out of the house. Make her alibi seem contrived. Drop the brooch.

Ah, the brooch. How did they get that? It had to have been stolen from the house while he and Joanna were gone. He had to get back to the house and look around.

"Well, it really doesn't matter. It's her brooch, isn't it? It was at the scene, and she had the opportunity. That's enough for the district attorney to hold her. And that's enough questions for now."

Cody could see he wasn't going to get any further with Andy, so he stood up. "Okay, Andy. Thanks for your time. Try to give my explanation some thought. I'll see you later."

With that, Cody walked out the door and into the bustling detectives' room. He wanted to talk to Harvey about his theory, and he had to get home to search for evidence of a break-in.

If he could find anything solid, he just might convince Andy that his ideas had some merit. He hurried to the consultation room. This was getting monotonous. Boy, could he use a cigarette right now. He fought the urge, but he was weakening.

CHAPTER 16

As Cody walked into the consultation room, Harvey and Joanna were sitting across from each other at the table. Harvey was wearing the same blue serge suit that he had worn the previous day. His wavy hair looked like it had been tossed around without much concern. That was Harvey. He was all business and didn't care much about his appearance.

Joanna was clearly in a state of shock. She appeared to be listening to Harvey, but Cody didn't believe that anything was sinking in. He sat next to Joanna at the table, put his arm over her shoulder, and said to Harvey, "What are our options, Harve? What you think is going to happen next?"

"Well, as I was just trying to explain to Joanna, with this new charge and the brooch as evidence, they can revoke the bail. That means she is going to have to go to jail. I don't think they have any recourse."

As he said that, the realities of the situation seemed to hit Joanna. She put her head on Cody's chest and began to cry. He tried to calm her but could see that it would be impossible at this point. The three of them just sat there for a few minutes, waiting for Joanna to settle down.

Finally, he said, "Harvey, I've been giving this a lot of thought. It seems to me that this whole thing is too slick. Everything is right there for the cops. I think Joanna's been set up. To my mind, it's just the kind of thing the mob would and could do. What do *you* think?"

"I kind of agree about the setup, but why would the mob want to set up Joanna?"

"It's not that they wanted to get Joanna, it's that she was just at the wrong place at the right time. Don't you see? Someone must have gotten wind of the fact that Hollowell was going to his favorite haunt with a date, which just happened to be Joanna. Once they knew that, they set the ball rolling. This allowed them, whoever they are, to drop enough clues to convince the cops that Joanna did it. The Johnston and Dupres murders were part of the cover-up. And now this brooch thing, it's all too clean."

Harvey was listening closely and nodding his head; Joanna was still crying but more softly.

"I guess that sounds reasonable, Cody. However, without some sort of proof, it's going to be hard to convince a judge to continue her bail."

"I know, Harve. I'm going to have to work faster. I must be on the right track though. Yesterday, I spoke with Lola Dupres, and today, she's dead."

Joanna had all but stopped crying and was only sobbing intermittently. Cody felt like he could talk to her now, so he turned to her.

"You've got to try to control yourself, honey. It looks like you're going to be in here for a while." He quickly added, "Not too long though because I'm going to find out who did this and get you out."

"I don't think I'll be able to stand it," Joanna sobbed into his shoulder. He hugged her closer to him.

"It'll only be for a little while. I promise. I'm on the right track. I'm sure of it."

He knew he was completely disregarding the fact that she certainly had the motive and opportunity to kill Hollowell. She also had the opportunity to kill the other two people. But by plugging away, he felt he would get to the bottom of it. He turned to Harvey.

"I'm sure they are going to want to interrogate her again before they incarcerate her."

"Absolutely. What are you going to do now?"

Cody looked at his watch and saw that it was now 10:00 a.m. They probably wouldn't be through with Joanna for another couple of hours. He decided his first order of business would be to go home and look for evidence that someone had broken into the house.

Then, he wanted to get to the motel where Lola was killed. He knew, however, that getting a look at the crime scene would be a problem, particularly if Andy were going to continue to play hardball. Detective Wilson would have to be visited again. And he must get back to the Hollowell house in order to find out about a private office. Then, there was Ms. Hastings.

Another busy day, he thought. He had to hurry because Joanna would get crazy if she had to stay in jail too long. After recounting his itinerary to Harvey and Joanna, he put his arm gently around her.

"Do what Harvey says, okay? I'll be back in a couple of hours. Try to hold yourself together and don't worry."

He could see that Joanna was trying her best to be strong, but he knew that she was not handling this too well. She didn't answer, only smiled weakly, and put her arms around him and held on tightly. If he was going to unravel this mess, he had to get moving. He stood up and turned to Harvey.

"Call me as soon as Andy is done. Here's the number of my cell phone. I'll keep it turned on." After scribbling the number on a scrap of paper, he looked back to Joanna.

"I've got to go now. The sooner I get started, the sooner I'll get done. Try to stay calm, okay?"

"I'll try, but please hurry. I won't be able to stand this too long."

"I'll hurry, don't worry. See you soon. And don't forget, Harve, call me just as soon as you're finished with Andy. I'll come right back."

"Okay."

Cody hurried out of the room without glancing back at Joanna. He knew if he had to look at her unhappy face again, it would be even more difficult to leave. Dashing through the station house and out to his car, he headed directly home. All he had on his mind was getting to the bottom of this case and restoring his and Joanna's life back to normalcy.

*   *   *   *

Jumping out of the car almost before he turned off the engine, Cody ran up the stairs to the porch and examined the lock for evidence of scratches. After careful inspection, he saw what appeared to be small thin scratches, which easily could have been made by a picklock or just from the house key. Using his key, he opened the door and went quickly to the bedroom. Joanna had said that the last time she had seen the brooch, it was in the jewelry box in the bedside table. He opened the top drawer and carefully examined the contents. Joanna kept her pajamas, handkerchiefs, and jewelry in this drawer.

The jewelry was in a large flat box on the bottom of the drawer. Joanna, being extremely neat and meticulous, had placed every pair of pajama tops and bottoms, one on top of another. The handkerchiefs were next in order, and then the jewelry box. He carefully lifted each piece and noted if any were out of place. As he lifted the third pajama top, he saw a handkerchief sitting on a pajama bottom. This was not right. Joanna would not have a handkerchief between a pair of pajamas. Someone had removed the box, and then put the contents of the drawer back hurriedly, misplacing a handkerchief.

He closed the drawer and looked through some of the other drawers. Although the thief had been careful, Cody could tell that the contents of most of them had been slightly rearranged. This must have been a professional job. Now, he was going to have to convince Andy that the brooch had been stolen. But how?

In the kitchen, he warmed up some stale coffee and tried to think for a minute. That old urge for a cigarette was back. Just as he was contemplating going out and buying some, the phone rang. He decided to let the answering machine take the call.

THE SOUNDS OF DEATH

After four rings, the machine played the taped message Joanna had recorded. Then a deep, scratchy voice came on.

"Thomas, we know who ya are. Quit yer fuckin' snoopin' around. If ya know what's good for ya, you'll keep your fuckin' nose to yourself, or it might get cut off."

The phone clicked off. Cody was flabbergasted. The comments on the phone sounded like something the mob would say. How had they found out about him? He thought for a moment, and then it hit him. It must have been Lola. She was the only connection between him and the mob. She must have called them and told them that he had been to see her. It wouldn't have taken much for them to find out where he lived.

Now, he was really in trouble. If they got the idea that he was somehow going to mess up their business, they would surely come after him. What the hell was he going to do now? He couldn't stop. Joanna had to be freed. If he took the tape to Andy, it might convince him that the mob was involved, and then he might go easier on Joanna.

He decided against the Dupres crime scene just now. Although the tape of the phone conversation might be helpful in convincing Andy of mob interest, he wanted to see Dan Wilson first. Maybe Wilson had turned up something he could use.

Cody took the tape from the machine and replaced it with a new one, quickly recording a new message. Hurrying to his car, he started for the twenty-eighth precinct station.

*　　*　　*　　*

169

Cody ran quickly through the first floor of the station house, went directly to the stairs, and ran up two steps at a time. Arriving at the desk-filled room busy with detectives, he searched for the balding head of Dan Wilson. Wilson was at his desk, talking on the phone.

This time, Cody went directly to him without waiting. When he arrived at the desk, Wilson was just hanging up. He looked up, somewhat quizzically, not appearing to recognize Cody at first. Then it was clear that he recognized the face and his mouth screwed up in unfriendly sneer. That didn't keep Cody from putting out his hand in a gesture of friendship. Wilson half-heartedly returned Cody's handshake.

"Hi, Sarge. Thought I'd come by and see what you've turned up."

"Ah . . . well . . . just the usual stuff. Nothing earth-shattering."

Cody was hoping Wilson wasn't going to "stonewall" him. He decided to blow a little smoke; it couldn't hurt.

"Ah, come on, Sarge. I know a good detective when I see one. I'll bet you picked up a lot of interesting stuff. What about hairs and fibers, and how about material for DNA examination?"

Wilson clearly wasn't anxious to talk to him. Maybe he'd heard about Cody's reason for leaving the force. He hoped not. Quietly, he waited for Wilson to answer. Finally, reluctantly, he spoke.

"Yeah, there was some hair that we thought didn't belong there. It was long and bleached blond. It could've come from Johnston's date that night, but we can't be sure."

Long and bleached blond, certainly not Joanna's, thought Cody. "That's good. Anything else?"

"We found some partial prints. Whoever it is tried to wipe them off. They must've been in a hurry, though, 'cause they left some."

"Does Andy Perone know about them?"

Cody felt that if they had no similarities with Joanna's prints, Andy might be persuaded to think about dropping the charges against her.

"As a matter of fact, I just faxed them over to the thirty-ninth today. I don't know if Perone made any comparisons yet."

"I sure as hell hope he has. My wife's hair is dirty blond, and it's not bleached. I don't think the prints will match, either."

"Yeah, so what's this got to do with the Hollowell case? I guess there are some similarities, but I don't see anything here that exonerates your wife."

Cody thought about what Wilson said. He supposed that from the detective's point of view, nothing had changed, but from where he stood, this was convincing new evidence that Joanna hadn't killed Johnston. Since, in his mind, the same person had killed both Hollowell and Johnston, it meant that she hadn't killed Hollowell either.

"Well, maybe," he replied. "But to my way of thinking, things are looking up. Have you gotten anything else about the gun?"

"No, nothing, just that it looks like a small-caliber gun, like I told ya that before." Then, while shuffling some of the papers on his desk, he said, "Look, I've got work to do now. I really don't have time to answer any more questions."

Realizing that it was useless to go on, Cody again put out his hand to Wilson and said, "Okay, Sarge, thanks a lot for your help. You don't know how good you've made me feel."

Wilson just about touched his hand and waved him off. "Yeah, yeah. It's okay."

Cody weaved his way through the many desks without glancing back at Wilson. His mind was on other things right now. The long blond hair intrigued him. If there were similar hairs at the Hollowell scene that would certainly be a connection, which Andy couldn't deny. If Joanna's hair didn't show any of the same characteristics, wouldn't that prove that someone else had done the killing? He had to go see Andy next. Between the tape and the new evidence, he had to be as convinced as Cody was of Joanna's innocence.

Cody nearly ran to his car. He hadn't felt this good since this whole thing began.

CHAPTER 17

When Cody arrived at the thirty-ninth precinct station, he virtually sprinted to Andy's office. As he scurried through the outer room toward Andy's cubicle, the detectives at their desks and filing cabinets stopped what they were doing to observe this wild man running among them. In fact, some moved toward Cody as if to try to stop him.

He continued on, however, since he thought some of them probably recognized him from his recent visits to see Andy. But one of the detectives sitting nearby got up from his desk and cut him off before he reached Andy's office.

"What's your hurry, pal? Where do you think you're going?"

"I've got to see Andy Perone right away. Do you know where he is?"

The detective replied with a tight-lipped grin, as he stood between Cody and Andy's door, "He ain't here, as you can plainly see. Who are you, and what do ya want?"

Cody was getting a bit exasperated, both with the attitude of the detective and the fact that Andy wasn't there. He felt himself start to tremble, his signal of anger. Trying to hold his temper in check, he answered, "I'm a private investigator, and I've known the lieutenant for a long time. We're working on a case together."

Cody was reluctant to say his name for fear that it would be recognized. If he did, this detective might really give him a hard time.

"Workin' on a case together? Are you shittin' me? What case?"

"The Hollowell murder. I've got some critical information for him, which I'm sure he'll want to hear."

"I'll bet he does," said the detective with even more sarcasm.

Cody knew this attitude. Many cops disliked private investigators. They seemed to resent the fact that some private investigators were competent and found clues or even solved cases when the police were stumped. They felt that all private investigators were nothing but keyhole peepers.

Then, in an obvious attempt to embarrass him, the detective turned to the room full of cops and said, "Hey, fellahs, this here's a private 'dick' who says he's workin' with Perone on the Hollowell case. I'll bet Perone's happy 'bout that."

The detective said this with a laugh, which was followed by scattered laughter around the room. Cody was on the verge of exploding but thought better of it. He kept himself under control and waited for the laughter to subside. Then, with a nod toward Andy's cubicle, "Look, detective, I promise you that I've known Andy Perone for a long time. I don't think he'd mind if you let me wait in his office till he gets here."

He remembered that Andy was probably still questioning Joanna. It was 12:45 p.m. He estimated that Andy should be finished soon.

"Yeah, how do ya know that, wise guy?"

"I happen to know that he's been interrogating a suspect since ten o'clock, so I'm assuming he'll be back soon."

The detective seemed surprised that Cody knew this, but after a few minutes contemplation, he said, "Okay, Mr. 'Private Eye.' Go ahead in and wait. But if you're bullshittin' me, it'll be your ass. Perone don't like bullshitters, ya know."

Cody opened the door to Andy's office and went in. He looked back and saw the detective staring at him intently. Sitting down in one of the chairs, he crossed his legs. A cigarette would be good right now. A quick look on Andy's desk revealed no cigarettes. Then he remembered Andy had given them up two or three years ago.

From his vantage point, Cody noticed a manila folder on Andy's desk. He pulled his chair closer to the desk to get a better look at it. The name on the front read "HOLLOWELL." *Hot damn!* he thought. He had to get a look at that file.

Cody looked over his shoulder through the glass window in the door to see what the detective was doing. He had returned to his desk, which was only a few feet away, and had his back to Andy's door, he was busy typing. No one else seemed to be paying particular attention to the office. *This is perfect,* he thought.

He reached across Andy's desk with as little movement as possible and picked up the folder. The coroner's report was at the top of the pile. His eyes quickly skimmed through it. There was nothing new there. The next page contained a listing of all the evidence found at the crime scene.

There were the cords, the bed sheet, and the contents of the vacuum cleaner that the criminalists had used as they went over the entire room. These vacuums can pick up pieces of evidence that are easily missed by the naked eye, such as minute pieces of hair and clothing fibers, as well as dirt and dust, that might have been deposited by the perpetrator.

Other pages included the fingerprint reports, the DNA reports, the report on the bullet fragments, and the report of the lipstick smudges that were found. Cody read through these reports hungrily. He was particularly interested in the one on the hair and the fingerprints.

The report on the hair said that there were many different strands of hair found, including some consistent with Joanna's. There were also some long blond ones that were bleached. A small smile spread across his face. "Long bleached blond hairs," he said to himself. It was imperative that these be compared to the ones found at the Johnston scene.

The prints were clearly Joanna's, but there were others, many others. There could be some that matched the partials found at Johnston's. The lipstick matched the color and manufacturer of Joanna's. The DNA report was incomplete, but the material found matched Hollowell's. There was none from Joanna.

Reading the DNA report brought back the pictures of Joanna and Hollowell on the bed. His seemingly secure marriage was now a tangled mess. All this was because of Hollowell. He tried to erase the thoughts, but it was difficult. There was nothing new on the bullet.

Engrossed in the file, he didn't notice Andy's approach. His heart jumped as the door flew open, and Andy walked in. When Andy saw him reading the file, he erupted with rage.

"What the hell d'ya think you're doin'? Who let you in here? Gimme that file."

Andy virtually ripped the folder from Cody's hands. Although flustered, Cody tried to remain cool. "One of your detectives let me come in and wait for you. I came to see you because I have some interesting new stuff that I thought you'd like to see."

"Really!" Andy said, drawing it out with great sarcasm. "Is this like the 'good stuff' you brought me the other night?"

Reminding him of his previous deception, Andy continued, "What do ya have that you think can help? I've just finished with your wife. And frankly, things don't look too good for her."

"We'll see how you feel after you look at what I've got for you this time. First, I'd like you to listen to this tape. After you've heard it, I think you'll agree that there's someone else involved here."

He handed the tape to Andy. Andy looked at it scornfully, as if to say "Nothing you have will help."

"What's this, another murder taking place?"

"Nope. It's a phone call I got this morning. I think you'll find it very interesting."

Andy looked at the tape, for a moment appearing totally disinterested. Cody had been apprehensive, fearing that Andy had already made up his mind about Joanna. Now, he was afraid that

Andy wouldn't be willing to objectively review any evidence which he felt could help change his mind. After all, wasn't there always an alternate explanation for things?

Finally, Andy put the cassette in his tape machine. They listened together to the rough voice as it spoke the warning to Cody. When it was over, Andy stopped the machine and said, "So what? You're getting a warning about stickin' your nose where it don't belong. I'd like to give you the same warnin' sometimes. What's this got to do with Joanna and the murders?"

"Come on, Andy. Isn't it obvious to you that somebody else has an interest in this thing?"

He wondered why Andy couldn't see what he was seeing. Wasn't it obvious that there were other people involved? Was Andy being forced to close this case quickly? Was he willing to railroad Joanna because of other pressures?

"All I hear is you're gettin' on somebody's nerves. You've been runnin' around town like a chicken without a head, talkin' to anyone who'll listen to you. It's no wonder you're getting warnings."

"Yeah, but who's giving the warnings, and why?"

"I sure as hell don't know. Do you?"

"You don't want to know, do you?" These words came out before Cody could stop them. "Andy, aren't you listening? Don't you recognize the routine? You've heard this kind of stuff before, haven't you?"

"Yeah, but how do you think this will help your wife's problem?"

"Okay, let me run it by you. First, if Joanna did this alone, why would anyone else get upset with my investigation? Second, why would Johnston and Lola be killed? Third, why would Joanna want to kill them?"

"Wait a minute!" Andy interrupted. "It's perfectly obvious to me, at least, that they were killed to cover somethin' up. Your wife certainly would have benefited from Johnston's death because he might've contradicted her story about the cab. As for Lola, she could've known about Joanna's sister's prostitution and drug problems. This made Lola a threat to drop that bomb at any time."

Cody was astounded that Andy was so fixed in his interpretation of the facts. It seemed like he wasn't interested in any other explanation. Why? He tried to think back to other cases. Was Andy always so closed-minded, or was he being told what to do? If the mob could control the politicians, like the councilmen or commissioners or even higher up, they could have pressure applied to the police commissioner, who could pressure Andy. He found that hard to believe, but he wondered.

"Andy, please try and open your mind a little. Why would the mob be involved if it were only Joanna? You don't believe she has anything to do with the mob, do you?"

Cody thought he could see the wheels turning in Andy's head. Was he finally getting the point? He continued, "Besides, I know you've gotten some new information from the Johnston case that could certainly be of tremendous importance to Joanna."

"What information are you talkin' about?"

"The fingerprints that Dan Wilson sent over, for one thing."

Andy's eyebrows shot upward, as if to say "How did you know about that? Besides, they're only partials. They won't be too much help."

"They can be, if there are no similarities between those and Joanna's whatsoever, right?"

"Maybe."

Is he beginning to soften a little? wondered Cody.

"And what about the bleached blond hairs that were found at the Johnston murder scene?"

"What about 'em?"

"There were long bleached blond hairs at the Hollowell crime scene too, weren't there? You can compare them, can't you?"

"You know hairs can't be matched exactly, they can only be compatible."

"I know, but if they're compatible, wouldn't that be too much of a coincidence to ignore?"

Again, Andy's face indicated that his mind was working. Cody pressed on, hoping he was getting through to him.

"And you remember that I told you I had something else for you?" He thought this was the right time to drop the earring on Andy.

"I remember," said Andy in a disgusted tone. "I remember that you haven't given me anything yet."

"Well, I will now."

Cody reached for his wallet. He had kept the earring in a piece of tissue in a compartment in his wallet since he showed it to Joanna. He took it out and gave it to Andy.

"What's this?" asked Andy as he pulled open the tissue.

"That's an earring that I found at the Hollowell crime scene. Actually, I found one piece in the room and one piece on the fire stairs. Remember, you caught me there?"

"I remember you said you didn't find anything."

"But I did. I just didn't want you to know. I didn't know Joanna was involved then, either."

"So you conveniently came up with it just now. How do I know where that came from?"

"I just told you where it came from, didn't I?"

It was unbelievable that Andy was being so hard-assed. But then, he knew that Andy was a cop, and cops were notoriously hardheaded about their own theories. He had been the same way. But Cody felt that didn't excuse Andy at this point.

"Cody, you could've had this earring in your wallet for two years. I don't know where you got it or whose it is. I have only the word of a man whose wife is suspected of murder. Ain't that true?"

Cody thought about it for a moment. He guessed he could see where Andy was coming from. Nevertheless, he still thought Andy owed him the benefit of a doubt.

"Andy, after all we've been through together over the years, can't you trust me on this?"

Cody saw Andy put his hands on his hips, drop his head, and let out a long sigh. They stood there for a long moment, looking at each other. Finally, Andy broke the silence.

"Okay, what about this earring?"

"It's from a woman who has pierced ears. Joanna doesn't have pierced ears. Now, if you put all this together, doesn't it put some doubt in your mind about Joanna's guilt?"

Another long moment of silence passed before Andy replied. "Lookin' at it from your side, I guess there's room for some doubt."

At last, thought Cody.

"That's all I'm asking, Andy. Just look at it my way for a moment. Look at the prints. Look at the hair. Think about the earring. Make some comparisons to the Johnston case. And give some thought to the mob. I think you'll have to agree with me."

"Okay, Cody, let me have a few days. I'll review all this stuff. I'm not makin' you any promises, but I'll consider your ideas."

Cody breathed a sigh of relief and put out his hand.

"Thanks, pal. I do appreciate it. I'll call you the day after tomorrow, okay?"

"Don't call me, I'll call you."

"Okay, Andy."

Even though Cody said okay, he knew he wouldn't be able to wait until Andy called. He turned to open the door, and then looked back to Andy.

"I really need your help, Andy. Don't let me down, please."

He walked out of Andy's office without waiting for a reply. As he walked slowly through the outer room, he began to contemplate his next move. It was 2:00 p.m. Getting back to Hollowell's house was important, but he should see Joanna first. He had to.

CHAPTER 18

As he waited in the visitation room for Joanna, Cody's thoughts wandered through the events of the past week. He found it almost impossible to believe that his beautiful wife could be in jail for not one but two murders. Joanna couldn't even stand the sight of blood.

He believed, with the recently surfaced facts, that Joanna was innocent of the murders. There was still the issue of her infidelity, however. Even though Joanna's motives for being with Hollowell seemed clearer, the fact that she admitted having sex with him was still devastating. It was something that he had never imagined could happen. He wondered how he would ever be able to erase the thoughts of Joanna in bed with that crude, disgusting two-timer.

Cody's thoughts once again drifted back to that first night in the hotel. He remembered the words Joanna spoke as they lay on their wedding bed.

"Cody, I'm so happy at this moment, I can't imagine ever making love with anyone else."

Those words sounded hollow now. She had made a decision to get Hollowell. That decision, however, led to her having sex with him. He was not sure how this act would affect their marriage from this point on. Trying to convince himself about Joanna's honesty, he thought back through their marriage. There was never anything to suggest that she was or ever would be unfaithful. There wasn't ever the possibility of another man. He had trusted her implicitly. Now, this event had put these vile thoughts in his head.

At this moment, however, his top priority was freeing Joanna. He felt confident he would solve the case. When that was accomplished, he would deal with all of the other issues. What would he expect from Joanna for the rest of their relationship? How would she regain his trust? He didn't know.

The sound of the metal door at the far end of the room awakened him from his thoughts. When he looked up, he saw Joanna, dressed in a plain light blue prison dress. Her hair was unkempt, and she had no makeup on.

As she came toward him, he noticed that her shoulders were slumped, and her face was drawn. There were dark rings under her eyes, and her cheeks appeared thinner. Her face had an almost skeleton-like appearance. It was clear that she had lost weight. Her dress hung on her like a drape. This was not his Joanna; this was a woman whom he didn't recognize. She was looking anxiously about the room for Cody.

Cody stood up and smiled at her as she approached. She gave a weak smile back, but he could tell her heart wasn't in it.

All the anguish and confusion of the past few minutes seemed to disappear as she approached him. How could he judge her when she looked so pathetic? He wanted to take her in his arms and comfort her, but the only way they could touch was to kiss as they stood on either side of the table. They were also allowed to hold hands across the table, and so he held hers gently.

Her palms were damp with sweat, and he could feel her trembling. He spoke softly.

"Hello, sweetheart. How're things going?"

"Cody, I can't stand it in here. I don't know how I'm going to last. You must get me out."

At a time when she needed him so much, he felt almost helpless.

"I will, honey. I'm on the right trail. I was just talking to Andy, and he's going to look at some new evidence that's turned up."

"What new evidence?"

Joanna seemed to perk up a little with that comment.

"There were hair strands at the Hollowell scene similar to some that were found at the Johnston crime scene. They won't match yours. I gave Andy the earring. He knows you don't have pierced ears. Also, there were some partial fingerprints found at the Johnston scene. We know they won't match yours, but they might match others that were found at the Apollo. So you see, we have a lot of new stuff. We'll have you out of here in no time."

Cody knew this was only a thin thread he was offering, but he wanted to give Joanna something to hang onto.

"I also found evidence that someone had broken into our house. That's how they got your brooch."

"Well, when do you think Andy will let me out?"

It was obvious that Joanna wasn't thinking clearly because she was scared to death. He knew it wouldn't be soon. And she would only be more frightened if he told her she would likely have to stay in jail until the case was solved. He tried to soften things a little anyway.

"It's going to be a little while yet. He's going over the new evidence as we speak. It shouldn't take much longer. Try to be patient."

"I'm trying, but it's hard. Some of the women in here are so tough. I try not to mingle with them, but they still come after me. They say such terrible things."

With that, she put her head down on their clasped hands and started to cry softly. Cody bent over and kissed the back of her head. The guard immediately called to them.

"Sit back, please. I must be able to see your hands at all times."

They sat upright with a jerk. Cody looked over at the guard through angry eyes. Couldn't he see what was happening? He looked back at Joanna.

"It's okay, honey. Don't cry, please. I'm going as fast as I can. I'll get you out of here in a couple of days."

Again, he was being overly optimistic, but he had to cheer her up somehow. Besides, he knew he was getting close. There were just a few loose ends to tie together, like solidifying Hollowell's connection with the mob. That part would be difficult, but it could be done. It had to be done.

In order to do this, he would have to see Hollowell's private papers. If Hollowell had been doing business with the mob, there would have to be some evidence of it in his office or at his home. Cody spent the rest of the time with Joanna, trying to make her feel better.

Finally, the guard said, "Okay, time's up."

As they stood up, the guard moved closer. He stood right next to them as they kissed.

"I have to go now, sweetheart. Stay as strong as you can. Just keep thinking that I'll have you home real soon, okay?"

"Hurry, Cody. I don't think I'll be able to stand it much longer."

"I'll see you tomorrow, honey."

Cody stood and watched as the guard walked behind Joanna to the door. As she went through it, she turned to him. Cody could see her lifeless eyes staring at him with tears flowing like never before. Her mouth drooped at the corners, and there was not even a hint of a smile that he could see. There was no hope left in her face.

Cody was worried about Joanna's mental state. He wondered if she would try to hurt herself somehow.

The door closed with a clank that echoed through the empty room. The smile that he had on his face faded.

There was no time for self-pity; he had work to do. It was 2:45 pm. His original plan had been to go to Hollowell's house and try to get into the old boy's desk at home. But now, he decided he had to go back to Hollowell's office. It was important that he do a couple of things there.

First, he wanted to talk to Ms. Hastings. He wanted to ask her some questions about her relationship with Hollowell. Maybe he could trick her into revealing some secret link between her and Hollowell. Second, he wanted to get a look at Hollowell's private files. There would have to be a way to get Hastings to let him into Hollowell's private office.

As he drove downtown, he picked up his cell phone and punched in the number to Hollowell's office. It had rung only once when the voice on the other end said, "Law offices of Hollowell, Strand, and Booker. Can I help you?"

"This is Mr. Thomas. May I speak with Ms. Hastings, please?"

"I'm sorry, sir, but she is out of the office at present. Do you want to leave a message?"

Cody's mind began to churn. If she were out of the office, could he somehow use this time to get at Hollowell's files?

After a moment, he continued, "Oh, has she left already?" he was acting as if he was aware of her plans. "She told me she was going out but that she would try to wait for me. We have some business to finish, and it has to be completed this afternoon. Did she mention that if she couldn't wait, it would be all right for me to come in and get started?"

There was a pause on the other end of the line. The voice came on again and said, "She didn't leave any message that you were coming in, sir."

"She didn't? Well, she must've forgotten. This is very important. I'm sure she would want me to get started."

"I'm sorry, sir. I don't know what to tell you."

"Do you expect her back today?"

"Yes, but I'm not exactly sure when."

Cody took a deep breath and prepared to make his pitch. *This had better be good,* he thought.

"Why don't I come over now? Maybe by the time I get there, she'll be back, and we can get to work. If not, maybe you'll let me wait there for her."

"I guess that would be all right. She may be back soon, and that would solve the problem."

"Okay, then. I'll be right over. Thanks."

Well, the first step was accomplished. Now, all he had to do was get into Hastings's office or Hollowell's files. It wasn't clear exactly how he would do either, but at least he had his foot in the door. Trying to beat Ms. Hastings to the office, he headed downtown as quickly as he could.

CHAPTER 19

Cody pulled into the underground parking lot of the Allworth Building, which housed Hollowell's offices. He located an open spot and parked his car. During the drive over, he'd had an uncanny sensation that he was being followed. Another car was pulling onto the entrance ramp as he got out of his car. Since it turned before getting close enough to identify, he shrugged, and tried to ignore the uncomfortable feeling. He told himself not to be so suspicious.

He entered the elevator and pushed the button for the lobby floor. When the elevator reached the lobby, the door opened, he hurried across the lobby to the building elevators and stepped into one that went to the seventeenth floor. The slowness of the car caused him to fidget. When the door finally opened, he got out and found himself again in the large reception room. He walked up the receptionist.

"Hi! I'm Cody Thomas. We were just talking on the phone a few minutes ago, remember?"

"Yes, I do, Mr. Thomas. Ms. Hastings hasn't returned as yet."

Perfect, thought Cody. *Now all I have to do is get into the main offices.*

"I see. Well, perhaps I can wait for her in her office. Or better yet, maybe I can get started on our project. I don't think she'll mind."

"Well, I don't know. She didn't leave me any instructions. I wouldn't—"

Cody interrupted her, hoping to overcome her reluctance. "Don't you remember me from my last visit here? If you'll recall, Mrs. Hollowell approved my appointment last time."

"I do seem to remember Mrs. Hollowell calling, but I'm not sure why."

"You remember Ms. Hastings meeting me that time, don't you?"

"Yes, I do . . . but . . ."

He kept on talking, trying to confuse her into seeing things his way.

"Mrs. Hollowell instructed Ms. Hastings to work with me on this problem. It has to do with Mr. Hollowell's death."

That wasn't a lie, thought Cody. *I am working on his murder after all.*

"Oh, Mr. Hollowell's murder? I didn't know that."

That seemed to strike a note. He continued.

"Yes, I'm a private investigator working with the police on this case. I need to review some of Mr. Hollowell's old cases since they may have some connection with his murder."

"And Ms. Hastings knows about this?"

"Absolutely. She's working right along with me."

Cody could see he was making headway. He wanted to get in before Ms. Hastings returned. The receptionist, silent for a while, finally said, "Since you're working with the police and Ms. Hastings, I suppose it will be all right. Where would you like to begin?"

Cody felt like a defense attorney who just got his client acquitted. He smiled a little.

"Maybe I could get a look at Mr. Hollowell's office."

"Okay, follow me."

She opened the door to the inner office and let Cody walk through. He walked behind her as she led him down a long corridor. They passed the offices of many attorneys. These were clearly junior partners, since the offices were small, with functional but inexpensive furniture. They reached the end of the hallway where there were two huge offices, one at each corner of the building. The receptionist pointed to the one on the left.

"That's Mr. Hollowell's office."

"Thanks." Cody turned and walked past her into the lavishly furnished room. It was at least thirty feet long and thirty feet wide. The floor rugs extended up the walls in one continuous piece. The desk was ten to twelve feet wide and six feet deep. A high-backed chair that stood behind the desk was covered with cordovan-colored leather. There were brass studs outlining the back and seat, fastening the leather to the wood. In the corner of the room, there was a large rubber plant, and there were many ferns hanging from the ceiling. Against one wall was a filing case. There was a lock at the top, which undoubtedly meant that it held very private material. Two large client chairs covered with black velour sat in front of the desk. The walls were covered by expensive-looking paintings. There were various awards which Hollowell had received from different societies and organizations.

The receptionist walked out of the office. Cody waited a few minutes and shut the door. There probably wasn't much time, so he was anxious to get started.

He went quickly to the desk first. Looking through the top drawer, he found only the usual items. The other drawers also yielded nothing of interest. This didn't surprise Cody since the police had most likely gone through the desk soon after the murder.

Moving to the filing cabinet, Cody tried the top drawer. To his surprise, it was open. There were many manila folders lined up neatly in the drawer. As he flipped through them, he noticed there were no identifying labels. They were, however, numbered with Roman numerals. Cody took a few folders out and opened them.

Inside, he saw the names of cities, maps of these cities, and locations circled on the maps. There were also lists of numbers. There were three- and four-digit numbers followed by lists of numbers from one on up through fifteen. He studied the pages for a while and concluded that it must be some kind of code.

In each folder, he also found stubs from airline tickets to its corresponding city. He looked through a few others and found the same kind of material. If this was a code, there had to be a key to it somewhere. He wondered if the police had found it. If they had, they certainly wouldn't tell him about it. But if they hadn't and he could decipher the code, it might lead him to the motive for Hollowell's death.

He decided to take the contents of one of the folders. Folding them carefully, he slipped them into his inside coat pocket. They would have to be examined more carefully later on. Other drawers contained similar folders. He saw nothing there that could be used to decode the pages in the folders. It seemed like there was nothing more of interest, so he closed the drawers and walked to the door.

Glancing at his watch, he noted that he had spent about half an hour in Hollowell's office. He wondered if he could possibly get into Hastings's office before she got back. Opening the door, he peered up and down the hall. He saw a few people busily walking from one office to another and some secretaries typing away, but there was no one who appeared interested in him.

He walked casually back through the long hallway, passing the offices of the less important attorneys. As inconspicuously as possible, he walked into the large room, which housed a typing pool, filing cabinets, water coolers, and desks.

On the right side of the hall beyond the typing pool, about halfway down, was Olivia Hastings's office. Walking purposefully toward her office, he tried not to seem out of place. No one paid much attention to him. Apparently, if someone was allowed access to the inner sanctum, no one questioned his or her presence.

When he reached Ms. Hastings's office, he looked around to see if anyone was watching him. He nonchalantly opened the door and stepped inside. Closing the door behind him, he immediately went to her desk.

The top of the desk was meticulously ordered. The pencils, paper clips, rubber bands, and filing cards were neatly lined up. He opened the top drawer to find similar tidiness. Quickly scanning the contents, he found a small black book containing phone numbers. Leafing through it, he saw a name and a number that he recognized. It was his.

He thought for a moment and remembered that she had said that she didn't know Hollowell had hired him. If that were so, why did she have his name and number in her private phone book?

A few pages later, he found another familiar name. Lola Dupres. Why did she have Lola's number? Had she set up dates for Hollowell? He put the book back, closed the drawer, and moved on to another.

In this drawer, he found personal items like tissues, a comb, lipstick, and some pieces of jewelry. The comb interested him because it had some of her hair in it. The hairs were long and blond. He couldn't tell if they were bleached. With a tissue, he carefully pulled the hairs from the teeth of the comb.

He looked through the jewelry. His heart jumped as he saw, in the corner of the drawer, a small diamond stud for pierced ears. He held it up to the light. It looked just like the one he had found in the stairwell at the Apollo Hotel. Could this be the mate? No, that would be too easy. He decided to take it with him for comparison.

With another tissue, he wrapped the earring and put it in his wallet. He closed that drawer and was about to look through another when he heard someone outside the door say, "Hello, Ms. Hastings."

A voice replied, "Hello, Sally. How are you?"

He quickly jumped around to the front of the desk and sat down in one of the chairs. The door opened and in walked the tall blonde Ms. Hastings.

"All right, wise guy. What is this nonsense you've been feeding Sally?"

"Sally? Oh, you mean the receptionist? I just told her the truth. I am working on Mr. Hollowell's murder and Mrs. Hollowell did let me in here before. And I did want to see you. So you see, it isn't such nonsense."

Cody was trying to be calm and professional. He could see that Ms. Hastings was clearly upset, but about what? Was she still angry from his last visit? Was she concerned he would find something she was hiding? Was she still trying to protect Hollowell in some way?

While these questions were flying through his mind, the phone rang. As Ms. Hastings picked up the receiver, she reached up and slipped off her earring. Cody looked at the lobe and saw that it wasn't pierced. He was confused. If she didn't have pierced earlobes, why did she have the earring he had found in her desk drawer?

It obviously didn't belong to her. Where did she get it? Was it even a match for the one he had found at the hotel? How did all this fit with his mob theory? How was Ms. Hastings involved?

"Hello," said Ms. Hastings curtly. "Oh, yes, Mr. Booker. I've just returned. How can I help you? The Phillips file? All right, I'll bring it right over."

She hung up the receiver and absently put on her earring. She looked over at Cody.

"I'd like you to leave my office now. I have work to do, and I don't want you hanging around. In fact, I don't want to see you again. I am going to leave word that you're not welcome here anymore."

Cody knew that any comment he might make would be useless. Besides, he had garnered some interesting clues. He would have to go over this material and try to make some sense out of it. Walking quickly to the door, he turned back to Ms. Hastings.

"I'm sorry you feel that way. I'm only trying to help catch Mr. Hollowell's killer."

"Oh, really. I thought the police had her in custody already. Kindly leave now."

It seemed to him that Ms. Hastings was very sure about Joanna. He left her office without closing the door. Hurrying to the waiting area, he passed Sally, the receptionist.

"Were you able to find what you needed?" She obviously hadn't been notified about him as yet.

"Why, yes. You have been very helpful. Thanks."

He continued to the elevator and pushed the button. A moment later, a car arrived; he stepped in and rode it to the lobby. Walking across the main floor to the parking lot elevators, he reached into his coat pocket to be sure the papers from Hollowell's files were safe. *Now*, he thought, *I really have to get into Hollowell's house again.*

It was now 4:35 p.m. Having spent a couple of hours upstairs, he wondered if it was too late to go over to Hollowell's. Maybe a phone call was in order to find out if Mrs. Hollowell was home. He took his cell phone from his inside pocket and dialed the number. After the phone rang three times, a voice answered.

"Hollowell residence."

"Is Mrs. Hollowell there? This is Mr. Thomas."

"No, I'm sorry, she's just gone out."

"Oh, I see. When do you expect her back?"

"Not until quite late, I'm afraid. Did you want to leave a message?"

Cody thought back to his surveillance of her. What did she do at 4:30 P.M. on Tuesdays? This was her workout night. She usually had a light dinner, went to the gym, and worked out until seven thirty. After a shower and coffee with some friends, she usually got home around ten or ten thirty.

"No, thank you. I'll call again."

He was trying to decide if he wanted to go to Hollowell's now and try to break in or if he should wait until tomorrow and call for an appointment. The question was how could he get the most information? *Probably by breaking in,* he thought. That would also be the most dangerous way.

Realizing he was hungry, he decided to get something to eat and contemplate his next move. He noticed a small restaurant at the far end of the main floor. He made his way to the restaurant, passing various shops that were renting space in the building. After waiting at the door for a few moments, a waitress led him to a booth in the back corner. As he sat down, she handed him a menu. After giving the waitress his order, he pulled the papers from his coat pocket and began to study them. This time, more carefully.

Cody ate his dinner while trying to decipher Hollowell's papers. He thought the cities might be places where Hollowell did business,

business for the mob perhaps? Hollowell could drop off or pick up drugs, or he might deliver money or any number of things. It would be relatively easy for him since he was a "respected" citizen.

He tried a few simple substitution codes, but these didn't work. Since there were many possible combinations, he wasn't discouraged. It was six o'clock and already dark outside. Sneaking into the Hollowell house tonight might be the best way. Putting the papers back into his pocket, he went to the cash register and paid his bill.

As usual, after a meal, he was dying for a cigarette. He looked through the items in the glass case under the cash register, hoping to find something to quench his desire. Remembering that the stale cough drop that he had used before had worked pretty well, he asked the cashier for a box. As soon as she gave it to him, he opened it and popped one into his mouth. It wasn't the answer, but it would have to do for now.

CHAPTER 20

Cody walked back through the lobby and took the elevator down to the parking lot level. After reaching his car, he unlocked it and hopped into the front seat. Anxious to get to Hollowell's house, he put the key into the ignition. When he turned it, there was a loud, high-pitched screech. An eardrum-shattering explosion quickly followed. The car shook and Cody was thrown backward, against the seat. He almost choked on the cough drop.

Billows of black smoke gushed from under the hood and into the car. The fetid stench of the smoke caused him to cough. He opened the door by reflex action and jumped out. As he jumped, he caught his foot on the brake pedal, which caused him to tumble onto the floor of the garage. He continued to roll, in order to get as far away from the car as he could.

When he came to a stop, he found himself in the middle of the exit ramp. Opening his eyes, he saw a large black car speeding toward him. He rolled off the ramp, back toward his smoking car. The car accelerated past him, missing him by only inches. It continued up the ramp and out onto the street. Despite all the confusion, Cody was able to discern the make and model. It was definitely a black Cadillac Sedan deVille.

Cody stood up, his entire body shaking. He looked over at his car. It appeared to be intact, although smoke continued to pour from under the hood. Absently reaching into his pocket for a cigarette, he was disappointed to find only the cough drops.

Holy shit! That was close, thought Cody, as he inched cautiously toward his car. He reached in and removed the keys. Pulling the latch, he released the hood. Carefully, he lifted it and looked at the motor. He could see that it was basically intact, although it was covered with a sootlike coating. There were pieces of cardboard and paper wadding scattered all over the motor, electrical wiring, battery, and everything else he could see.

He wondered why he was still alive. Whoever had placed that bomb could easily have made the charge substantial enough to disintegrate the car and him as well. Was this another warning?

The black Cadillac appeared to be the same car that Gino's boys were driving earlier at Lola's. They were telling him to terminate his activity. Cody thought the use of the word "terminate" was appropriate here. He must really be getting close if they were trying so hard to scare him off.

He decided against trying to start the car. The visit to the Hollowell residence was off for now. Getting home was going to be a problem. He decided to call Harvey. Maybe he could give him a lift, and they could go over the new information, as well as this close call. Cody also needed to call Andy. After seeing this, he couldn't deny the mob was involved.

Brushing himself off, he took his cell phone from his pocket and dialed Andy's private number first. He was usually around at this time of night, cleaning up his desk. Andy answered the phone after only one ring.

"Perone."

"Andy? This is Cody."

"Thomas? I thought I said I would get in touch with you."

"You did. But that was before I was almost blown to bits."

There was a moment of silence on the other end. "Blown up? What the hell are you talking about?"

"You heard me. Someone put a bomb in my car just now and tried to kill me."

"If someone wanted you dead, you wouldn't be talking to me. Where did this happen?"

"In the parking lot of the Allworth Building. Can you get your people to come over and examine my car? Maybe you can get a line on who did it, though I'm pretty sure I already know."

Again, there was silence on the other end. Cody was sure Andy would be reluctant to acknowledge probable mob involvement. His suspicions were confirmed.

"I suppose you're going to tell me it was Buononotti's boys, aren't you?"

"Who else? When you see my car, you'll know. Can you send someone over?"

Cody was really getting fed up with Andy's resistance to the possibility of criminal involvement. He was ignoring the obvious.

"All right, I'll have the forensic people come over."

"Aren't you coming?"

"No, I'm investigating another murder. Hollowell's not the only dead guy we've got, you know. I'll talk to forensics when they're finished."

Cody was too tired and shaken to argue with Andy anymore.

"Thanks a lot, Andy. Will you give me a call when they're finished?"

"Aren't you going to wait for forensics to get there?"

"No. I'm too tired. I want to get home."

"All right, then, I'll be in touch in a couple of days."

The phone clicked off. Cody was so upset at Andy's attitude that he never mentioned the hair, the earring, or Hollowell's secret files. He wanted to cool off for a little while before he tried to convince Andy that there was enough new evidence to release Joanna.

He dialed Harvey's number and waited. After a few rings, he heard a disinterested voice. "Law office of Harvey Whitcomb. Mr. Whitcomb's answering service."

"Could you contact Mr. Whitcomb, as soon as possible. This is an emergency. Tell him Cody Thomas must talk to him immediately." He was trying to stay calm, but after all he had just been through, it wasn't easy.

"Please ask him to call 215-240-3259. That's my cell phone. I'll wait here till he calls back. And hurry, please."

"I'll call him, sir." The operator disconnected.

Cody sat down in the front seat of his car. Most of the smoke had cleared by this time. He tried to think things through while waiting for Harvey to call back.

It seemed obvious that Hollowell must have been connected to Gino. The fact that they were trying to scare him off pointed in that direction. Hollowell must have screwed up somehow, which pissed off Gino; therefore, he was killed.

Because they knew he was a lady's man, they probably arranged for a woman to kill him or set him up for someone else to do it. Johnston had to be killed because he knew who had sent the cab for Joanna. If he was found and talked, it could lead right back to them. And Lola had to be killed because she could connect Hollowell with Gino. They couldn't have Lola shooting off her mouth to the cops about Hollowell, the mob, drugs, and prostitution.

While he was running through this scenario, the phone rang. He answered, "Harvey?"

"No, it's not Harvey."

Cody recognized the voice as the same one that had left the message on the answering machine.

"We told you to stop fuckin' around, didn't we? This is your last fuckin' warning. The next fuckin' time, you'll find yourself dead. Now, leave it alone." The phone clicked off.

These guys aren't kidding around anymore, thought Cody. But he couldn't stop now. He had to get Joanna out of jail, and that meant nailing whoever is in the way, even if he was putting his life in danger. The phone rang again, and when he answered this time, it was with some trepidation.

"Hello?"

"Cody, this is Harvey. What the hell's going on now?"

"Harve, you're not going to believe it. Could you come down and pick me up at the Allworth Building parking lot?"

Harvey's voice revealed his confusion as he said, "The Allworth Building! What're you doing there?"

"It's a long story, Harve. I'll tell you all about it when you get here."

"Okay. I'll be there in about twenty minutes."

"Thanks, Harve. I'll be waiting."

Cody disconnected and went back to his thoughts. Things seemed pretty clear to him except for the things he had found in Olivia Hastings's desk: the earring, the hair, and his and Lola's phone numbers. Could she somehow be involved with Gino and the mob?

Andy still had to be convinced of all this. To do that, he would need solid proof. The answer to the code had to be in the Hollowell house; therefore, getting in was crucial. He was hoping there would be other things to help him satisfy Andy and the district attorney.

Twenty minutes seemed like two hours. When he finally saw Harvey's car come down the ramp, he waved him over. Harvey pulled up and stopped. As he got out of his car, Cody could see Harvey's amazement by the expression on his face.

"What the hell happened to your 'caah'?" Harvey still said "car" like a New Englander.

"This is a warning from Gino. He wants me to stop getting in his hair."

"Gino? Do you mean Buononotti? You think they're trying to kill you?"

"No. If he wanted me dead, I wouldn't be talking to you right now. He just wants me to stop nosing around."

He walked over to Harvey's car. "Let's get out of here. We'll talk about it on the way to my house."

Cody described the entire picture, as he saw it, to Harvey as they drove to his house. Harvey listened closely without venturing an opinion until he was finished.

"It sounds like you have it pretty much figured out, except for the business of the blond hair and earring. Don't they bother you a little?"

"Yes, but isn't it possible that Hastings could be involved with the mob?"

"I guess she could. But it seems to me that if she knew all about Hollowell and his connections to Buononotti, he would have had her killed too. After all, they usually don't like loose ends."

Cody thought for a moment. "I suppose you've got a point, Harve. But that might still be coming. She did seem a bit edgy to me today. She may suspect something's going to happen."

But Cody thought, Gino hadn't fooled around with Lola or Hollowell. Why would he wait to kill Hastings? Harvey was probably right. If he were, then he would have to explain Hastings's possible involvement in another way. That is, if the hairs turn out to be hers and the earrings are a match. Things were getting a little confusing. It would be much simpler if she were part of the mob.

Harvey was turning into the driveway.

"Why don't you come in for a cup of coffee or a drink, Harve?"

"I'd like to, but I've got to get home to my wife and kid. I've been so busy lately, I'm 'haadly' ever at home anymore. My wife's about to divorce me."

"I know what you mean, Harve. Okay, I'll talk to you just as soon as I get things straight in my head. I'm going over to see Mrs. Hollowell tomorrow. Hopefully, I'll find something to help me out. See you later."

"See you later, Cody."

Cody got out of the car and headed for the house as Harvey pulled out of the driveway. He practically dragged himself up the stairs to the porch and opened the door to the house. It seemed very lonely without Joanna there to meet him. He realized just how much she meant to him now that she wasn't around.

He suddenly felt very tired. Forgetting the coffee, he decided to go straight to bed. Tomorrow would be another long day. After taking a shower, he brushed his teeth, got into his pajamas, and went to bed. He was asleep in seconds.

CHAPTER 21

Cody woke up at eight o'clock feeling rested and ready to go. Dressing quickly, he went downstairs for a cup of coffee and some toast. The paper was on the porch when he went outside. He read it as he ate his breakfast. Nothing new was being reported, which usually meant the police were being tight with their information.

His major task of the day was to go to Hollowell's house and try to get at his private files. Since his car was at the police garage, he would have to rent one. Taking out the phone book, he looked up a rental agency. There was one nearby. He called and ordered a medium-sized car, which this agency was able to deliver to him in half an hour. By the time he had finished his coffee and toast, the car had arrived.

It was still kind of early to call Mrs. Hollowell. But being too anxious to sit around the house, he decided to ride over to Hollowell's and wait outside until a reasonable hour. At that time, he could call her on his cell phone.

He drove to the mansion and parked in the street outside the gate. From where he was parked, he could see the front of the house through the iron gate. Parked in the driveway was a white convertible Mercury Cougar. *Nice car,* he thought. He wondered who owned it.

Mrs. Hollowell was probably up since she had a visitor. Glancing at his watch, he saw that it was nine o'clock. He popped a cough drop into his mouth and waited. At nine thirty, the front door opened, and Mrs. Hollowell's visitor came out. It was Olivia Hastings.

She must have come here to report me to Mrs. Hollowell, thought Cody. He wondered if this would screw up their relationship. As Olivia Hastings was leaving, she leaned over and kissed Mrs. Hollowell on the cheek. After she drove away, Mrs. Hollowell waved and went inside.

He slumped down in the front seat, so Ms. Hastings wouldn't see him as she drove out of the gate. After waiting a few minutes, he dialed Mrs. Hollowell's number.

The maid answered, "Hollowell residence."

"Hi! This is Cody Thomas. May I please speak with Mrs. Hollowell?"

"Just a moment, please. I'll see if she's at home."

A few minutes later, she came back on the phone and said, "I'm sorry, sir, she's not at home."

Not at home? Hadn't he just seen her? What's going on here?

"Ah . . ." Cody stuttered, "When *will* she be at home?"

"I'm not sure, sir."

It certainly seemed like Mrs. Hollowell was trying to avoid him. The Hastings visit must have had something to do with this. What was he going to do now? If Mrs. Hollowell were going to avoid him, he would have to wait until she was out of the house and sneak in.

Once again, he thought back to her routine. Today was Wednesday. During the day, she usually hung around the house until noon. Then she would attend a weekly meeting of the patrons of the arts league. These meetings typically lasted two hours. She would then attend her weekly one-hour karate lesson, then a quick shower, and home for a light supper.

In the evening, at seven o'clock, she went to her bridge club and played cards until eleven o'clock. She would then get home at around midnight. That was how he could do it. He would go over at seven thirty and break in.

Being his typically compulsive self, Cody thought he should look the place over for the best way to get in. He decided to come back later that afternoon to inspect the house. His experiences as a policeman had taught him a great deal about security systems. He remembered the motion sensor he had seen in the foyer during his first visit. That knowledge should help him.

He decided to use the rest of the morning to see Andy. This idea didn't excite him all that much, but he wasn't about to give up just because Andy was being hardheaded. Joanna had to be visited also. He drove off to the station.

Arriving at the station, Cody went to Andy's office. He was busy at his desk. There weren't many detectives in the outer room at this time of the day, so it was relatively easy to get back to Andy's cubicle.

He knocked cautiously on the door. Andy looked up and a look of resignation appeared on his face as he saw Cody through the window of the door. He waved him in.

"What're ya doin' here at this hour?"

"I needed to talk to you about a few things. I thought this might be a good time."

Andy sat back in his chair and put his hands together across his chest. He looked Cody straight in the eyes, and for a change, seemed almost friendly.

"I know how upset you must be about Joanna. I also know you were a good cop. But you've gotta let me handle this case without any more interference."

"I don't mean to bust your balls, but I do have some new and very interesting stuff for you."

Andy parted his hands, gave a half grin, and breathed a long sigh through his nose.

"Okay. What've you got this time?"

"First, have you had a chance yet to compare those hairs and the prints from the Johnston case with the ones from the Hollowell case?"

"As a matter of fact, we have. And both samples of hair are compatible. This is not saying they're a perfect match, just that they could be from the same person, understand?"

That piece of news, understandably, excited Cody. He managed to keep himself under control, however, because he wanted Andy to keep going. As Andy continued, he kept his mouth shut.

"As for the prints, you know they were only partials, but we couldn't find any that had similarities with Joanna's. Of course, that only says she wasn't at the Johnston scene. We never suspected her of that one anyway."

"Then, don't you think, since the modus operandi were so similar, it makes it less likely that Joanna did either?"

"That's not likely to stand up in court, is it?"

Cody, of course, was now convinced that Joanna was completely innocent. All he had to do was convince Andy.

"If I were to give you more convincing evidence that someone else could be involved, what would you say then?"

Andy sat up straight in his chair. "Have you got some?" he asked in a half-mocking, half-sincere tone.

"What if I gave you some hairs that match with the ones you have? And what if I gave you an earring that matches the one you have? What would you say then?"

"Do ya have them? If you do, you'd better hand them over."

"And what about the bombing of my car? How can you explain that away? Joanna sure as hell didn't do that."

Cody knew he was on a roll now. He wasn't ready to let Andy off the hook so easily. It was time to hit him with all the ambiguities that he recognized and that Andy seemed to want to ignore.

"Okay, okay. Show me what you have. If you really have all this evidence, maybe I will be able to do somethin' for Joanna."

"All right," Cody replied, as he took his wallet from his pocket. He carefully removed the tissues containing the earring and the hairs from Ms. Hastings's comb.

"Take a look at these. That earring should match the one I've already given you. And the long, blond hairs should compare with those from both crime scenes."

Andy accepted the two tissues, placed them on his desk, and unfolded the one containing the earring. After looking at it for a moment, he put it on the desk and opened the other tissue. He studied the hairs briefly, and then looked up.

"Where'd you get these?"

"They came from Olivia Hastings's desk."

"Olivia Hastings! You mean that tall blonde from Hollowell's office?"

"That tall *bleached* blonde."

Andy appeared genuinely surprised. Cody thought Andy must not have considered her a suspect at all. Maybe he wasn't as smart as he thought he was. She should have been included as a possible candidate, if only because of her proximity to Hollowell.

"Didn't you give her any consideration?"

"Not really. Why should we? She was only his assistant. We found nothing suspicious about her. Did you?"

"Well, when I talked with her, I had the distinct impression she was going out of her way to protect Hollowell. It went way beyond the usual employer-employee relationship."

Andy did not seem to be persuaded by this argument.

"Okay, so you were impressed. How'd you get into her desk?"

"I went over to look through Hollowell's private files. When I was finished, I just walked back to her office and went through her desk."

"Just like that, huh? You really have iron balls. Where was she when all this was goin' on?"

"I don't know. But she did come back while I was there and read me the riot act. Aha! But not before I collected these babies," he said, pointing to the earrings and hair.

Andy seemed skeptical. He sat back in his chair and picked up the earring again. Pulling open the top desk drawer, he took out another folded tissue. Cody recognized it as the one that contained the first earring. Andy held them side by side. Cody's impatience escalated.

"Let me have a look at them, will you."

Andy looked up, clearly annoyed. He looked back at the earrings, completely ignoring Cody. Andy's comparison continued for another minute or so. Then he handed them to Cody, who was about to jump out of his skin. He eyed them like a kid looking at a barrel of candy.

After squinting at the earrings for a long moment, Cody looked at Andy. "Well, what do you think? They sure look alike to me."

"Yeah, I'll have to admit, they do. But I'm not sure what it proves about the Hastings woman."

"I'm not sure about that myself because she doesn't have pierced earlobes either."

That bit of news seemed to surprise Andy. He sat back in his chair and spread his hands.

"Then I guess they're not hers. Well, whom do they belong to? And what're they doin' in her desk?"

"Exactly. Whose are they, indeed? But if one was at a crime scene, doesn't that suggest it has something to do with the murder?"

"I'm not sure what I think right now. What about these hairs? Where'd they come from?"

"From a comb in Hastings's drawer. As you can see, they're long and blond, and if I haven't missed my guess, bleached."

Cody could see this was getting through to Andy. At long last, he was beginning to see things his way. He let Andy mull things over for a while.

"If these hairs compare with those at the two crime scenes, she'll have a few questions to answer, won't she?"

"The problem is this stuff you took from her desk was obtained illegally. We couldn't use it in court."

Cody knew all along that was the case, but he also felt that Andy or the district attorney could somehow get back to Hastings's office and get some of her hair legally.

"Isn't there some way to get some hair samples from her, legally?"

"I can't think of any right now. Besides, we're not sure if these are compatible with the others. And we're not sure what these earrings mean."

"At least you can get the lab boys to compare them, can't you? Then we'll figure something out."

"Yeah, I can do that right now."

Cody could see that Andy was completely intrigued by this new evidence. He acted, for the first time, as if someone other than Joanna could be guilty. This was the old Andy.

"There's something else, Andy."

Andy looked up quickly, as if anxious to see and hear more. Cody waited a few moments to build up the suspense.

"I've got these papers from Hollowell's private files."

He took the pages from his coat pocket and handed them to Andy, who took them, opened them, and scanned them quickly.

"Oh, yeah, we've seen these. We thought they probably had something to do with clients he didn't want anyone to know about. They may represent some business dealings that he was keeping from his partners. Besides, since everything seemed to point toward Joanna, we didn't think they had anything to do with his murder."

"I guess I'm a little bit more suspicious than you. I thought they might have something to do with Gino Buononotti and the drug racket."

"Gino Buononotti? Why him?"

Andy's reluctance to consider the mob was surfacing again. Why was he so unwilling to even consider the mob? This bothered Cody tremendously.

"Why not? I know Hollowell was involved with cocaine and hookers. Gino is involved with cocaine and hookers. Hollowell defended some of the mob in court. Lola Dupres was involved with Gino. Hollowell was involved with Lola. Don't you think this is all too coincidental?"

"Okay, but how does this Hastings dame fit into the puzzle? You can't have it both ways, you know."

Andy, of course, had hit upon the same problem Cody was having—how to connect Hastings to Buononotti and the murders.

"I haven't quite figured that out yet, but I will. Don't worry. All I know is, somehow or other, the mob must be involved."

Andy sat silent for a few seconds, and then appeared to try to change the subject.

"What do you think these files represent?"

"I think they're drop-off and pickup spots for drugs. My feeling is that Hollowell was a bagman for Gino and that he somehow screwed up, and they killed him or had him killed."

"I see, but what about Hastings?"

"Maybe she was the come-on. Perhaps she set him up for the boys."

Andy thought for a while. "Where do the earrings fit in?"

"I'm not sure yet. Somehow, they will. Anyway, are you still convinced Joanna is a murderer?"

Andy sat back in his chair and ran his fingers through his hair.

"I must admit, you make a strong case against it. However, I'm still not sure any of this will hold up in court. We'll have to get more solid proof."

Andy had said "We'll," thought Cody. *He's on my side again. It was about time. Now, maybe, we can make some headway and get Joanna out of jail.*

"I'll be working on that today. I'm going over to the Hollowell place and see if I can find any connection between Hollowell and the mob."

"How do you intend to do that?"

Cody was not about to tell Andy that he intended to break into the house. He wouldn't go for that at all.

"I'm going to call her and get permission. She thinks I'm working with you on her husband's murder. I think she'll let me into his home office. She's been very nice to me."

"Don't take anything without her permission. If you find something, we need to be able to use it in court."

"Don't worry. I'll be extra careful."

Cody felt optimistic. Andy was being cooperative. Things were falling into place. And he had some good news for Joanna.

"Can you get me in to see Joanna?"

"Sure, I can do that. I'll call over and tell them she has a visitor."

"Thanks, pal. For everything."

Andy picked up the phone and called the captain of the guard to tell him Cody was on his way to visit Joanna. When he hung up, Cody grabbed his hand and shook it warmly.

"Thanks again. Oh, by the way, is there anything on my car yet?"

"Nothing yet. Give us a break, it only happened last night, you know."

"I know, just thought I'd ask."

Cody walked out of the office as if on air. He hadn't felt this good since this whole thing began. Joanna would be excited by the news.

CHAPTER 22

During his visit with Joanna, Cody told her all the good news. She, naturally, was excited but still quite depressed. This spurred Cody's eagerness to work even faster. Joanna's whole personality was changing. Her voice showed no emotion, and her eyes were dull and lifeless. She wasn't smiling as she usually did when they were alone, and her answers were without feeling, her questions pointless. She had not been wearing makeup in days, which was not like the Joanna he knew. He had to do something about that as soon as possible.

He decided it was time to drive back to the Hollowell residence. It was 11:30 a.m., and by the time he arrived, Sarah Hollowell should be off to her meeting. He knew the house would be empty because this was the maid's day off. She didn't usually return until the next morning. The only thing he would have to contend with was the groundskeeper.

Arriving at the house, he drove by the gate. Mrs. Hollowell's car was in the driveway. She apparently hadn't left yet. He drove around the block and studied the house from all sides. The wall surrounded the house completely. Since it stood seven feet high, Cody thought he could climb over it by standing on the roof of his car. The most advantageous point to get over the wall appeared to be the back side. There were many trees and the shrubs stood almost as high as the wall. Once he got over, they would help conceal him.

Screens enclosed a tile-roofed porch that extended from the back of the house. Once on the porch roof, he would be able to climb up to one of the gabled windows just above. Hopefully, he would then be able to get into the house through the window. His only concern was the alarm system.

He drove around the block and arrived back at the gate. Mrs. Hollowell was just coming down the driveway. As she waited for the gate to open, he continued past. By the time she drove onto the street, Cody had reached the intersection and was heading around to the back of the house. He found a satisfactory spot and parked only a few feet from the wall.

After waiting a few minutes to be sure she was some blocks away, he stepped out of the car. Calmly, he surveyed the area, carefully looking up and down the street for anyone who might be able to see him. About a block away, he saw a car coming in his direction. He casually walked up the street as if heading for somewhere specific. After the car had passed, he strolled back to his car, and again, looked cautiously around.

Feeling comfortable, he climbed on top of the rented car. Since he stood six feet tall and the car was almost five feet high, it was easy to see into the garden area behind the house. He leaned over as far as he could and scanned the area. Seeing nothing or no one, he placed his hands on the top of the wall and gave a short leap. This landed him on the two-foot wide cement coping that topped the wall.

He steadied himself and, again, looked around. The coast was clear. Sitting on the edge of the wall, he turned slightly and placed his hands on the edge of the coping. In one motion, he pushed away from the wall and turned to face it. At arm's length, his feet were only a few inches from the ground. He released his hold and fell softly to the grass below.

Rubbing his hands together, he cleaned off the loose sand and dirt. He separated some of the bushes, which were growing about a foot from the wall. These were giant spreading yews, with large branches that, he estimated, would be able to hold him if necessary.

After making sure the groundskeeper was nowhere in sight, he stepped from behind the bushes and ran at full speed to the porch. Upon reaching it, he waited for a moment to catch his breath. Since he was sucking air with great difficulty, he remembered why he wanted to stay away from cigarettes.

Regaining his composure and breath, he tried the screened door that led to the porch. It was locked. He walked to the corner of the porch where he found a large post. Wrapping his large hands around it, he tested it to see if it would hold his weight. This post could be used to get to the roof of the porch.

The stones that made up the wall of the house extended slightly from the cement. He tested their ability to hold him by grasping the higher stones with his fingers and placing the toes of his shoes on the lower ones and found that they extended far enough from the cement and were strong enough to allow him to climb the wall.

Next, he inspected the windows. The alarm system, luckily one with which he was familiar, had couplers attached to each window and to the frame. When these couplers are separated, the circuit is broken, setting off the alarm. These are usually placed on the windows and doors that are accessible to burglars.

Cody pulled himself up to look through the window to see the type of system that was in place. He could see the couplers on each window and frame. It was a standard alarm system. This meant he would have to deactivate the couplers in order to get in.

This could be done using a pair of small alligator clamps with a wire extension between the clamps. By placing one clamp on the wire supplying the coupler on the window and the other clamp on the wire supplying the coupler on the frame, the window could be opened without breaking the circuit. Of course, he would first have to remove a piece of the windowpane in order to get at the couplers. For this, he would need a glasscutter.

As he was peering through the last window, his heart jumped as he saw the maid coming into the library. He jumped down to the ground and hugged the wall, hoping that she hadn't seen him. She wasn't supposed to be at home.

Until that moment, he had given some thought to breaking in right then and there, but for one thing, he didn't have the right materials. And now, the maid was home. He waited for what seemed like an hour, but was really only a few minutes, before trying to look into the library to see if the maid had gone.

Raising himself up to the window slowly, he saw that she had left the room. He didn't know where she was, but he thought he had better get out while the getting was good. After making sure the groundskeeper was not around, he ran straight for the bushes. When he reached them, he pushed his way through and, again, waited to catch his breath.

In a few minutes, he was ready. He climbed back to the top of the wall using the branches of the largest bush he could find in the vicinity. After reaching the top, he was able to step to the roof of the car easily. Jumping to the ground, he got into the car and rested a minute.

All this had taken about an hour. Since he hadn't planned on coming back until around seven thirty that night, when Mrs. Hollowell was playing bridge, he had a lot of time to kill. He decided to try to talk to Harvey to fill him in on the latest news. Harvey had often acted as a sounding board. He was the voice of reason while Cody frequently was ready to barge right in.

Cody called Harvey from his cell phone. Luckily, he didn't have to be in court today and said to come right over. It was about a twenty-minute ride to Harvey's office, which was in a small office building downtown. Because of Harvey's conservative nature, neither the building nor his office was very flashy. With Harvey, everything was functional—no wasted motion or money.

The office was on the first floor about halfway toward the back. Cody opened the door and stepped into a small waiting room. Harvey had no partners. The room was furnished like Harvey, very simply. Thelma, Harvey's long-time secretary, was sitting behind her desk, typing.

"Hi, Thelma. Harvey's expecting me."

"Oh, hi, Cody. Yes, I know. He's in his office. Go right in."

She waved Cody toward the door to her right. Thelma had been with Harvey since his days with the district attorney's office. She was both discreet and loyal. The door led to Harvey's consultation room.

"Hi, Harve," Cody said, as he closed the door behind him and sat in one of the client chairs in front of Harvey's desk.

The room was typical of all lawyers' offices with volume after volume of law books covering the walls. The one thing that was not typical about Harvey's office, however, was the distinct lack of flamboyance. There was an average-sized desk made of mahogany. On it, there was a simple lamp and in and out boxes. A small calendar booklet was set in the corner. There was a paperclip holder, alongside of a pen and pencil box, off to the right. Sitting in front of Harvey was a laptop computer, which was on.

Harvey was dressed in his usual vested three-button suit. This one was gray. He wore a white spread-collared shirt and a gray tie with maroon and black designs.

Harvey stood about five feet ten inches tall. His nose was broad but not too long. He wore no facial hair, and his sideburns were neatly trimmed. His hair was wavy but, as usual, not combed well. His dark-rimmed glasses were pushed up on his forehead since he didn't need them for close work.

"Hello, Cody. What's up?"

"Oh, nothing critical this time. I have some time to kill, so I thought I'd run some new things by you."

"Okay, 'staat' talking."

The way he said "staat" instead of "start" again betrayed his New England years. He leaned back in his chair and folded his hands across his chest.

"Well, to begin with, there's no doubt about Joanna's innocence. Even that skeptic Andy Perone can't deny it anymore." He said this with conviction and some pride. There was nothing like proving somebody wrong.

"I've found so many clues pointing to the involvement of other people, it can no longer be denied."

"That's great. What've you got?"

He went through the business of the hair, the earrings, and the coded files, and how he thought they exonerated Joanna and incriminated Hollowell, Buononotti and, probably, Hastings. And there were the similarities between the Hollowell and Johnston murders. However, when he tried to make the connection to the mob, he again fell short. Also, Ms. Hastings's hairs continued to give him trouble.

"What do you intend to do with those coded files?" Harvey asked.

"I'm going to try to find the key to the code and decode them. And if they show what I think they'll show, I'm going to shove them up Perone's nose."

"How do you propose to do that?"

"I'm going to go to Hollowell's house and find it."

With a quizzical look on his face, Harvey asked, "You mean that Mrs. Hollowell is going to let you go through her late husband's private things?"

"Well, not exactly."

"What does that mean?"

Cody squirmed in his seat because he knew how Harvey would react to the news of his intended break-in. He paused for a moment and reached into his pocket for a cough drop. Putting one into his mouth, he continued, "She was being very cordial to me until Hastings got her ear. Now, she won't accept my calls."

"So?"

"So I'm going to break into her house tonight while she's out."

Cody said that last part very fast, like a kid explaining to his parents something he was ashamed of.

"Break in? Are you nuts? What if you get caught?"

"Oh, I won't get caught, Harve. I know all the tricks."

"That's what all the burglars think, right before they go to jail. This could really hurt Joanna, you know."

"Only if I get caught. But if I'm not caught, it can really help her."

Now, it was Harvey who was squirming in his chair. Cody tried to allay his fears.

"Look, Harve, I've got to prove that Hollowell was dirty. I think those coded files will do that. The key to those files must be in that house. Mrs. Hollowell will be out of the house for five or so hours tonight. The maid is off, and the groundskeeper doesn't work at night. With my experience, I'll be able to get in and out unseen. I'm sure of it."

"I still think you're crazy, Cody. What if you don't find the key? Will it be worth the risk?"

Cody knew that was possible, but he didn't want to hear it. He ignored Harvey's cautious remarks.

"Crazy or not, I've got to try, for Joanna's sake. Of all people, Harve, you should know, I've got to get solid proof that will stand up in court."

"I do, I do. But you can't get proof illegally."

"If it's there, I'll find a way to get it legally."

They continued to argue the merits of the plan for at least another half hour. Then they discussed Ms. Hastings and her role. Then Mrs. Hollowell's name came up. Cody was trying to cover all the bases.

"You know, Harve, I've even given some consideration to Sarah Hollowell, although I found nothing suspicious when I was following her for her husband. The thought has crossed my mind that the spouse is always the most likely suspect."

"That's true, but don't you think you would have seen something suspicious in all that time?"

"Yeah, but she's a very smart lady. She has a PhD in psychology and, for a while, actually had a practice. She is definitely smart enough to plan and execute something like this."

Cody could see Harvey trying to think this idea through. He knew he had come up with a thought that Harvey hadn't considered. Trying to outthink Harvey was always fun. It was like a game for them to see who could come up with the best theory.

"Isn't it possible that she knew about me following her? If she did, she could easily have kept her best foot forward. Then, when she knew I was finished tailing her, she could have killed him. Getting Joanna would have been the icing on the cake."

"I guess that's possible. But don't you think the police have thought of her?"

"Probably, but just in passing. They've been convinced of Joanna's guilt from the beginning. That was the beauty of this whole thing."

They argued about Mrs. Hollowell for another fifteen or twenty minutes. Cody couldn't convince Harvey. It was getting toward five o'clock, and Harvey had work to do. Besides, Cody wanted to get something to eat before he went home to change. He thanked Harvey for listening to him and headed toward the door.

"Keep an open mind about Mrs. Hollowell, Harve. Anything's possible, you know?"

"You're not really serious about her, are you?"

"Well, maybe only halfway."

"Okay, I'll think about it."

Harvey smiled and waved good-bye as Cody left the office.

CHAPTER 23

Cody had eaten a burger and fries from McDonald's on the way home. He went through the plan, in his mind, over and over again. That was his nature. Leaving things to chance didn't appeal to him.

At home, he dressed in a pair of jeans and a black sweatshirt. On his feet, he wore a pair of lightweight boots with thick rubber soles. The soles had heavy ridges, making it easier to get a grip on various surfaces and climb with some security.

The glasscutter and small jumper cables were tucked safely into his pants pocket, along with a pocket flashlight and a small suction cup. The suction cup was needed to attach to the piece of window that would be cut so that it would not fall.

The papers he had taken from Hollowell's filing cabinet were in his back pocket. He would need them, in case he found the key to the code. A black knit cap, which when pulled down became a facemask, was tucked under his belt. It may not have been necessary, but he was just trying to be prepared for every contingency.

It was 7:45 p.m. Cody planned to arrive at the Hollowell mansion around 8:00 p.m. That should give Sarah Hollowell plenty of time to be out of the house. It would also be dark at that time, giving him his best shot at not being seen by the groundskeeper if he was out and about. Fortunately, it was a cloudy night, and the moon was crescent-shaped, making things even darker.

When Cody arrived, he drove slowly by the front gate, so as to be able to look up the driveway and see the front of the house. He could see large floodlights at each corner of the house, which brightly lit up the property; however, the light faded as it got closer to the wall.

The groundskeeper's house was dark, except for one room, which faced the main gate. The keeper was probably relaxing in front of the TV set. With any luck, he'd be tired from a hard day's work and dozing in his chair. During his surveillance, Cody had never seen him around the property at night.

Cody drove around to the back of the house, just as he had rehearsed earlier in the day. He pulled up as close to the wall as he could. The streetlight was half a block away and, therefore, shed little light where he was parked. He got out of the car and looked around. There were no cars moving or parked, and the street was quiet. Climbing to the roof of the car, he hoisted himself to the top of the wall and repeated his earlier actions.

Dropping to the ground, he looked about quickly and saw no activity. He ran as quickly and quietly as he could until he reached the porch. There was a small yellow bug light illuminating it and the surrounding area, giving the night an eerie dreamlike glow.

Moving to the corner post, which he had tested earlier and found quite secure, he began to pull himself up to the roof. He used both his hands and his feet, like a young boy climbing a tree. Having strong hands made this job much easier. Once on the roof, he went to the wall just below one of the gables, which was a good ten feet above him.

Grasping the protruding stones, he began to climb up the wall. He was glad he wore those rubber-soled boots, since they made his footing more solid. About halfway to the gable, his hand slipped off the stone he was reaching for, causing him to fall five feet to the porch roof. Even though he landed on his feet, he still made a loud thud. His leg had scraped along the wall on the way down, tearing his jeans and bloodying his right knee. Cody cursed silently. This was not going to be as easy as he had thought.

Why, he wondered, had he decided to break into the house by an upper floor? Actually, it made sense. For one thing, an upper room was the most likely place for Hollowell's office. Second, he knew there were motion detectors downstairs, and he wanted to avoid them at all costs. That was why he was risking his neck climbing the walls of the second story.

Gathering himself, he started up the wall again and used greater care. He reached the gable in a few minutes this time. Making sure his footing was secure, he took the glasscutter and suction cup from his pocket. Putting the suction cup up to his mouth, he wet it thoroughly with saliva and stuck it to the window. He began cutting the glass around the cup, making sure the hole would be large enough for his hand to fit through. He tapped the cut portion of glass with the end of the glasscutter while holding the suction cup. The piece came free; he removed it, and placed it on the roof of the gable.

The jumper cables were next. Putting his hand through the hole in the window, he carefully clipped one set of small alligator jaws to the wire above the coupler on the window. Then he clipped the other set to the wire above the coupler on the frame. This kept the circuit unbroken when he lifted the window, thereby fooling the alarm system into thinking the window was closed.

Turning his hand upward, he reached up and opened the lock. He carefully removed his hand and arm from the hole and pushed the window open. When it was fully opened, he was able to climb into the room. He knew there would be no motion detectors in a room that was protected by a window alarm system.

It was very dark, so Cody took out his penlight and turned it on. He looked around the room and saw that it was a spare bedroom. The fact that the curtains were hanging loosely caught his attention. The door that led to the hallway was closed but not locked. Even though he knew no one was home, he was as quiet as he could be when he opened the door.

Slowly, he put his head out. He moved ever so slowly, in case there was a motion sensor in the upstairs hall. Sensors were usually set to detect normal motion but, if one moved very, very slowly, the alarm would not be tripped. He looked carefully up and down the hall and saw no motion detectors. Thank goodness!

He stepped out into the hall, flashing his penlight up and down. The large, wooden railing, which he had seen from the foyer during his first visit, was about five feet from the door. To his right, he could see two doors and, to his left, there were two others.

Including the room he had just left, these were the five doors he also remembered seeing.

At each end of the hall, he saw two large doors, at the top of the right and left staircases. He thought these most likely led to two larger bedrooms, perhaps master bedrooms with their own baths, walk-in closets, sitting rooms, and fireplaces. These rooms were probably for the Hollowells, one for each. They more than likely hadn't shared the same bedroom for a long time.

He moved slowly down the hall, trying each door as he went. The first two were also bedrooms. They were each furnished similarly. There was a bed, a bedside table, closet door, TV set, and chair. The windows all had the same treatment, only in these rooms, Cody noticed that the curtains were tied back with cords.

The third door he tried led to what appeared to be a den or an office. There was a desk and a chair, which sat near a window. In this room, in contrast to the others, the windows were covered with blinds. He noticed a small filing cabinet and an enclosed bookshelf with glass doors. On the desk were a phone and a Tiffany-type lamp with a stained glass shade that had gold fringe. Cody became excited because he thought this was the most fertile room in which to find Hollowell's secret things. He stepped into the room and closed the door. Going to the windows, he made sure the blinds were closed tightly.

Turning on the desk lamp, he went first to the filing cabinet where he felt Hollowell would probably hide his most secret things. There were four drawers in the cabinet. All four were unlocked.

Cody looked through the drawers and found many manila folders, similar to the ones in Hollowell's business office.

He opened one of the folders and found it empty. He opened a few more, and they, too, were empty. *This is strange,* he thought. Why would Hollowell keep these empty folders? Had the police emptied them? Had Sarah Hollowell disposed of their contents in order to protect her husband? Had Olivia Hastings convinced her to get rid of any suspicious evidence?

Cody closed that drawer and looked through the others. He found nothing of note. Going to the desk, he tried those drawers. They, too, were basically empty. He turned and looked back to the wall at the bookcase. As he walked toward it, he could see that it was filled with what appeared to be old law books. He tried the doors. They were locked.

The books looked like antiques. Hollowell must have been a collector. Perhaps this bookcase held the key. He noticed a small letter opener on the desk. Picking it up, he tried to open the lock. After he fooled with the lock for a few minutes, he decided to force the doors. He jammed the opener between the doors and rocked it back and forth with great force. Suddenly, the doors popped open.

The books were bound in red leather. Each book had a Roman numeral printed in gold leaf on the spine. Cody picked up the first book, opened it, and leafed through the pages. As he did this, he noticed they were filled with old cases. A number identified each case. Depending on how close they were to the front or back of the book, the numbers could be two, three, or four digits long. The cases were also identified by the names of the plaintiffs, the defendants, and the dates they were adjudicated.

Then he noticed that each line of the report was numbered in pencil, and every word in each sentence was also numbered. After looking at the page for a moment, it struck him. This was the key to the code! He nearly screamed out loud. Hollowell had used these old law books to secretly code his clandestine meetings.

Cody took the papers out of his pocket and opened them on the desk. On the first page of the papers, he read the sequence of numbers. First, there was a Roman numeral. It was VI. He looked on the bookshelf for a book marked with the same Roman numeral. When he found it, he took it off the shelf and put it on the desk.

The next number on the page was a three-digit number: 432. Cody turned to that page in this volume. The case number on that page was 9601 and the date was 9/6/84. He looked at the wrinkled page from Hollowell's office papers and, sure enough, those were the next set of numbers.

The case was "State of New York v. Cornwell." He read through the case quickly. It had to do with a narcotics officer, Cornwell, being prosecuted for stealing drugs from the dealers and selling them. Each line of the report was numbered and certain words in each line were highlighted. Looking back on Hollowell's papers, he found a progression of numbers which read 3, 4, 10, 14, etc. He located line one and found word three. It was "New" and word four was "York," word ten was "narcotics" and word fourteen was "officer."

As Cody continued on down the page, following the numbers, the code became clear. It was rather ingenious. It was picking out the pertinent words, and when they were all put together, it identified someone in New York named Cornwell who had narcotics and was selling them.

Then Cody looked at the map that accompanied the page. He could find circles around certain locations in the city. These were probably pickup spots for Cornwell, who was the bagman for the mob.

Cornwell didn't have to be the guy's real name, but just the way Hollowell identified him. Cody went through a few other books and pages, using the same method, and found other locations in other cities associated with other names. This certainly appeared to tie Hollowell in with some kind of narcotics arrangements.

It didn't tie him to the mob, per se, but it did suggest that he was involved with narcotics. He knew that this was not conclusive evidence, and Andy would be the first to remind him of that. In his own mind, however, this information showed Hollowell to be dirty, and that was probably the reason he was killed. It didn't take a great stretch of the imagination to tie this to Buononotti and his racket.

It certainly appeared that there was enough here to, at least, make Andy think about Hollowell and the mob. How was he going to get this stuff to Andy? He knew Andy would never accept it from him since it was obtained illegally. Maybe he could get Andy to search the house again. Andy could use the fact that the case was unsolved as an excuse to come back and search for more clues. He folded the papers and put them in his pocket.

Just then, Cody could hear what sounded like cars coming up the driveway. He quickly turned off the desk lamp and went to the door.

Since he was in a room facing the back of the house, he couldn't see who drove up. He opened the door slightly and waited for the front door to open.

In a few minutes, the door opened and in walked Sarah Hollowell and Olivia Hastings. Mrs. Hollowell went to the alarm panel, punched in her code and deactivated the alarm. Together, they walked into the library, and Mrs. Hollowell closed the sliding door.

He was confused. Surely, he hadn't made a mistake about Mrs. Hollowell's itinerary. This was "bridge night." He stood there quietly for a few seconds, trying to understand what was going on. How come she was home at this hour and accompanied by Olivia Hastings? When he had more time, he was going to have to give this a lot of consideration.

Since they were in the library, he thought it would be a good time to get out of the house. He hurried out into the hall and back to the bedroom through which he had entered. When he got there, he decided to wait for a while to see what happened next. Leaving the door slightly ajar allowed him to look through the banister into the foyer.

Cody was becoming frustrated. He had to know what was going on between these two women. *This has to be more than a pure business relationship,* he thought. *But what?* He decided to try to get closer to the library. Crawling on his knees, he moved toward the banister. He could hear voices, but they were muffled, making it impossible to understand what was being said.

He was just about to try to go down the stairs to get closer, when the doors slid open. Sarah Hollowell and her "guest" came into the foyer. Cody quickly slumped to his belly and slowly crawled back toward the bedroom. The women were busy talking, so he was able to get back to the bedroom unnoticed.

Through the slightly opened door, he could hear them coming up the stairs. Mrs. Hollowell was saying, "You may as well stay the night, Livvy, dear."

"I'd like that very much."

"Stay the night?" he repeated to himself. What the hell was going on here? How well did these women know each other? He closed the door quickly for fear they might notice that it was open.

Cody could hear the door to the large bedroom on the right open. Since he heard no other door opening, he concluded that they both went into the same room. They obviously knew each other very well. He wanted to get closer to their bedroom door so he could hear what was going on, but he didn't want to take the chance of getting caught. Maybe he could try to climb across the outside wall and look into the window of their bedroom.

He went to the window and climbed out onto the wall, again grasping the protruding stones. Slowly and quietly, he edged toward the gable that led to the bedroom where the women were talking. His hands were sweating, making his grip tenuous at best. He continued moving closer until he was just below the gable.

Reaching up, he took hold of the frame of the window and slowly pulled himself up so he could peer in. The curtains were pulled back and shade was partially up. He could see everything, but couldn't hear too well. What he saw shocked him to the core.

There were Sarah Hollowell and Olivia Hastings locked in an embrace and kissing each other. He could see their tongues exploring each other's lips hungrily. They were pawing at each other like two long-lost lovers. Tearing off their clothes frantically, they tossed them haphazardly around the room.

Cody couldn't believe his eyes. Obviously, these women were lovers. How long? Was this going on while Hollowell was alive? Did it start after he died? What did this have to do with his murder, if anything?

There was no talking going on now. His hands were beginning to strain as he tried to hold onto the stones. He decided he'd better call it a night. Carefully, he inched his way back until he was over the porch. He climbed down to the roof, then down the post to the ground. The grounds were quiet, so he ran to the wall. Using a bush with thick large branches, he climbed to the top of the wall. From the wall, he jumped to the roof of the car, then to the curb.

Sweating profusely, he got into the car and absently began looking for a cigarette. When he realized there wouldn't be one, he almost exploded. He started the car and drove off down the street.

His head was spinning. His mind was having trouble trying to comprehend what he had just seen. Suddenly, he realized he had left the house so hastily, he had not cleaned up after himself. The jumper cables were still on the alarm wires, the bookcase was open, the old law book was on the desk, and the window was left open.

He began hoping that Mrs. Hollowell or the maid didn't visit that room too often. Even if they did go in, how could they know who had broken in? He couldn't worry about that now, it was too late. The clock on the dashboard read 10:34 p.m. He was exhausted. All he wanted to do was go home, take a shower, and lie down. He needed time to figure this whole thing out.

He was so agitated when he arrived home that he had to have three double shots of bourbon before he could shower. After the shower, he lay in bed, thinking about what had just transpired. His craving for a cigarette was at its peak, but there were none to be had in the house, not even an old butt. He settled for another double shot of bourbon. After that, he was feeling mellow and ready to sort things out.

First, he was elated that he had found the answer to the coded files. These files appeared to indicate that Hollowell was travelling around the country, meeting certain people in different cities. The meetings must be illegal or else the files wouldn't have been coded. The trips seemed to have something to do with drugs. To his mind, that would connect Hollowell to Buononotti, who was the drug kingpin of the whole city and, maybe, the state.

If Gino killed Hollowell for some screwup, how did that tie in with the other murders? Gino would seem to have no reason to kill Johnston unless he had some information he shouldn't have had. Lola could be connected to Gino since she was undoubtedly paying him a kickback. She might have tried to put some pressure on Gino when she heard about Hollowell's death and ended up dead herself. Lola knew Hollowell because he used her service. Therefore, Hollowell, Lola, and Gino were connected.

Then came the big fly in the ointment. What was this business between Sarah Hollowell and Olivia Hastings? How did Hastings's hair end up at both crime scenes? Whose earrings did he find? Why did Hastings have one of them? Could she be somehow tied up with Gino? If she was, how did Mrs. Hollowell fit in? Why had he not picked up on the relationship between these women during his surveillance? When did it actually begin?

His mind was awash with thoughts, but it was also becoming muddled due to the bourbon. He was thinking he probably shouldn't have drunk so much. All those unanswered questions were on his mind as he drifted off to sleep. His last thoughts were of Joanna. He knew she was innocent. All he had to do was get enough evidence together to convince Andy and a jury. He would go to see her in the morning.

CHAPTER 24

Cody woke up with a brutal headache. He sat up at the side of the bed and felt waves of nausea roll through his stomach. Staggering down to the kitchen, he took a tray of ice cubes from the freezer, emptied it into the sink, turned on the faucet, and filled it with cold water. Plunging his face and most of his head into the icy combination, he held it there as long as he could. After repeating this four more times, he got a towel and dried his face and hair.

Next, he went to the coffee maker and began to brew some coffee. When it was finished, he poured himself a large mug full and drank it in large gulps. He hoped it would somehow, magically, make him feel better. It didn't work; for when he was finished, he still felt nauseated and still had a headache. Whoever said coffee was a cure for hangover was obviously dead wrong. What he really needed was some of the "hair of the dog that bit him." He poured another mug of coffee, only this time he added a shot of the same bourbon that he had last night. Sipping it slowly, he gathered his thoughts.

He planned his itinerary for the day. First, he would go to see Andy and tell him the latest news. He had to try to convince him to go back to the Hollowell house and get the books Hollowell had used for the code. Then, he would see Joanna. About the thing between Sarah Hollowell and Hastings, he wasn't sure what to do. Maybe he would run it by Harvey first.

He finished his "medicine" and weaved his way up to the bathroom for a shower and shave. When he was finished, he dressed and tried to call Andy. It was nine forty-five as he dialed Andy's number. Luckily, Andy was there and answered the phone.

"Lieutenant Perone."

"Hi, Andy. This is Cody."

There was a slight pause at the other end, and then a soft sigh. "Hello, Cody. What's up?"

"Well, for one thing, I've solved the mystery of the Hollowell coded files."

There was another short pause before Andy said, "You did? How the hell did you do that?"

"It's a little too complicated to tell you over the phone. I was hoping to come down there and tell you in person. Then I'd like to see Joanna. What do you think?"

"Okay, come on down."

Cody was gratified to hear Andy sounding so friendly. He certainly had a change of heart.

"I'll be right there. See you soon."

He hung up the phone and, for a moment, forgot about his hangover, until he turned to get his jacket. The sudden spin brought back the waves of nausea and the thumping in his temples. But nothing could slow him down, now. In the rented car, he started for the station. He had to remember to ask Andy about his own car.

On the way to see Andy, he recounted the events of the previous evening. He wondered about the apparent love affair between Sarah Hollowell and Olivia Hastings. There had been no inkling that either one had lesbian tendencies. Could this have been the motive for murder?

Since the hairs found at the two crime scenes appeared to belong to Hastings, did that mean she alone was the murderer? Why would either of these women want Lola Dupres dead? How does Gino fit in with these ladies? There was a lot of work to do if he was going to make a case against either women or Gino Buononotti. Since there was conflicting evidence, Andy was sure to recognize that fact and point it out.

Cody pulled up to the police station and parked in the lot next to the building. He hurried through the station and up the stairs to Andy's office. The outer office, where the detectives' desks were, was relatively quiet. No one paid him much attention as he walked back to Andy's small cubicle.

Once again, when Andy saw him through the window of his door, he waved for Cody to come in. As Cody opened the door, Andy stood and greeted him with a smile and a handshake, a distinct change in attitude. Could he finally believe in Joanna's innocence? Has all this work paid off? He wasn't sure, but it really didn't matter as long as it was true.

"Sit down, Cody. What've you got for me today?"

He didn't know where to start, but the code was as good a place as any.

"As I told you on the phone, I've cracked the code. I think you'll be interested in the outcome."

"Okay, let me have it."

"The answer can be found in some old law books at Hollowell's home office." Cody went on to explain about the numbers and how they related to secret messages that pointed out drug and money exchanges.

Andy was sitting back, taking this all in without comment. When Cody had finished, he said, "Well, what do you think it all means? Do you think it has anything to do with the murders?"

"As I've told you many times since this all began, I think Hollowell was a mule for Gino Buononotti, picking up and dropping off drugs or whatever the mob needed."

Andy rubbed his chin and tipped his head back to look up at the ceiling. He seemed to be thinking about what Cody had just said. Then he sat forward.

"How does your wife tie in with this theory?"

"My wife? She doesn't. She was just a victim of circumstances."

"What circumstances, Cody? She admits to being in the room around the time of Hollowell's murder, doesn't she?"

Cody took a deep breath and thought, *Are we back to that stuff again?* It seemed like every time he brought up the mob, Andy brought up Joanna.

"I've explained it to you, at least a hundred times. Yes, she was there, but for her own personal reasons. And she left before he was killed."

"Okay, okay. Let's not go through that again. What have you got that connects 'the mob,' as you call them, to Hollowell's death?"

Cody knew he had nothing concrete to connect Buononotti to Hollowell's murder, but he pushed on anyway.

"Only the fact that Hollowell probably worked for them, and you know how they operate when someone screws up."

"How are you so sure Hollowell worked for Buononotti?"

"Because of the coded files."

"There's no proof those files have anything to do with Buononotti or anything illegal for that matter. Only Hollowell knew what they meant, and he's dead."

Back to square one, thought Cody. Because of Andy's apparent reluctance to implicate the mob, Cody decided to get off that subject and go in a different direction.

"Okay, then, let's try this on for size. Last night, I saw Sarah Hollowell and Olivia Hastings making passionate love."

He stared at Andy, waiting for his reaction. Andy didn't even flinch.

"Cody, we knew they were seeing each other, shortly after the murder. What of it? What has that to do with anything?"

This time it was Cody's turn to react. He was astounded. They knew about the women and never said a thing to him. He couldn't believe his ears. After a moment, he stammered, "You knew about that? Why didn't you tell me?"

"In the first place, it's none of your business. In the second place, it has nothing to do with the murder. Don't they have a right to see each other if they want to?"

Cody was having difficulty processing what Andy was saying. It seemed perfectly clear to him that this affair could constitute a motive for these women.

"Andy, I can't believe you can't see a connection. Don't you think it gives at least one of them a motive?"

"What motive, Cody?"

"To get Hollowell out of the way, what else? They could have found out about me and realized Hollowell was trying to get something on his wife. My information potentially could have made a divorce a whole lot cheaper."

Cody had remembered finding his phone number in Olivia Hastings's personal phone book.

Andy smiled weakly, folded his hands on the desk, and dropped his head. In a moment, he raised it.

"She wouldn't have had to kill him for that. She could've gotten enough on him to win in any court."

"Well, what about the hair and the earring?"

"The hair could've gotten on Hollowell at the office, and I don't know who owns that earring."

Cody was completely exasperated. He didn't know where to turn next. The apparent significant evidence he had dug up was, according to Andy, not so significant. He thought Andy had been coming around, but his attitude was just as negative as before.

"Andy, what's going on? The last time we talked, you seemed to believe in Joanna's innocence. What's changed your mind?"

"My mind hasn't changed. I'm just tryin' to show you how tough it'll be to prove your point in court. I do believe, now, that Joanna didn't kill Hollowell, but I don't have enough to convince the district attorney."

Cody breathed a huge sigh of relief. At last, Andy was on his side. He jumped up from his chair and leaned over the desk to grab Andy's hand. "Thank God, thank God. I was about ready to go nuts. I just couldn't understand how you couldn't see it my way."

"Take it easy," said Andy, as he tried to get his hand free. "Remember, just because I believe, that doesn't mean we can get a jury to believe."

"I know. But at least you're on our side."

"I've always been on your side, asshole. But I'm a cop, and I must have proof positive. And so must a jury."

Cody sat down again. He now realized he was going to have to provide more solid proof. Andy had forced him to see this from all angles, not just as Joanna's husband. Nevertheless, he felt much better knowing Andy thought Joanna was innocent. He wanted to see Joanna now. He asked Andy to fix it for him, and he did. He thanked Andy and left, not knowing if he was as happy as he had been on the way over. Things were looking up though. He still had a slight headache, and he wanted a cigarette more than almost anything. He put a cough drop into his mouth.

*   *   *   *

Joanna slouched through the large metal door into the visiting room. She looked more haggard and forlorn than the last time he saw her if that were possible. It looked as if she hadn't combed her hair in days, and she wore no makeup. The circles around her eyes were blacker, and she was not smiling. It appeared as though she had on the same dress, for it was wrinkled and smudged with dirt. He could see that her fingernails were long and unpolished. This was definitely not the careful and meticulous woman he had married.

He stood as she approached him, kissed her briefly, and held her hand as they sat down. The guard looked on impassively.

"How are you, sweetheart?"

"Terrible. When am I going to get out of here?"

"Soon, baby, soon."

This was all he could say. He didn't quite know how to console her. After his visit with Andy, his optimism of this morning had waned a little.

"How soon?" she persisted. "I can't stand it in here much longer. I'm going crazy."

"I know it's tough. Just try to hang on for a little while longer. I've got some terrific new evidence. Even Andy thinks you're innocent?"

"Well, why am I still in here?"

Her eyes flared as she spoke those words. Cody could sense a distinct change in her demeanor. She was angry and combative, which was a distinct difference from her usual calm and even temperament. He had to get her out of there, and soon, he thought. This place was killing her.

"It'll just take a few more days, I promise you, just a few more days."

"I can't see how I'll last a few more hours, let alone days."

"I know, but I've got to get just a few more facts together. That takes time."

Joanna dropped her head onto her hands and started to cry. Cody was grief-stricken. He had to make this easier for her. But how?

"Just keep thinking about us and the times we'll have together when this is all over."

"Will it be over, Cody? Will it? When?"

"Very soon, now. You'll see."

He tried to tell her about the code and the two women, but he could see she wasn't really paying attention. Then the guard stood up and motioned to him. It was time to go. Cody didn't know how to leave her. He leaned down and kissed her on the top of her head and said it was time to go. The look that spread across her face was unbearable. Once again, tears welled up in her eyes. That same drawn, haggard look appeared on her face, and those circles around her eyes darkened.

"I'll be back tomorrow. There's no doubt about it now. I'll get the evidence today that'll get you out of here. I promise."

He knew he had to give her some kind of hope. He was fearful, however, of the consequences if he didn't come through on his promise.

"Good-bye, sweetheart, and try not to worry."

Joanna turned away from him without saying a word. With her head down, she shuffled back through the large door that led back to the cells. Cody's heart was breaking. His headache came back with a vengeance. With his temples throbbing, he left the visitation room, wondering what to do next.

It was eleven thirty. When he got to the car, he tried to call Harvey, but he was in court and would be there until two o'clock or two thirty that afternoon. His head was thumping painfully, so he decided to go home and try to take a nap. Perhaps Harvey would be free later. As he drove home, he remembered that he had forgotten to ask Andy about his car.

CHAPTER 25

When Cody arrived home, he first went to the telephone and turned off the bell. He didn't want to be disturbed while he was sleeping. Then he went to the kitchen and took three aspirins. He had to get rid of the lingering headache. Finally, he went upstairs, got undressed, and went to bed. Sleep came rather quickly. He slept about two hours, awaking at 1:30 p.m.

He sat up slowly at the side of the bed, testing whether the headache had gone away. The familiar thumping and accompanying nausea that had been present for the last sixteen hours were no longer there. Sitting quietly for a moment or two, he gathered his thoughts. The stinging from his knee reminded him of the events of last night.

He limped into the bathroom and took a shower, carefully washing the scraped area. Afterward, he dressed it with some iodine and a large adhesive strip. Feeling much better after he was dressed, he recognized some mild hunger pangs. In the kitchen, he prepared a sandwich and a cup of coffee. Cody loved coffee with cold cuts sandwich.

Before starting to eat the sandwich, he decided to call Andy. When he reached the phone, he noticed that the answering machine light was blinking. He pushed the replay button and heard a beep followed by a soft female voice.

"Mr. Thomas, this is Sarah Hollowell. It is 12:15 p.m. I am calling because I think we must talk. I know that you are pursuing my husband's killer, and I think I have some important information for you. I will be tied up all afternoon, so do you think you could meet me this evening? I don't think it's a good idea to meet at my house because I am sure I am being watched. Please meet me at the Holiday Inn on the interstate highway at seven o'clock this evening. I'll be waiting for you in the cocktail lounge. Please don't disappoint me."

Cody's mouth was left half open as the machine stopped. This had taken him completely by surprise. What could she possibly have to tell him? Was this some kind of trap? It certainly could be, but he felt he had to meet her, no matter what. Even if she was trying to fool him, he felt he was smart enough and would be vigilant enough to outsmart her.

Looking at his watch, he saw that it was two forty-five. He decided to call Harvey and get his input on this latest incident. He dialed Harvey's number, and Thelma picked up the phone on the other end.

"Law office of Harvey Whitcomb."

"Hi, Thelma! Cody Thomas here. Is Harvey there, by any chance?"

"You're in luck, Cody. He just walked in. I'll ring his phone. You're not in trouble again, are you?"

"No, not this time. I just need to talk to him."

Cody waited impatiently for Harvey to pick up. He was thinking about Sarah Hollowell and her request when Harvey came on the line.

"Cody? What's the 'matta'? You didn't get caught in Hollowell's house, did you?"

"No. I told you I'd be fine. Just listen to this. I got a message on my answering machine from Sarah Hollowell, asking me to meet her this evening. She says she has some important information about her husband's murder, and I'm to meet her at the Holiday Inn on the interstate. What do you think of that?"

There was a long pause on the other end of the line while Harvey was thinking. Cody could see, in his mind's eye, Harvey rubbing his brow, as he did when in deep thought. Finally, Harvey spoke.

"That's a strange request, don't you think?"

"I sure do. That's why I called you. What do you think she's up to?"

"I'm not sure. Do you think she really has something new?"

Cody liked it when Harvey didn't have an immediate idea. It made him feel a little superior.

"I have the feeling that this may be a trap, although I'm not sure what she's trying to accomplish. Perhaps I'm getting too close, and she's trying to get me off the track."

"How would she know how close you're getting?"

"She may be getting the information from Olivia Hastings. They're lovers, you know."

There was an even longer pause at the other end this time. Cody could hear Harvey's chair squeak as he sat back suddenly.

"What did you just say?"

"They are lovers." Cody emphasized these words.

"How the hell do you know that?"

"Because I saw them making love last night when I was at the house."

Cody went on and told Harvey about the events of the previous night. He described how he had seen them while hanging on the wall outside the bedroom window.

"Wow! That's a shocker. This certainly puts a new slant on this thing, doesn't it?"

"Absolutely! The most remarkable thing is that I never suspected a thing while I was tailing her."

More silence from Harvey. Finally, he spoke.

"What about the code? Did you find anything?"

"You bet! I found the answer to it all. Those files spell out meeting places, people, what took place, and money transactions, just as I suspected."

"Does it tie Hollowell to the mob?"

"I think it does, but I don't think that Andy's convinced or that the courts will agree."

Cody and Harvey talked about the code and its meaning for a while longer. Both agreed that Hollowell was involved with the mob up to his teeth, but they would need more solid evidence. Then Harvey asked, "What are you going to do about tonight?"

"I'm going, of course," answered Cody emphatically. There wasn't ever any doubt in his mind.

"Shouldn't you let your cop friend know what you're doing?"

"I've already given that some thought, and I've decided to lay out my entire plan for him. He's probably going to advise against it though. He doesn't think Mrs. Hollowell could be involved in any way."

"Do you think he'll give you some help?"

"I don't know, but I think if he listens to me, we'll be able to work something out."

Cody knew that if his theory about the women were correct, he would need backup help. From his days on the force, he knew that it was important to have backup when entering a particularly dangerous situation. Being meticulously careful about those situations kept you alive. He wasn't going to leave anything to chance, not with something this important.

"Even though I'm not a cop anymore, I think he'll be there for me. Don't worry, Harve, I'll be on the lookout for anything suspicious."

"You'd better be."

"I'll be extra careful. I'll call you when it's over, okay?"

"Okay. Take it easy."

Cody heard the click of Harvey's receiver as he hung up. *Harvey's a good man,* he thought. As usual, he slowed Cody down a bit and made him think things out a little better. A phone call to Andy was next to tell him about Sarah Hollowell's phone message. To his surprise, Andy was receptive. Together, they worked out a plan that was mutually satisfactory.

Cody decided to get out to the Holiday Inn a little earlier than the appointed time in order to look the place over. He always liked to be aware of his surroundings so as to be better able to protect himself in case of an emergency.

His stomach growled, reminding him that he hadn't eaten yet. He could smell the coffee that was brewing. He picked up the huge sandwich he had made and ate it voraciously. When he finished, it was four thirty-five. The drive to the Holiday Inn would probably take about forty-five minutes, maybe longer, since there would be people coming home from work. He grabbed his jacket and went out to the car. He was still driving the rented car.

It took him longer to get there than he thought it would. It was six o'clock when he pulled into the parking lot. It also took him a while to find a parking spot since the lot was crowded with many cars, mostly of the sports variety. This was the happy hour, and many yuppies had obviously come here to drink and mingle.

That's good, thought Cody; it would be more difficult to notice him. After parking, he walked into the lobby and looked around. It was relatively empty, except for a few people talking near the registration desk and one man sitting in a lobby chair smoking a cigarette. The urge to walk over to him and ask for a smoke was enormous, but he thought better of it. He turned and walked slowly into the cocktail lounge through the door on the left side of the lobby.

There were no stools left at the bar. After struggling through the crowd toward the far corner where the bar joined the wall, he tried to get the bartender's attention. It took a few minutes, but eventually, he was able to order a club soda. He wasn't about to put any alcohol into his body after last night. He paid for his drink and stepped back against the wall, trying to blend in with the crowd.

There were at least thirty or forty people crowded around the bar. It was a large room with a long bar, perhaps twenty to twenty-five feet long. The people were crushed up against one another, drinking and talking, paying little or no attention to anything, except what they were trying to accomplish—making out.

Cody thought that Mrs. Hollowell knew what she was doing when she suggested that they meet here. There would be no way anyone could listen in on a conversation in this madhouse. He looked over the room and carefully scanned as many of the faces as he could clearly see. No one's face was familiar to him.

He hung around for the next hour, drinking club soda until it seemed as if he was about to explode. Suddenly, he became aware that he had to go to the bathroom. He put his glass on the bar and pushed his way to the men's room, which was on the other side of the room. People were slowly sifting out of the lounge either to eat or, if they were lucky, to get a room.

As Cody was making his way through the crowd, a young well-built dark-haired woman pressed herself up against him and said, "Where are you going, handsome?"

Startled by the incident, he tried to step around her. It wasn't because he was a prude, but because his mind was somewhere else. The woman stood her ground.

"What's the matter? Are ya bashful?"

"Er . . . ah . . . well, no," he stammered.

"Well, then, why don't you slow down and buy me a drink?"

"I'm just on my way to the head. Maybe when I come back, okay?"

He didn't need this kind of thing right now. Besides, he was accustomed to making the first move. Stepping around her, he continued on to the washroom. She called after him.

"I might not be here when you get back. It'll be your loss."

Cody turned to her and shrugged. When he finished in the bathroom, he washed his hands and stepped back into the lounge with caution. Since meeting someone other than Sarah Hollowell wasn't on his agenda, he carefully avoided Little Miss Aggressive. His mind was focused on the job at hand. Looking around, he saw her talking to another guy who looked like he was a lot more interested in the encounter.

He pushed his way back to his position near the bar and ordered another club soda. He needed a cigarette desperately but fought off the urge to bum one from someone at the bar. He put a cough drop into his mouth and waited.

*   *   *   *

It was about six forty-five when he saw Sarah Hollowell step into the lounge through the door. He moved back out of the light so as not to be seen by her. The lounge was decidedly less crowded. Sarah found an empty table at the far corner of the room. Three women who were going in to dinner had just vacated it.

In a few minutes, the waiter went over and took her order. She settled into her chair and began to look around. It was still crowded and dark enough that he felt she wouldn't be able to see him. The waiter finally brought her drink, and she began to sip it. It was then that Cody decided to walk to her table. He looked around carefully and saw nothing suspicious.

As he approached the table, she caught sight of him, put her drink down, and sat up straight. She appeared nervous, but he thought that was to be expected. He stood at the table for a moment, just looking around. When he was satisfied nothing was irregular, he sat down.

"Well, Sarah, here I am. What is it you have for me?"

She hesitated for a while and appeared to be trying to gather herself.

"Mr. Thomas, you startled me for a second." She paused, and then continued, "You see, I think Samuel was involved in something dirty and illegal."

This opening surprised Cody. He hadn't expected her to attack her dead husband in this fashion.

"What makes you think that?"

She took a deep breath, looked around as if worried someone might be listening in, and continued. "Someone was in my house last night, looking through Samuel's office. Whoever it was went through some of his private books, which he kept under lock and key. I think those books were used by Samuel for something illegal."

"Why something illegal?"

Cody was watching her very closely and could see that she was looking around as she spoke. He wondered if she was expecting someone. He, too, looked around and saw no one suspicious.

"Because he only used those books before and after a business trip. And he never allowed me to see them or even go into his office when he was working on them."

"Why should that bother you now? How come you didn't suspect something before he was killed?"

She sat up straight and looked around. Then, ducking her head down slightly, she said softly, "Because it never occurred to me until this morning when I saw the office has been ransacked. Then I wondered why anyone else would want to see those books. They must be important to someone, now that he's dead."

She looked straight at Cody and spoke with such sincerity that he began to think maybe her husband, too, fooled her. Then he wondered if she suspected that he was the one who was in her house last night. After all, hadn't he been anxious to see that room? Maybe this meeting was simply a ploy to force him to admit that it was he who was there last night.

"Why are you telling me this? Why didn't you call the police?"

"We did call the police."

Cody took note of the "we." Had she slipped and included Olivia Hastings?

She continued, "However, I thought since your wife is a suspect, you might be better motivated than the police. They seem to be quite satisfied that she did it."

Cody sat back to think about those comments for a moment. That reasoning did not ring true. His years on the force had taught him to view all statements with suspicion. He usually had a "sense" about these things.

As he sat back against his chair, he suddenly felt something between his shoulders. He turned his head and saw the face of Olivia Hastings smiling at him. In her gloved hand, he could see a nickel-plated small-caliber pistol equipped with a silencer. Since she was bent over, her breasts were pushed up against his back. The gun was between her breasts and Cody's back. It was almost completely hidden from sight except from Cody's position.

She put her face next to his, as if to kiss him on the cheek, and said, "Good evening, Mr. Thomas. Please sit quietly, and don't make any fast moves. If you do, I will surely shoot you."

Cody was frozen for a second or two. He had let his guard down and had been taken completely by surprise. Sarah Hollowell had done her job well. She had gotten him interested enough in her bullshit story that he had lost concentration and allowed Hastings to sneak up behind him. Where had she been hiding? He hadn't seen her in the lounge. He gathered himself and said with bravado, "You're not going to shoot anyone right out here in the open," trying to bluff his way out.

"Oh, but you are mistaken. You see, this gun has a silencer, in case you hadn't noticed. I can fire it in this place, and no one would be the wiser. So please don't tempt me."

She was right; the place was still crowded enough for the muted sound to go unnoticed. A shot could be fired, and they could leave before even the employees found him. He continued to try to bluff his way out.

"You don't have the nerve to kill me. I could get up right now and walk out, and you would do nothing about it."

"I'm warning you, Mr. Thomas. Don't try me. I *will* shoot, and no matter what happens afterward, you'll end up dead. I assure you of that."

Cody wanted to test her will but thought better of it. She didn't sound like she was kidding. Besides, she had the gun against him right now, and maybe he would get a better chance later.

"Okay, what do you want me to do?"

"That's better. Just get up and walk slowly toward the door. And please, don't make any fast moves."

CHAPTER 26

Cody stood up as directed and turned to face the door. Sarah Hollowell stood up at the same time and moved up beside him. She put her arm through his and smiled, as if they were companions. All three of them walked casually to the door. Olivia Hastings had put the hand with the gun in it into the pocket of her black London Fog raincoat. She wore a large wide-brimmed hat, which was pulled down so as to hide most of her face. Her long bleached blond hair must have been pulled up under the hat, because it could hardly be seen at all.

When they reached the door, Sarah Hollowell stepped forward and opened it. Ms. Hastings, using the hand in her pocket, which held the gun, gave Cody a slight shove. He walked through the door into the lobby. The women followed closely behind.

When Cody stopped for further directions, he was urged to move forward again, by the hand in the raincoat.

"Walk toward the elevator, Mr. Thomas," said Ms. Hastings through her clenched teeth.

Cody looked around the lobby as he walked and saw some people checking in and out of the inn. No one was paying any attention to a man and two women walking toward the elevators. When they reached them, Mrs. Hollowell reached over and pushed the up button. A few minutes passed before the next car arrived.

By the time the doors slid open, another couple had arrived. Ms. Hastings stepped closer to Cody and pushed the gun in her pocket up against his side, just to remind him to behave. She smiled at him as she turned her face away from the other couple. They were too busy staring into each other's eyes to notice anyone else right now.

"Push the button, dear," Ms. Hastings said to Sarah Hollowell as they entered the car. She didn't mention the floor number, but Sarah knew which button to push.

They stood quietly as the car rose slowly. It stopped at the third floor where the other couple got off. Since neither of the women moved, Cody stood motionless. A man and a boy wearing bathrobes and slippers got on. They had towels wrapped around their necks and were talking about the nice swim they just had at the indoor pool.

Cody gave some thought to trying to escape, but was concerned that Hastings would shoot him and the other two people. The man and boy got off at the fourth floor, and no one else got on before Cody and his companions arrived at their destination.

"Get out, please," said Ms. Hastings as she pushed Cody out of the car. "Walk to the right."

They walked down the long corridor. When they got to room 824, they stopped. Sarah Hollowell took a card from her purse. It was perforated and fit into a slot above the doorknob. A small green light appeared, and Cody could hear a click. Mrs. Hollowell pushed the door open, and Olivia Hastings pushed him inside.

"We're here, Mr. Thomas. Please make yourself comfortable." She pushed him toward the bed. The two women took off their coats. Ms. Hastings had given the gun to Sarah Hollowell while she removed hers.

"Now, Mr. Thomas, please remove your clothes," said Olivia Hastings, having taken the gun back from Sarah.

"Remove my *what?*" said Cody, astonished by the order.

"You heard me. Take off your clothes. Right down to the skin." She waved the gun to emphasize the order.

As he reluctantly started to undress, he saw Sarah Hollowell take four pieces of cord from her handbag. Cody could see that these were similar to the curtain cords that were found at the Hollowell murder scene. He also had recognized the gun as a 25-caliber Beretta, no doubt the same gun used to kill Hollowell, Johnston, and Lola Dupres.

The picture was very clear now. These two women had killed all three, although he wasn't quite sure why as yet. While removing his clothes, he decided to ask them, feeling he had nothing to lose at this point.

"Tell me, ladies, why did you kill all those people?" he asked as nonchalantly as he could while getting naked in front of these women.

"Well, I guess we can tell you the story, since you won't be around to repeat it to anyone," Olivia Hastings said with a sarcastic half smile on her face. Cody thought she was particularly cold and ruthless.

"You see, Mr. Thomas, Samuel T. Hollowell was not a very nice man. First of all, he treated Sarah like a dog for most of their married life. He cheated on her repeatedly. He often embarrassed her in front of friends, and he physically and sexually abused her.

Cody had gotten down to his underwear at this point and was sitting on the bed listening. He didn't find anything she said hard to believe. Ms. Hastings was so engrossed in telling the story that she apparently hadn't noticed he had stopped undressing. She went on.

"My reasons are a little different. You see, in my younger days, I worked for Lola Dupres. It was a way to make money for my education."

As she said that, Cody's head snapped up in amazement. *So,* he thought, *Ms. Hastings was a hooker.* That was a real shock. He thought Hollowell had been seeing her but never suspected she had hooked for Lola. He could see her smile in that tight-lipped way that revealed her inner viciousness.

"That's right, Mr. Thomas. I was a paid whore. In fact, that's how I met our beloved Samuel T. He dated me frequently and paid well. When I graduated college, he offered me a job, which I took because it got me out of a profession that I hated.

"You see, basically, I despise men, and that job only made me hate them more. I've hated men since I was a little girl, and my beloved father forced himself on me."

Cody could see by her expression that she was becoming very agitated. He wondered if he had done himself a favor by stirring her up.

She continued, "That son-of-a-bitch Hollowell held that over me like a whip, forcing me to do things for him that I detested as much as prostitution, especially forcing me to help him with his dirty drug business."

Drugs, thought Cody. "I knew it," he said to himself. And he was no doubt connected to the mob. He ventured another question. How could it hurt?

"Was he working for Gino Buononotti?"

"Yes, he was one of Buononotti's mules. He made pickups for him all over the country. For that, he got all the drugs he wanted. He used them for his women."

"Didn't Buononotti get pissed off when you killed him?"

"No because I got his permission. Gino never liked Hollowell anyway. So you see, we actually did him a favor."

Since she was answering his questions, Cody just pushed right on. "Why didn't you just let Buononotti take care of him?"

"Because then we would have been indebted to him. And when you owe him, he never lets you forget it."

Hastings was on a roll now, so he just went right on asking questions. "Why did you kill Johnston and Lola?"

"Ah, Johnston and Lola. I did them all by myself. Johnston was potentially dangerous to us because he could possibly identify Sarah's voice and connect us to the murder. It was Sarah who sent the cab for your wife. We had to send the cab because we had to get her away from the Apollo quickly. As for Lola, that bitch had a big mouth and was about to spill the beans. She was getting scared because you and the cops had been around asking questions."

"How did she know you were the killers?"

"She found out from one of Gino's boys, who also has a big mouth. Besides, I never liked her from the time I worked for her."

So there it was, almost exactly as he figured it. Though, truthfully, he had never guessed about Mrs. Hollowell and Olivia's prostitution. As he looked over at her, he noticed for the first time that she had pierced earlobes. He asked, "Were those diamond earrings yours, Sarah?"

She had been sitting quietly in the chair by the window. He noticed she hadn't said anything up to this point. Obviously, Olivia Hastings was the leader of this twosome.

"Ah, why, yes."

"Oh, I *thought* you were the one who took that earring from my desk," said Ms. Hastings. Cody could see her eyes light up with that piece of information. He needed a few more answers to questions that were bugging him.

"Tell me how and why you picked my wife for a patsy."

"She actually picked herself. When we found out that she was seeing the old prick, we tried to find out what we could about her. I have a few friends at the courthouse that gave me a copy of her file. It told of a dead sister, and when I ran that down through the coroner's office, I found that she died of a drug overdose."

Cody marveled at the efficiency and thoroughness of their research. *No one's life is a secret anymore,* he thought.

Ms. Hastings continued. "It also said your wife's sister was a prostitute. When we checked it out with Lola, we found that she had worked for her and that old man Hollowell had known her. This gave her a perfect motive. So we just waited for their date, and there it was. Clever, huh?"

Cody found himself getting angry at the coolness with which this woman toyed with people's lives.

Ms. Hastings went on, "Okay, Mr. Thomas. Continue getting undressed, please. We have some business to attend to."

He decided to go for a few more questions while he still had the time. "When did you ladies become lovers?"

"That's really none of your business, but it was two years ago," said Mrs. Hollowell, who appeared to be slightly embarrassed that Cody knew about them. She continued, however. "We met at the health club. Frankly, it was Olivia who brought me out. I have never felt this fulfilled in my whole life."

She looked over at Olivia Hastings with a smile, and Olivia smiled back. Then Hastings said, "All right, Mr. Thomas. That's enough questions. Lie on your back on the bed, and put your hands over your head against the bed posts."

Cody decided on one more question, what the hell, he had nothing to lose. "Why go through all this trouble with the tiring with the cords and the white scarf?"

"We thought we'd make it look like some sort of serial killer and keep the police looking somewhere else."

As Cody obeyed, Sarah Hollowell began to tie his wrists and ankles to the four bedposts while Olivia Hastings held the gun pointed at his head. He knew that if he didn't try something right now, it would be too late. Quickly pulling one of his hands from Sarah Hollowell's grasp, he made a grab for the gun. But Ms. Hastings was too fast for him and pulled it away. Then she brought the pistol swiftly down on his head.

Cody felt the thud of the gun and became disoriented. He heard ringing in his ears, and everything went blank for a moment. When his head cleared up in a few seconds, he was aware of something warm and wet running down his forehead and into his eye. It was probably blood. He shook his head a couple of times to clear out the cobwebs.

It was then that Ms. Hastings said, "That was stupid, Mr. Thomas. I told you to behave yourself. Now you have a split head. Oh, well, they'll just think you like rough sex."

She said this in that same cold-blooded voice. *Well,* thought Cody, *it looks like this is it.*

His mind was racing, trying to come up with an idea that would keep him alive a few more minutes. He was wondering what was taking Andy so long. It was for just such an emergency that he had made his plans.

As Olivia Hastings moved closer to him, he blurted out, "No one's going to believe this was a sex party gone bad if there's no evidence of sexual activity."

He could see Ms. Hastings contemplating his remark. Then she said, "I guess I can fix that." She took Cody in her hand and began to stimulate him. But he was certainly in no mood and was not responding. She had put the gun on the bed beside him and was concentrating on the job "at hand" when the door crashed open.

Andy Perone and three uniformed police came rushing into the room. Olivia Hastings was completely startled by the noise and stood up from the bed. She reached for the gun but was subdued by one of the officers. Sarah Hollowell was so stunned that she stood frozen in her tracks.

When Cody finally realized his plan had worked, he began to laugh, first because he was happy to be alive, and second because he was naked and embarrassed. His heart was pounding as if it was going to erupt from his chest.

In a few minutes, Andy and the other officers had taken Olivia Hastings and Sarah Hollowell into custody. Cody was sitting on the chair in the room, holding a wet towel on his head with one hand and another towel around his waist with the other. He was still trying to clear his thoughts as he turned to Andy.

"Am I glad you got here when you did. What the hell took you so long?"

"We were outside the door the whole time. We had to wait till she answered all your questions. You actually did a great job for a guy who was about to get his head blown off."

Andy said that with a wide grin. Cody, who didn't think it was all that funny, answered, "You cut it pretty damn close." He shook his head. "I told you Hastings was your killer, didn't I?"

"You sure did. I've got to hand it to you, Cody. You almost had this figured to a tee," he said still grinning. That was the look that Cody remembered from their days together.

Then Cody said, "How do you feel about Buononotti, now? I knew he was somehow involved."

An expression of guilt spread across Andy's face. He dropped his head and turned away briefly. When he turned back, he said, "Cody, you know how it is on the force. There are times when you do what you are told and keep your mouth shut. This was one of those times."

"Even when it means screwing a friend?"

"I wouldn't have let Joanna take the fall if it came down to that. You believe me, don't you?"

"I guess I do." This was said without too much enthusiasm.

"Believe it. Now, get your clothes on. You look ridiculous."

Cody knew what Andy was talking about, and he laughed. It was the first time in a week that he felt like laughing. Now, it was time to get Joanna.

"Andy, can we go over to the jail and get Joanna?"

"Sure. We can go there right now. I'll get the district attorney to drop all the charges, and you can take her home today."

"That's great, Andy. Let's get going."

Cody, who had finished dressing, grabbed Andy by the arm and began pushing him through the door. They drove to the station in Andy's squad car.

*   *   *   *

When they arrived, Cody virtually flew through the station to the cells. He waited impatiently in the area where the prisoners came to retrieve their belongings. When the door came open and he saw Joanna, he ran to her and took her in his arms and squeezed her tightly. Neither spoke for what seemed like hours. Finally, Joanna broke the silence.

"Am I really free, Cody?"

"Yes, you are, sweetheart. I'm here to take you home, for good this time."

"I was beginning to think this day would never come."

"I'm sorry I took so long. But it's over now and we can go home."

They hugged again and, this time, kissed for a long moment. Andy had provided a police officer to drive them home. They got into the patrol car and started home. Joanna was holding Cody's arm so tightly it was going numb. Neither said a word.

Cody sat quietly and thought about the events of the last week; he could hardly believe they had really happened. His mind quickly reviewed all that had taken place: Joanna being accused of murder, of her being in jail, and most of all, of her having sex with Hollowell. He wasn't sure he was ever going to be able to completely erase that from his mind. That was going to be his biggest test.

He also thought his relationship with Andy would not be the same. Andy had practically admitted he was covering for the mob. No doubt, there was pressure from above. The mob obviously had a strong hand in city government.

He could understand that, but he was saddened and disillusioned by Andy's response to the pressure. He had expected Andy might have made a stand for honest. But then he thought, *I guess, Andy's pension means more to him than honesty.*

Then he sat back with his arm around Joanna and smiled. He'd had enough excitement to last for the rest of the year. Maybe a couple of run-of-the-mill cases would give them time for some relaxation and allow their relationship to heal. He sure hoped so.

CPSIA information can be obtained at www.ICGtesting.com
Printed in the USA
LVOW040721021212

309626LV00002B/9/P